I0648824

Murdoch Mackenzie

Nautical Descriptions of the West Coast of Great Britain from Bristol Channel to CapeWrath

Murdoch Mackenzie

Nautical Descriptions of the West Coast of Great Britain from Bristol Channel to CapeWrath

ISBN/EAN: 9783741183850

Manufactured in Europe, USA, Canada, Australia, Japa

Cover: Foto ©Andreas Hilbeck / pixelio.de

Manufactured and distributed by brebook publishing software
(www.brebook.com)

Murdoch Mackenzie

Nautical Descriptions of the West Coast of Great Britain from Bristol Channel to CapeWrath

NAUTICAL DESCRIPTIONS

OF THE

WEST COAST

OF

GREAT BRITAIN,

FROM

BRISTOL CHANNEL to CAPE-WRATH

(The most North-western Promontory of SCOTLAND);

ADAPTED TO

The several Charts in the MARITIM SURVEY of the West of GREAT BRITAIN.

CONTAINING

A particular Account of the TIDES, ROCKS, SHOALS, CHANNELS, ANCHORING-PLACES, and HARBOURS, along that COAST, with suitable SAILING-DIRECTIONS interspersed.

To which is prefixed

The Principal OBSERVATIONS and MEASUREMENTS, on which the SURVEY was grounded.

By MURDOCH MACKENZIE, Sen.

LONDON:

Printed for the AUTHOR; and for KENNETH MACKENZIE of New London-Street, Hart-Street; and his eldest Son MURDOCH MACKENZIE; and sold (together with the Charts) by MOUNT and PAGE, on Tower-Hill; SAYER and BENNET, in Fleet-Street; JEFFERYS and FADEN, in the Strand, near Charing-Cross; and DURY in Duke's-Court, Leicester-Fields.

MDCCLXXVI.

Observations *of the Sun, and actual* Measurements *on the West Coast of* GREAT BRITAIN, *on which the Survey of it was grounded.*

Meridian Zenith Distances of the Sun's upper Limb.

			Deg. Min.	Latitude.
1770,	*July* 2d.	Middle (nearly) of *Lundy Island*, the meridian zenith distance of the ☉ upper limb was	27° 48'	51° 7½'
	July 7th.	At *Warren* church, on the south side of *Milford-haven*	28° 47'	51° 39½'
	March 18.	At *Trevan Head*, near *Cardigan Island*	53° 13½'	52° 8½'
1769,	*June* 19th.	At the old abbey of *Bardsey Island*	29° 15'	52° 47½'
1767,	*June* 8th.	At the east end of the town at *Holy Head*	30° 6'	53° 17'
1766,	*June* 10th.	At the top of *Snaefell Hill*, in the *Isle of Man*	30° 50'	54° 15'
	September 6th.	At *Carsethorn Head* in *Kirkcudbright*	48° 13½'	54° 51'
1756,	*October* 11th.	At the house *Tynacraigs*, near the small isles of *Jura*	66° 31'	55° 45'
1753,	*May* 5th.	At *Dunvegan Castle*, in *Sky Island*	40° 45'	57° 21'
1755,	*July* 13th.	At *Flowerdale*, in *Gerloch*	35° 40'	57° 37'
	May 30.	At *Gailrum*, in *Ru-Stoir*	36° 9'	58° 16'
1748,	*April* 11th.	At *Stornoway*, in the *Lewis*	49° 49'	58° 15'
1750,	*June* 4th.	At *Ru-Wrath*, in *Strathnaver*	35° 41'	58° 24'

These Observations were made with *Bird's* twelve-inch quadrant; which, for the most part, was adjusted immediately before, within one minute of a degree.

Measurements on the West Coast of GREAT BRITAIN.

Measured in *Long Island*, in *Scotland*, on the sand between *South Uist* and *Benbecula*, from the beach of Gold, eastward to a rock near the middle of the Strand, whose top is always above water, 3½ miles.

Measured on the sand of *Melbost*, in the *Lewis*, on the north side of the *Aird*, two miles 350 yards; from the corn ridges, at the head dyke, on the S. end of the sand, to the grass on the north side of it.

Measured on *Barnard's Wharf Bank*, in *Wyre-water*, in *Lancashire*, three miles thirty-six yards, from the watch-house at the mouth of the river, eastward.

Measured on the *Red sand*, in the river *Clyde*, 3½ miles; from that part of it, which is over-against *Gilgher* in *Cardross* parish, eastward to the banks of *Hewel*.

Measured along *Formby Sand*, in *Lancashire*, from the land-mark on that point, southwards to the point of *Crosby* 3½ miles and three yards. Also from *Crosby Point* southward to the end of the sand near *Rock-hall* (forming an obtuse angle with the other line measured) 4½ miles.

Measured on the sand in *Ramsey Bay*, in the *Isle of Man*, 2½ miles, and 110 yards; from the end of a dike, nearly eastward to *Shellal Point* below *Ballivanby*.

Measured along the sand at the head of *Holy Head* bay two miles and 146 yards; from the edge of the grass on the east side of the bay, in the direction of a kern, on a hill above *Rofcolen* church, bearing S. W. ½ W.

These Measurements were made with a substantial iron chain, fifty feet long; the straight line marked on the sand by upright poles, and small rods stretched between them, and the number of chains counted by pins set at the end of each chain.

The *fundamental* angles, at each extremity of the above base-lines, for ascertaining the positions of distant hills, or other conspicuous objects, and the angles at these hills or objects, formed by aerial lines, connecting them and remarkable points, promontories, or rocks on the coast, were taken with a Theodolite; the distances of other intervening stations along the shore, and of rocks and shoals off it, were determined by the magnetic intersections of these points, promontories, and distant hills.

The variation of the magnetic needle was found by the Stars, by setting up a light in the direction of ε in Ursa Major, when it and the Pole Star were on the same vertical circle; or when the Pole Star was at its greatest azimuth, and a proper allowance made for its distance from the meridian at that time.

How to accommodate any future Variation of the Compass to the following Descriptions, and their respective Charts.

If the variation of the compass shall, at any time hereafter, be *westward of the variation in a Chart*, write the difference of the two variations, and a W. on the margin of the Chart, and of its description, to be referred for use. Then, North in the Chart, being so much eastward of North by the compass; and South in the Chart, so much westward of South by the compass; all bearings and courses in that Chart, and in its description, that are on the *West side of the magnetic meridian*, are to be reckoned, or steered by the compass,

as

as if they were *nearer to the North by that difference:* and all bearings and courses *on the East side* of the magnetic meridian in the Chart, or its description, are to be reckoned, or steered by the compass, as if they were *farther from the North* by that difference.

But if the variation of the compass, any time hereafter, shall be *eastward of the variation in a Chart*; write the difference, and so E. on the margin of the Chart, and of its description, to remain there for use. Then, North in the Chart being so much westward of North by the compass; and South in the Chart so much eastward of South by the compass; all the bearings and courses in that Chart, and in its description, that are on the *East side of the magnetic meridian*, must be reckoned, and steered by the compass, as if they were *nearer to the North*, by the difference of the two variations; and all bearings and courses *on the West side of the meridian in the Chart, or description*, as if they were *farther from the North* by that difference.

Note. The *Welsh* and *Earse* (or *Gaelic*) names of places are, for the most part, spelled in the Charts and descriptions agreeable to the common pronunciation: it may not therefore be altogether unnecessary to observe, to an *English* Reader, that, in order to pronounce them intelligibly, *(ch)* and *(gh)* must always have a guttural sound; that *g* is pronounced hard before *e* and *i*, as well as before *a*, *o*, and *u*; that *a* is pronounced open, as in *(war)*, or in *(all)*; and *i* sharp, as in *(image)*, or in *(bit)*, with very few exceptions.

NAUTICAL DESCRIPTIONS

OF THE

COAST of SOUTH WALES.

COMPREHENDING

From WORMS HEAD, *in* BRISTOL CHANNEL, *to* BARDSEY ISLAND.

CARMARTHEN BAY.

A Description of the Tides, Rocks, Shoals, Channels, Anchoring-places, and Harbours, in CARMARTHEN BAY, *between* WORMS HEAD *and* CALDY ISLAND.

CHART II.

Tides between WORMS HEAD *and* CALDY ISLAND.

TIDES.

ON the full and change days of the moon, it is high-water on the shore in *Carmarthen Bay*, at 5½. A league or two out on this Bay, the stream does not turn till an hour or two later. In *Caldy Sound* the stream begins to run westward at four hours of flood on the shore, and to set eastward at four hours of ebb.

In *Carmarthen Bay* ordinary spring-tide rises twenty-one feet perpendicular, and neap-tide twelve.

Flood-tide, along this part of the coast, runs eastward; and ebb westward.

In *Carmarthen Bay*, the stream, when strongest, runs about one mile an hour; in *Caldy Sound* it runs about three miles an hour, and neap-tides one.

Rocks, Shoals, and Sand-banks in CARMARTHEN BAY.

ROCKS and SHOALS.

Cefnsidan Sand extends from the entry of *Barry* harbour northward to the channel leading to *Carmarthen*: the S. part of this Sand dries with spring-tide only; great part of the north half of it dries with neap-tides.

Middle-patch is a bank of sand about two miles long, from N. to S. and three-quarters broad; which divides the *Bar of Carmarthen* into two channels; the E. and W. and dries with spring-tide only. The channels are described with *Carmarthen River*.

Drift Rock is a small rocky shoal, which lies about two miles and a half S. S. E. ½ E. from the S. end of *Caldy*. The least water on it is four fathoms, and therefore not dangerous; except by a great breaking sea that rises on it, when it blows fresh from the W. or S. W. Leading marks to it are, the spire of *Tenby* church, about a ship's-length shut in over *Small-ord Point*, near *Spur Island*, in *Caldy*: sail in that direction till you open the sandy hillocks in *Leadstep Bay* with *Red-ord Point*, and you will be then on the shallowest part of *Drift Rock*.

The *Spaniel* is a small rocky shoal, on which the sea often breaks in blowing weather. It lies about a mile E. ½ S. from *Caldy Chappel*, and S. E. ½ E. from *Small-ord Point*: the least water on it is two fathoms. There are no land-marks for avoiding this shoal, which can be distinguished by a stranger: the best way is to keep within three quarters of a mile from the S. end of *Caldy*; or else above a mile and a half from it.

Woolhouse Rock lies about two miles N. E. by E. from the eastmost point of *Caldy*, and two miles S. E. from St. *Catherine's Island*, and dries a little after half ebb. Half a cable's-length from the E. and W. sides of it, there are three fathoms at low-water; half a cable from the S. and N. sides, there are but four feet. To avoid it on the E. or W. sides, keep part of a small sandy bay, which is between St. *Catherine's Island*, and the houses of *Tenby*, open to the E. or W. of that island: or to avoid it along the E. side, keep *Monkstone Head* N. To avoid it on the N. side, keep the old wind-mill in *Caldy* open, or in a line with the west extremity of *High Cliff* in *Caldy*.

ANCHORING-PLACES. Carmarthen Bay.

Carmarthen Bay is, for the most part, clean sand, and a moderate depth of water. In it a vessel may stop a tide almost any where (the forementioned shoals and sands excepted) when the wind is off shore, or the weather

they

CARMARTHEN BAY.

Rossilly Bay. Caldy Sound. Near Tenby.

than moderate. The best parts are in *Rossilly Bay*, about a mile from the shore, on 2½, or three fathoms at low-water; especially when the wind is S. or eastward of south: in *Caldy Road*, when the wind is from the S. S. E. westward to the N. N. W.; and near half a mile eastward of *Tenby Harbour*, on 3½ fathoms.

CALDY ROAD.

Caldy Road is by far the best stopping-place in *Carmarthen Bay*; because it is sheltered from all winds but what blow from the easterly quarter; and if there is hard raking with such winds, a ship may slip her cable about half-flood, and sail to the westward, through *Caldy Sound*, for *Milford haven*.

Anchorage.

The best anchorage in *Caldy Road*, is where the old windmill on *Caldy* appears in the middle, between the spire of the church, and the ruinous chapel at the S. end of the Island; and *Old-castle Point*, on the main westward of *Caldy*, a ship's-length open of *St. Margaret's Island*: there you will ride on 5½ fathoms, sand and small shells, near half a mile from the shore; and between two sandy shoals, one extending N. E. from *High Cliff*, about three-quarters of a mile; and the other extending N. from *Eel Point*, at the W. end of *Caldy*, towards a-cross the Sound. The least water on these shoals is nine feet, except near the shore, where there is but six feet at low-water. The extremity of *High Cliff Bank* is extended, where *Old-castle Point* is half a sail's-breadth open to the N. of the W. end of St. *Margaret's Island*.

High Cliff Shoals. Eel Point Shoals.

Setting of Tide in Caldy Road.

In *Caldy Road*, the stream of tide sets to the westward, through *Caldy Sound*, when it is four hours of flood on the shore; and continues so till about four hours ebb; and then sets eastward for six hours. Spring-tides, when strongest here, run about three miles an hour; neap-tides one mile.

To sail through Caldy Sound from the W.

To sail from the westward, through *Caldy Sound*, for *Tenby*: in sailing from the westward, through *Caldy Sound*, for *Tenby* harbour, or road, the shoals to be avoided, are *White-hart Sand*, and *Woolhouse Rock*: to sail clear of these, keep *Old-castle Point* (which is on the main, westward of *Caldy*) about half a sail's-breadth open of the W. end of St. *Margaret's Island*, till you bring the old windmill of *Caldy* in a line with *Caldy* chapel: keep that mark on, till you bring *Old-castle Point* about a sail's-breadth open of *Giltar Point* (opposite the W. end of *Caldy*), then steer E. N. E. keeping *Old-castle Point* without *Giltar Point*, till you bring the middle of *High Cliff* on *Caldy*, in a line with the spire of *Caldy* church; keep that mark on, steering about N. N. W. till you bring a white cliff, which is at the N. end of the land at *Tenby* harbour, open with the E. end of St. *Catharine's Island*, which will lead you about a cable's-length from that Island: when you are past the Island, you may steer for *Tenby Road*, off the entry of the harbour: or, if there is tide to go in, keep about a cable's-length from the shore all along to the Pier-head, and go in.

HARBOURS.

BURRY *Harbour*.

Scar Sand. Hunter's Overfall.

Burry is fit for small vessels only, that draw not above ten or twelve feet water, and can take the ground easy. The entry to it is between *Holmes Island* and the *Scar Sand*: the *Scar Sand* dries with spring-tide only. On the W. side of *Holme's Island*, there is an over-fall, or breaking sea, which extends W. by N. from the Island, about three quarters of a mile, where the sea is very rough in blowing weather, especially with W. and S. W. winds; which, to a stranger, has the appearance of being very shallow; but there is no less water on it than 2½ fathoms. Also within the entry, about a mile eastward of *Holme's Island*, the breakers run quite a-cross the channel with ebb-tide and westerly winds.

To sail into Burry Harbour.

To sail into *Burry* harbour: at three or four hours of flood, take *Holme's Island* E. by S. or E. S. E. and keep it a cable's-length, or a cable's-length and a half, on your starboard hand, to avoid the *Scar*, then keep *Landly* church a sail's-breadth open of, or just on by *Whitford Point*, till the highest top of *Rossilly-down Hill* bears over the top of *Lanmadock Cliff*, which is about two miles eastward of *Holme's Island*, and the most remarkable Cliff there (here a buoy has been several times placed, to direct vessels the fairest where to steer north-eastward between the *Scar* and *Middle-patch*; but it has as often broke away): then keeping these marks on, sail north-eastward, and they will lead between the *Middle-patch Bank* and the *Scar Ledge*, till *Landfaint* chapel (in *Kidwelly* parish) is in a line with the W. shoulder of *Penbray Hill*, then steer S. E. along the E. side of the *Scar*, till a small white house below the *Banks of Lanmadock*, is in a line with the extremity of *Whitford Point*; there drop anchor on 2½, or three fathoms, at low-water. If it is necessary to sail farther up the harbour, take a *Pilot*; for the channel, from this anchorage eastward, is almost dry at low-water; and the sand on each side of it begins to dry at half ebb. The places where vessels most commonly lie, are at *Penclow*, or *Castle Lougher*.

Time of High-water, and Rise of the Tide.

In *Burry* harbour it is high-water, on the full and change days, at six o'clock. Spring-tides rise twenty-one feet perpendicular; neap-tide eleven or twelve.

CARMARTHEN *River*.

Large vessels may go into *Carmarthen River*, when wind and weather are favourable; but the sand and shallows lie so far from the shore, and when it blows fresh from the S. or S. W. there is so rough and breaking a sea on the bar, that it is often difficult and hazardous, even for those who are best acquainted, to sail over it. The bed of the River is all clean, and soft for vessels to ground on wherever the ebb-tide obliges them to stop, when going up to the town of *Carmarthen*: but the most convenient places are, a bight in St. *Ishmael's* parish, near the mouth of the River, opposite to *Langhaftle*, the E. end of the town of *Caedy*, *Black Pool*, and *Ginnam's Pool*.

To sail into the River through the W. Channel.

To sail into *Carmarthen River*, through the W. channel: first get sight of *Langhaftle Castle*, which is pretty remarkable, and may be seen two or three miles before you come up with the bar; at four hours of flood, take that Castle a sail's-breadth open of *Worm Head*, and keep them so, till *Laughharne* church, in *Lawn* parish, be a little eastward of *Gingam Head* there; then steer S. E. till *Landfaint* chapel bears E.; then steer E. N. E. up the channel, about a mile and a half, till *Cowcliff* appears on *Lanshyle Ward*, and bearing N. there, if unacquainted, you may stop at anchor for a Pilot, on three fathoms water; for there are no distinct marks to direct a stranger farther up, except the channel is plainly perceived. This channel is easier kept than the E. channel is, and therefore preferable to it.

To sail through the E. channel.

To sail through the E. channel: keep *Lawn* church on, or a little open of, *Gingam Head*, till *Landfaint* chapel bears E. then steer E. N. E. about a mile and a half, till *Cowcliff* is on *Lanshyle Ward*; then bearing N. there stop for a *Pilot* on three fathoms. These channels are liable to shift a little; and therefore the fore-mentioned directions will not always serve.

TENBY

From TENBY to CARDIGAN.

TENBY *Road.*

Ships that draw not above fifteen feet water, may stop in *Tenby Road*, with the wind from S. W. westward to the N. The deepest water is when the small tower, near St. *Catherine's Island*, called the *Castle of Tenby*, is in a line with the spire of *Tenby* church, then bearing about W. and the E. end of St. *Catherine's Island*, is in a line with the W. end of St. *Margaret's Island*, or *Caldy Sound*; you are then on 5½ fathoms sandy ground. Vessels that draw little water, may anchor nearer *Tenby Point*, on three fathoms.

TENBY *Harbour.*

Vessels that draw not above thirteen or fourteen feet water, may lie safe within *Tenby Pier*. They should not attempt to go in before the last quarter of flood, and should enter head and stern; because there is sometimes a great run of sea within the Harbour, particularly when the wind has blown fresh from the S. E. quarter, and then shifts suddenly to the N. W.

A Description of the Tides, Rocks, Shoals, Sand-banks, Channels, Anchoring-places, and Harbours, between TENBY *and* CARDIGAN.

C H A R T III.

Tides between TENBY *and* CARDIGAN.

TIDES. High-water, full and change, at Caldy, Milford, Grasholm, St. David's Head, and Cardigan.

On the full and change days of the moon, it is high-water, at *Caldy Island*, at 5¼; in the mouth of *Milford-haven*, at 5¾; at *Grasholm*, at 5½; at St. *David's Head*, at six; at the *Bar* of *Cardigan*, at 7½.

Rise of the Tide.

Ordinary spring-tides, from *Caldy* to *Milford haven*, rise on the shore twenty feet perpendicular; neap-tides twelve; from *Milford* to *Cardigan*, ordinary spring-tides rise thirteen feet perpendicular, neap-tides six or seven; at *Grasholm*, spring-tides rise sixteen feet perpendicular.

Directions of the Streams.

Between *Milford* and *Caldy*, the stream of flood runs eastward; from *Milford* to *Ramsey Island*, the stream runs northward along the coast, from three hours of flood on the shore, till it is three hours ebbed; between *Grasholm* and the *Smalls*, the stream turns northward, when it is four hours of flood on the shore, and continues till it is four hours ebbed; then it turns southward: the northward stream shifting gradually, as the tide advances, from N. N. W. to N. E. and the southward stream from S. S. E. to S. W.; from *Ramsey Island* to *Cardigan*, the flood sets eastward.

Velocity of the Streams.

From *Caldy* to *Long Head*, near *Milford-haven*, within a league of the shore, spring-tides, where strongest, run about three miles an hour, neap-tides one: from the N. *Bishop*, along the *Bais Shoal*, five miles an hour; along *Strumble Head* four miles an hour; between *Grasholm* and the *Smalls*, six miles. The northward stream forms an eddy on the N. side of *Grasholm*, half a mile long, within which there is very little stream of tide.

Eddy near Grasholm.

Rocks and Shoals along the Coast, from TENBY *to* CARDIGAN.

ROCKS and SHOALS.

Stackpool Shoal.

Off *Stack-pool*, and St. *Govan's Heads*, there is a sand-bank, which extends from the shore a mile and a half southward, on which, with spring-tide, and when the stream runs against the wind, there is a rough breaking sea. The greatest part of this bank has from seven to fifteen fathoms water over it; but there is one part, said to be about a mile S. W. from *Stackpool Head*, on which some say, there is not above two fathoms at low-water. This part was searched for in a fair day, but could not be found; nor could any one give marks, or particular directions for finding it.

Crow Rock.

The *Crow* is a small rock, which lies three-quarters of a mile south of *Long Head*, at the mouth of *Milford-haven*, and dries at four hours of ebb; three quarters of a mile S. E. from *Crow Rock*, there is a rock which dries with very low spring-tides only, called the *E. Crow Tar*; and another small rock, called the *W. Crow Tar*, which lies one-third of a mile N. W. by N. from the *Crow*, and S. S. W. from *Long Head*, and dries with low spring tide only. To sail without these three Rocks, or along the S. and W. sides of them; keep above a mile from the coast, near *Long Head*; or keep the E. extremity of *Scomar Island* half a sail's-breadth open of St. *Ann's Point*, or *Midlan Island* open. When *Long* bears N. E. then you may stand northward for *Milford-haven*. When the *Crow* can be seen, keep it on the W. end of *Scomar Island*, till *Long Head* bears N. E.; then you are to the westward of them all. To sail between the *Crow Rocks* and the land, keep *Pal-staar Head* a little without *Hempton Head*; which will carry you about a cable's length from *Long Head*. Vessels, however, should not attempt this Sound, when it is not necessary, in case the Heads should be mistaken; or sudden calms, or squalls of wind from the cliffs, should affect their sailing.

E. Crow Tar. W. Crow Tar.

Crow Sound.

Turbot Bank.

Turbot Bank lies about two miles W. by N. from *Long Head*, and S. from St. *Ann's Light-houses*. The least water on it is six fathoms. In moderate weather a ship may stop a tide on this Bank.

Rock near Scotsbow-island.

Near a cable's-length N. N. E. ½ E. from the *Stack*, or E. point, of *Scotsbow Island*, there is a small rock, which dries with spring-tide only: there are four fathoms water between it and the *Stack*, and five on all other sides, at half a cable's distance.

Rocks in Jack's Sound.

Jack's Sound is the channel, near *Scheamer*, between *Midlan Island* and the main, about one-third of a mile wide. In this channel there are two rocks that dry with ebb-tide daily; one of them lies more than a third over from *Midlan Island*; the other above a cable's length from the main: the common channel for small coasting vessels, is between these two rocks.

Rock always above water.

Jack's Sound, dangerous to a Stranger.

There is a small rock, always above water, which lies near the N. entry of *Jack's Sound*, on the E. side, about half a cable's-length from the point; this rock must be taken on the larboard-hand sailing from the North. Such as are not very well acquainted, ought not to attempt sailing through *Jack's Sound*, except in necessity; and then they must have a leading wind, and favourable tide, to avoid the danger that will be

occasioned

occasioned by the narrowness of the channel between the two rocks near the middle, and the rapidity of the tide there.

Rocks off Grasholm. The Smalls.
The *Smalls* are a cluster of *Rocks*, that lie about two leagues W.N.W. from *Grasholm*; one of which is always above water, and remarkable; the three rocks nearest to it are covered only at high-water with spring-tide; the other rocks dry with spring-tide only. The greatest distance of any of these rocks from the highest one is not above a mile. There is no better mark for avoiding the *Smalls*, than by keeping above a mile from the highest of them on all sides.

Hats-and-Barrels.
The *Hats-and-Barrels* lie about three miles W. from *Grasholm*, and dry about the fourth hour of ebb. To sail along the E. side of them, keep within a league of *Grasholm*. To sail along the W. side of them, keep about one-third from the highest of the *Smalls*, and two-thirds from *Grasholm*. To sail along the S. side of them, keep the highest top of *Brasdie Hill* (the highest visible in *Pembrokeshire*) out to the southward of *Grasholm*. To sail along the N. side of them, keep the southernmost light-house at St. *Ann's Point*, on the W. end of *Scoulow Island*.

Carbarthen Rocks.
Clarbarthlan Rocks lie westward of *Pencloglar Point* in *Chlearion* parish, and about a quarter of a mile N. and N. W. of *Barnberry Rocks*, which are always above water. That rock, which is N. of *Barnberry*, dries with spring-tide only; the other rock dries about the last quarter of ebb. There are two other rocks, about a mile westward of *Clarbarthlan Rocks*, off *Abergeel*, and about half a mile from the shore: to sail without, or along the N. side of these, keep three of the *Bishop Rocks* in sight, without St. *David's Head*.

About three-quarters of a mile N. from *Abercastle Creek*, there is a rocky shoal, on which the least water is three fathoms. To avoid it on the N. side, keep St. *David's Head* a sail's-breadth out by *Pencloglar Point*.

Mafras, an alleged shoal.
The *Mafras* is said to be a small shoal, or overfall, lying two or three leagues N. W. or N. W. by N. from the northmost *Bishop Rock*. In that direction and distance, and a league or two round that distance, I sounded, two several days, and found the depth from forty-two to sixty fathoms. Several ripples, or swirls of tide, were met with that had some appearance of being shallow; but on sounding them, found only eight or ten fathoms less water there, than in the neighbouring parts. *Lewis Morris*, in his draught of this coast, has given the name of *Mafras* to the *Bass Shoal*, but seems not to have examined the *Bass*. It is reported, that some have seen the sea-weeds adhering to the *Mafras*; but none now alive say so, or that any one ever sounded over it, or that any vessel ever touched it; an unusual ripple, or breaking sea, may perhaps have given rise to the opinion of a shoal being there, to which Mr. *Morris* has given the name of *Mafras*.

The Bishop Rocks.
The *Bishops* are four remarkable Rocks lying westward of *Ramsey Island*. About half between the middle of these Rocks and *Ramsey*, there are three rocks that dry before low-water; and two about three-quarters of a mile E. S. E. from the northmost *Bishop*, that dry about half-ebb. If a vessel would sail between the *Bishops* and *Ramsey*, she should keep within half a mile of *Ramsey*, to avoid the first three rocks, if they are not seen; and within a mile and a half of St. *David's Head*, to avoid the two that lie eastward of the northmost *Bishop*.

The Bass Shoal.
The *Bass* is a sand-bank, where there is an over-fall, and in blowing weather a rough breaking sea. It lies about a league northward of St. *David's Head*, is about four miles long from W. S. W. to E. N. E. and about a quarter of a mile broad. The least water found on it was 3½ fathoms at low-water, which was near the south end of the shoal; on other parts there are five or six. About the middle of the *Bass*, *Strumble Hill* bears E. ½ S. St. *David's Hill* S. the N. *Bishop* S. W. ½ W. and the W. end of *Scomar* is seen through the middle of *Ramsey Sound*. To sail between the *Bass* and the N. *Bishop*, keep within a mile of the *Bishops*; or keep St. *David's Head* N. W.

Spring-tide on this shoal, when strongest, runs about five miles an hour. It may be perceived at any time almost, by a ripple and smooth in calms, and by a high breaking sea on it in blowing weather.

Abercastle Shoal.
Abercastle Shoal lies about three-quarters of a mile north from *Abercastle Creek*: the least water on it is 3½ fathoms; to avoid it on the N. side, keep St. *David's Head* a sail's-breadth out by *Pencloglar Point*.

STOPPING PLACES. Fresh-water-west Bay.
In *Fresh water-west-Bay*, between *Stackpool Head* and *Oldcastle Head*, a ship may stop, in moderate weather, or when the wind is off the shore, on eight or ten fathoms water.

Tarbet Bank.
Or, on *Tarbet Bank*, off *Lewy Head*.

Bay N. of Lewy Head.
Or, in the middle of the Bay next northward of *Lewy Head*, about a mile from the shore, on ten or twelve fathoms.

Mufsled Bay.
Or in *Mufsled Bay*, on the S. side of St. *Bride's Bay*, on five or six fathoms water.

GOLDTOP *Road*.

Goldtop Road.
Goldtop Road is a bight on the S. side of St. *Bride's Bay*, where ships that draw not above twelve or fifteen feet water may ride safe, while the wind is any how from the E. N. E. southward to the W. The best part is about a quarter of a mile E. ½ N. from *Goldtop Head*, when the second Head westward of *Goldtop* (which has two small rocks off it) is shut in by *Goldtop Head*, and *Roch Church* bearing N. E. by N. and in a line with the S. side of the first sandy shore southward of *Newton*: there you will have 3½ fathoms sandy ground, with clay below it. Small vessels may ride more south-eastward, on two fathoms, where they will be better sheltered from W. winds.

Porthclaiy Bay.
In *Porthclaiy Bay*, E. of *Pennanmilian Point*, near *Ramsey Sound*, ships may ride safe on the N. side of *Carigrafied Island*, on seven fathoms water, with any wind, except from the S. to the W. The best anchorage is when the W. end of *Carigrafied* bears S. and in a line with *Mullen Island*, near *Scomar*. It is not advisable to anchor much farther eastward in this Bay, because the bottom is rocky near the E. end; and if the wind shall happen to freshen at the S. W. a great sea will set in, and make very hard riding, and difficult turning out.

RAMSEY *Sound*.

Ramsey Sound.
Vessels may stop a tide in *Ramsey Sound*, especially with westerly and southerly winds. The best anchorage is about one-third of a mile northward of the *Bitches Rocks*, at the middle of *Ramsey Island*, about two cable's-length from the shore, off a small bight, when *Ugenshot* (the N. E. point of *Ramsey*) bears N. N. E.; here there are seven fathoms sandy bottom. Vessels should make no unnecessary stay in this place; for the ground is in some parts foul; and there are such irregularities in the stream of tide, that if you ride by a single anchor, it is scarce possible to keep it clear; or to keep a clear hawse when moored.

Setting of Tides in Ramsey Sound.
In the middle of *Ramsey Sound*, the stream of tide begins to set northward, when it is two hours and a half flowed on the shore, and continues so till about half-ebb; then sets southward till about half flood. But near the shore, on each side of the Sound, the stream runs contrary to the stream in the middle. With spring-tide

the

the northward stream, in the middle, runs about six miles an hour when strongest; and the southward stream about four miles.

Horse-shoe Rock lies at the S. entry of *Ramsey Sound*, on the E. side, about a cable's-length and a half southward of *Penmaenmelyn Point*, and dries at half-ebb. Rocks in Ramsey Sound. [illegible] Great-horse Rock.

The *Great-horse Rock* lies about half a mile N. by E. ½ E. from *Penmaenmelyn Point*, and dries with spring-tide only. To sail along the W. side of it, keep the westmost part of *Ramsey Island* a sail's-breadth, or pull out, by *Penmaenmelyn Point*.

The *Little-horse* is a rocky shoal, which lies about a quarter of a mile N. by E. ¾ E. from the *Great-horse*; the least water on it is sixteen feet. It is avoided (as the *Great Horse*) by keeping the W. point of *Ramsey* out by *Penmaenmelyn Point*; or by keeping near the middle of the Sound. Little Horse.

In the Bay on the S. side of St. *David's Head*, when the wind is off the land, a vessel may stop a tide on five fathoms clean ground, a quarter, or half a mile, from the shore. Stop at St. David's Head.

Carrigwastad Bay is at the extremity of *Strumble Head*; and is sheltered on the N. by a peninsula, and a small island. This place is convenient to stop a tide in, when the wind is eastward of N. The best part is on seven fathoms water, about a cable's-length southward of the island, when the Sound of the island is open; in most other parts the bottom is foul. If the wind begins to breeze from the westward, a vessel that draws not above twelve feet, may sail out southward, between the island and peninsula, by keeping the middle, or somewhat nearer the island. Carrigwastad Bay.

The stream of flood, along *Strumble Head*, sets in from the westward; and, when strongest, runs about four miles an hour, making a rough breaking sea, especially when the stream runs against the wind. Stream along Strumble Head.

FISCARD *Road and Harbour*.

Fiscard Road is safe anchorage with any wind, except from the N. to the E.; the ground holds well, being clay below the sand. The best anchorage is about a quarter of a mile southward of the *Cow Rock* (which is always above water), on three fathoms at low-water; that Rock bearing N. ½ E. and a White House, which stands a little eastward of the town of *Fiscard*, S. ½ W. and open to the W. of *Penmawrrer Point*, near *Fiscard Key*. A vessel that draws ten or eleven feet water, may go up to *Fiscard Key*, at high-water spring-tide; one that draws six or seven feet may go at high-water with neap tide. Fiscard Road.

On the full and change days, it is high-water in *Fiscard Bay* at 6½. Spring-tides rise fifteen feet perpendicular; neap-tides seven. High-water in Fiscard [illegible]

Porthgwgan anchorage is on the east side of *Fiscard Bay*, near *Dinas*, and about a quarter of a mile S. of a remarkable rock, which is always above water. Here vessels may stop with easterly winds, a little northward of a small sandy cove, about 1½ cables-length from the shore, on five fathoms gravel ground, when the remarkable rock before-mentioned, bears N. ½ E. and open of the point near it. Near this anchorage, westward and southward, the bottom is clean sand, but not quite so well sheltered. [illegible] Porthgwgan anchorage.

Aberdinas anchorage is on the E. side of *Dinas Head*, off the middle of the bight where *Dinas* houses are. Here a vessel may stop, with westerly winds, on three or four fathoms water, clean ground, above two cables-length from the high-water mark, without running into the Bay. Aberdinas anchorage.

On the E. side of *Newport Bay*, a vessel may stop off *Pwll*, on clean sand, near half a mile from the shore, on three or four fathoms at low water. Newport road stop and Harbour.

The bar and channel, to *Newport Harbour*, lie about half a cable's-length from the shore, directly below the village of *Newport*. On the bar, there are thirteen feet at high-water, with spring-tide, and seven or eight at high-water neap tide; so that this harbour is fit for small vessels only. When a vessel has got over the bar, and within the mouth of the river, she may there take ground on clean sand, and lie safe, easily sheltered all weathers. There are no marks for the channel; but it may be distinguished, for the most part, by the appearance of the water on it. Entry in it.

MILFORD-HAVEN.

HARBOURS.

Milford-haven is a spacious and well sheltered arm of the sea, where fleets of the largest ships may ride in safety; the bottom, almost every where, is clean and good. There are two lights kept on St. *Ann's Point*, on the west side of the entry, to shew ships in in the night-time.

To fall in with the entry of *Milford*, keep *Lundy Island* S. ½ E.; or *Preseley Top* (the highest, or most remarkable hill visible in *Pembrokeshire*) N. E. or *Caldy Island* east, till you make *Linny Head*; about a league northward of which is the entry. In the night-time, sailing from the S. or E. take St. *Ann's* lights N. or N. ½ W. (to avoid *Crow Rock*), then steer for the lights of the entry. In sailing from the westward, the lights must be kept northward of E. until they bear N. then steer for the entry. To fall in with Milford.

The rocks and shoals to be avoided in sailing into *Milford-haven* are; the *Crow Rocks* near *Linny Head* (described page 3), *Rat Island Shoal*, *Thorny Island Shoal*, and a Shoal said to be near St. *Ann's Point*. The three last Shoals can hurt none but large ships going in, or out, about low water. Rocks near the entry of Milford.

Crow Rocks are avoided, by keeping *Caldy Island*, or St. *Govan's Head*, E. till *Linny Head* bears N. E. or St. *Ann's* light-house N. or N. ½ W. then you are westward of all the *Crow Rocks*, and may steer northward for *Milford*. Crow Rocks avoided.

Rat Island Shoal is a small rocky Shoal, which lies about a third of a mile W. of *Rat Island*, and has sixteen feet of water over it at low spring-tide. Leading-marks to it are, the *Stack Rock*, just shut in by the land of *Nangle*, near *Thorny Island*, and the houses of *Linny*, a little open of the W. end of *Sheep Island*. To sail along the W. side of this shoal, keep mid-channel, or keep *Flimston Chapel* (which is eastward of *Linny Head*) a sail's-breadth open of the W. extremity of *Sheep Island*. To sail along the N. side of it, keep the *Stack Rock* a sail's-breadth open to the N. of *Thorny Island*. Rat Island Shoal.

Thorny Shoal is a small rocky Shoal, which lies about two cables length W. by N. ½ N. from *Thorny Island*, on which the least water is seventeen feet. Leading-marks to it are, that part of the N. coast of *Nangle*, which is next to *Thorny Island*, just out by the N. side of that island; and the highest top of *Sheep Island*, at the W. end, just shut in by *Rat Island*. Therefore, to avoid *Thorny Shoal* on the W. side, keep the W. end of *Sheep Island* open of *Rat Island*; to avoid it along the N. side, keep any part of *Nangle Head* a ship's-length out to the N. of *Thorny Island*. Thorny Shoal.

There is a rocky shoal, said to lie about two cables-length south-westward from St. *Ann's Point*, and that the least water on it is about ten feet. This shoal was searched for carefully, for several hours in a calm day, but could not be found; the person, who said he had seen it, had neither sounded over it, nor taken marks on it, but seemed a man of veracity. Shoal near St. Ann's Point.

From CALDY ISLAND *to* CARDIGAN.

Anchorage in Milford, Dale Road.

The first place of anchorage in *Milford*, is *Dale Road*; this is a convenient place to stop a tide at, when the weather is moderate, or to wait a wind in the summer-time. The best anchorage for large vessels, is about a cable's-length and a half N. N. E. from *Dale Point*, where *Stacy Island* is two or three ships-length open of the Point, and *Dale* church steeple is in a line with an uneven beach, a little beyond it, called the *Castle*; there is then three fathoms muddy ground. Small vessels may ride nearer the W. side, when *Dale Point* is just on *Stacy Island*, and the steeple and castle in one, in two fathoms water. Here it is high water on the full and

High water at Dale, and rise of the tide.

change days, at 5¼; and spring tides rise fourteen feet, sometimes twenty feet perpendicular, and neap-tides twelve.

Anchorage near Nangle.

Ships may stop a tide off the E. end of *Nangle Head*, and off *Nangle Bay*, on from five to eight fathoms water: only there are some patches of foul ground to be avoided near the *Head*, and off the W. side of the Bay. The rocky ground off the W. side of *Nangle Bay*, is when *Nangle* wind-mill bears S. W. ½ S. and the *Stack Rock* N. E. ½ N. and *Bulwell Point* E. by S. ½ S. Leading marks to it are, a cross-hedge, a little westward of *Nangle Point*, in a line with the wind-mill, and a grove of trees at *Pennermouth*, in a line with *Bulwell Point*.

Hubberston Road Anchorage.

Hubberston Road is the usual, and most convenient anchorage for ships of burden. Large ships ride about mid-channel, on ten or eleven fathoms water, where there is a visible stream of tide; when *Thorny Island* appears on *Blockhouse Head*, and *Hubberston Key* N. ½ E. or *Bulwell House* S. ½ W.; or they may ride any where in the channel, within a mile or two eastward of that. Smaller ships may ride nearer *Hubberston*, on

To sail to Hubberston.

two or three fathoms, where there is smoother water, and less stream of tide. To sail to *Hubberston Road*, take *Stack Rock* on the starboard-hand, and keep about mid-channel; or keep *Thorny Island* on *Block-house Head*, till *Hubberston* bears N. by E. and *Bulwell House* S. by W. then drop anchor. To avoid the shallow

Shallow water avoided.

water and sand-bank on the *Hubberston*, or N. side, keep St. *Ann's* light houses, and the N. point of *Thorny Island* in one, till you are near a-breast of *Gellyswick*, then steer in the light-houses by *Thorny Island*. To avoid the sand bank, which is on the S. side, between *Nangle Bay* and *Pennermouth*, keep at least a cable's-length and a half from the shore of *Bulwell*, and, between *Bulwell* and *Pennermouth*, stand no nearer the shore than till the *Stack* appears in the middle of *Dale Valley*, which is a remarkable saddle, or gap in the hills above *Dale*.

Banks between Hubberston and Neyland.

In sailing from *Hubberston Road* to *Neyland*, the shoals and rocks to be avoided are, the bank between *Bulwell* and *Pennermouth* (mentioned in the end of the last paragraph); a ledge extending a cable's-length southward from *Ware Point*; the *Cars Rocks*, and a sand-bank northwards and eastwards of them; and a ledge extending south-westward from *Neyland Point*, about a cable's-length.

Neyland Bank.

The sand-bank, on the S. side of the channel, between *Bulwell* and *Neyland*, is avoided (as was said before) while the *Stack* is on the middle, or a little southward of the middle, of *Dale Valley*.

Ware Ledge.

The *Stack* on, or a little northward of, *Dale Valley*, clears *Ware Ledge*.

The Cars.

The *Cars Rocks* lie about a quarter of a mile N. ½ W. from the tower, or watch-house, on the fort, and dry at the fourth hour of ebb. To avoid them, and the shoal northward of them, on which the least water is nine feet, keep *Ware Point* just on, or a little eastward of the *bluff Head* at *Bulwell*. You are abreast of the *Cars*, when the W. end of the fort is in a line with the E. end of *Peter Church*, near the fort.

Bank E. of the Cars.

About a quarter of a mile E. of the *Cars*, there is a sand-bank, about a cable and a half long, on which the least water is nine feet. There are no marks to lead along the N. side of this bank, and that off the *Cars*; therefore, ships sailing in this channel, should take care to have sufficient tide to go over them.

Neyland anchorage.

The best place of anchorage off *Neyland*, for large ships, is when *Ware Point* is about a ship's-breadth open of *Neyland Point*, and *Barnlake* bearing N. ½ W. and *Neyland Key* W. by N. ½ N. on eight fathoms, muddy ground. Between that anchorage and the shore, there is some foul ground, which must be avoided; it lies about half a cable's-length from the shore at *Barnlake*, when *Neyland Key* bears W. by S. and a lime-kiln at *Barnlake* N. by W.

Ferry Anchorage.

Small vessels, that have no business at *Neyland*, may anchor in the Bay, on the side opposite to *Neyland*, about a cable's length from the shore, when the *Ferry Point* bears E. by S. ½ S. and *Barnlake* N. by W. ½ W. on three fathoms at low-water; where they will have less tide.

There is water sufficient for the largest ships to go six or seven miles above *Neyland*, and the anchorage good most of the way. Small vessels, with spring tides, may go up to the town of *Haverford-west*.

SOLVACH *Creek*.

Solvach Creek is on the N. side of St. *Bride's Bay*, about three-quarters of a mile N. E. from *Stiches*, a high remarkable rock in the sea. About high water, vessels that draw ten or twelve feet, may go up and lie a-ground near the key. In the mouth of this harbour, vessels may ride on three fathoms at low water, when the wind does not blow between the S. and W.; but, from that quarter, a great swell and run of sea sets in,

Shoal within out of ... ;

which makes it very hard riding. Sail in along the E. side of *Stiches*, to avoid a rocky shoal that lies about half a mile W. by S. ½ S. from that rock; on this shoal the least water is six feet. A leading mark to it is, the highest part of *Skerdi*, and *Stiches Rocks*, in a line. The entry of *Solvach* is near two cables-length wide; and about half a cable's-length from the shore, on each side, there is a small rock always above water; between

Best channel in.

that on the E. side and the shore, is dries at low-water. The safest and best channel into the harbour is, to take the rock, which is on the W. side of the entry, on the starboard-hand, and to keep rather nearer the shore than to the rock: the least water in this channel is three fathoms. The channel between the two rocks is a little nearer the westmost of them than to the eastmost; here two fathoms is the least water.

PORTCLAIS *Creek*.

Portclais Harbour is the mouth of a rivulet, near St. *David's*, where very small vessels, that draw not above six or seven feet, may go in about high-water, and lie a-ground, sheltered from all winds, but those from S. to S. W. which set in a swell and run of the sea into this Creek. Off this Creek, about half a mile from the

Carreg-draggen, and Carreg-... ;

shore, there are two small rocks, *Carreg-fraeder* and *Carreg-trey*, which lie about S. E. from *Carrickgrenan Island*; the first about a quarter of a mile from it, and dries with spring-tide only; the other about three-quarters of a mile, and dries at the last quarter of ebb. A leading mark to *Carreg-trey*, is a hummock, or heap of stones, on the highest hill of *Ramsey*, W. by N. ½ N. and in a line with the highest part of *Carrickgrenan Island*. To sail along the S. side of *Carreg-trey*, keep the hummock on *Ramsey Hill*, in a line with the W. extremity of *Carrickgrenan Island*.

CARDIGAN *Road and Harbour.*

In moderate weather a ship may stop in *Cardigan Road*, in any part thereof, without the bar, above two cables-length from the shore: with easterly winds the E. side should be preferred; and the W. side with westerly winds.

High-water at Cardigan Bar. Rise of the Tide there.

It is high-water, full and change days, at *Cardigan Bar*, at 7¾.

Ordinary spring-tides rise thirteen feet perpendicular, neap-tides six or seven.

Cardigan Harbour is fit for small vessels only, that draw not above ten feet water, and can lie aground easy. The channel over the bar is now a little nearer the E. than to the W. side of the Bay, and is liable to shift. In this channel there are fourteen feet at high-water with spring-tide, and eight or nine with neap-tides; but before a vessel gets into sufficient shelter over the bar, there is not above ten feet in that channel with spring-tide. A leading-mark over the bar is, *Penrergid Point* (a low sandy Point on the E. side of the river, about three-quarters of a mile above the bar), bearing S. by E. ½ E. and a small hedge, about three miles off, just open with the Point: keep the hedge and Point so till you are over the bar, and in smoother water. To sail from thence up to *Penrergid*, where the channel turns south-westward, take *Penrergid Point* a little on the E. end of the hedge. A little westward of that Point, you may stop for a tide, or for a pilot to carry you higher up to the Pool, near *St. Dogmael's Village*, or to the town of *Cardigan*. In the Pool a vessel, by making fast to the trees on the W. side, may ride on 4½ fathoms the least water.

A Description of the Tides, Rocks, Shoals, Anchoring-places, and Harbours, between CARDIGAN *and* ABERISTWITH.

CHART IV.

Tides between CARDIGAN *and* ABERISTWITH.

TIDES. High-water, full and change.

On the full and change days of the moon, it is high-water on the shore, near *Cardigan*, at 7¾; at *New-key Head*, at 7½; at *Aberistwith*, at 8½: a league or two from these shores, the stream is an hour, or an hour and a half, later in turning.

Rise of the Tides. Direction of the streams.

Along this part of the coast, spring-tides rise thirteen feet perpendicular, neap-tides six or seven.

The stream of flood here comes from the westward, along *Strumble Head*, and from thence sets eastward toward the *Patches Shoal*, off *Aberistwith*; and then northward along the coast.

Velocity.

Near *Strumble Head*, spring-tides, when strongest, run about four miles an hour; along other Heads and Points, not more than two miles; and, on the *Patches*, three miles an hour.

ROCKS and SHOALS.

Along the S. coast of *Cardigan Bay*, there are several ledges, or rocky flats, which dry every ebb-tide; and extend above a quarter of a mile from the shore; but there are no rocks, nor shoals, without the head-lands, except the *Patches* and *Sarn-gwrtha Shoals*.

Patches and Sarn-gwrtha Shoals.

The *Patches* and *Sarn-gwrtha* may be reckoned but one shoal, though they go under two names, and are divided by a swash, or narrow channel, between them; *Sarn-gwrtha*, which is the E. part of this shoal, extends about three miles W. by N. from the shore, at the fishing house in *Warchley*, and, with spring-tides, dries for above a mile from the shore; the rest of it has from four to twelve feet water over it, at low spring-tide.

The *Patches* extend about six miles farther westward; the E. end of which is called the *North Patch*, of which a small part, near the *South*, dries at low-water with spring-tide: the rest of this shoal, to the westward, has from seven to twelve feet water over it, at low-water; except near the N. W. end, where there is but a foot and a half. The *Sarn* and *Patches* consist, for the most part, of stones, like large paving-stones. The channel, that divides them, is near half a mile broad, and has three fathoms the least water in the middle: to sail through this swash, or channel, keep the custom-house of *Aberistwith* just open with *Pengrub-ugan Point*, which is at the N. side of the castle of *Aberistwith*. The custom-house is at the W. end of the town, and appears whiter, and more distinct, than other houses there.

To sail through the Swash.

At that part of the N. *Patch*, which dries with spring-tide, *Dinas Hill* bears S. E. ½ S. *New-key Head* S. W. and the fishing-house E. ½ S.

Bearings at N. Patch.

To avoid the W. end of the *Patches*, sailing along it northward, or southward; keep *New-key Head* S. W. by S.; or *Sarn-badrig Point* in a line with the N. top of *Snowdon Hill*, and bearing N. E. by N. ½ N. *Snowdon Hill* is the most remarkable mountain at the E. end of *Caernarvonshire*. To avoid the W. end of the *Patches* sailing along it on the S. side, to or from *Aberistwith*; keep *Aberistwith Castle* E. by S. where it will be in a line with a remarkable hummock on one of the remotest hills.

To avoid the W. end of the Patches.

On the *Patches*, spring-tide runs about three miles an hour when strongest. Flood sets N. N. E. and ebb S. S. W. each beginning an hour and a half later than the stream along the shore.

Tide on the Patches.

ANCHORING-PLACES. Aberporth Road.

In *Aberporth Road*, with the wind between S. and W. N. W. vessels may stop in three fathoms water, clean sandy bottom. The best part is about a cable's length and a half from *Ogovraith Head*, when *Crabbeth Head* bears N. W. by W. In this Road a vessel should not continue long, lest the wind should freshen between the N. W. and the N. E.; for then there is a great sea in this Bay. S. E. winds make a ground-swell, which does not break but on the shore.

New-key Road.

In *New-key Road*, a vessel may ride pretty well sheltered, while the wind is from the W. N. W. westward to the S. E. The best part to anchor in, is where *Penrwgle Point*, and the house which is a little westward of it, are in a line, and bearing W. by N. about a cable's-length and a half from the shore, on 2½ fathoms at low-water. It is not advisable to lie long in this Road, lest the wind should blow between the N. W. and N. E.; for such winds make a great sea in this Bay; S. E. winds make a great hollow sea, or ground-swell in it. About half way between this place of anchorage, and the mouth of *Chwinimo Rivulet*, there is a rock which dries with spring-tide only.

Rock in New-key Bay.

ABERISTWITH

ABERISTWITH *Harbour*.

HARBOURS.

Aberystwith Harbour is a narrow creek, not fit for vessels that draw above nine or ten feet water; and these must have spring-tide to go over the bar. The bar lies very near the shore, a-cross the entry; so that when there is a swell on it, a vessel has the sea right a-stern, and is soon over it and out of danger. There is a perch placed, about a cable's-length within the bar, and a white moveable board on the land beyond it; which being taken in a line, they lead right over the bar. If a vessel is seen off this coast in the evening, the people of the place always take care to put up two lights; one on the perch, and another on the white board, for a direction over the bar when it is dark. *Aberystwith Harbour* may be distinguished at four leagues distance by *Dinas Hill*, which rises steep on the S. end: also by the ruinous castle at the N. W. end of the town; and, when nearer the bar, by a black tapering rock, which stands at the confluence of the two rivers, *Ridol* and *Istwith*.

Leading marks in.

Distinguished at a distance.

A Description of the Tides, Rocks, Shoals, Channels, Anchoring-places, and Harbours, on the E. and N. Sides of CARDIGAN BAY, *between* ABERISTWITH *and* BARDSEY ISLAND.

C H A R T V.

Tides between ABERISTWITH *and* BARDSEY ISLAND.

TIDES.

Time of High-water.

On the east, and north coast of *Cardigan Bay*, it is high-water on the full and change days of the moon, at eight o'clock.

Rise of the Tide.

Ordinary spring-tides rise thirteen feet perpendicular, and neap-tides six or seven.

Directions of the Stream.

The stream of flood along the E. side of *Cardigan Bay* runs northward, and the stream of ebb southward. Along the N. side of *Cardigan Bay*, the stream of flood runs eastward, and ebb westward.

Velocity of the Stream.

In *Cardigan Bay*, the stream of tide does not run above one mile an hour, when strongest, except over the shoals, where it runs two or three miles.

ROCKS and SHOALS.

The *Patches*, and *Sarnginnolis Shoals*, are described in the preceding chart, to which we refer.

Sarn-bad Shoal.

Sarn-bad Shoal is composed of large stones, and extends about three miles westward from *Sarn-bad Point*, at the mouth of *Sound Harbour*, in *Merionethshire*. At low-water, with spring-tide, it dries in scattered stones for near a mile from the shore: the rest never dries; but in some parts has only two feet; and toward the west end six, eight, or twelve feet water over it at low spring-tide.

How avoided.

This shoal is avoided along the N. side, while the top of *Cardervidrish Hill* is seen over the tops of the high hills, next W. of it; if *Cardervidrish* appears over the low hills, next S. of these, it will lead on *Sarn-bad*. It is avoided along the W. end, sailing northward or southward, while *Aberdovy Point* bears S. E., or when a high hill up *Barmouth River*, with a conspicuous hummock on the top of it, is seen without *Penglas Point*: *Penglas* is a low green Point, on the S. side of *Barmouth Bay*.

Sarn-badrach Shoal.

Sarn-badrach, or the *Causeway*, is a long narrow shoal, which begins about a mile from the shore of *Llanbedrog* parish, and extends W. by S. about three leagues. For the most part it consists of small stones, like paving-stones, and is not above a cable's-length broad, except toward the W. end. On the W. end there are several large stones, or rocks, that dry at low-water with spring-tides, one of which appears as large as a small yacht. The E. end dries, with very low spring-tides, for two or three miles. On the edge of this shoal, all along, where a ripple, or over-fall appears, there is not above two or three feet of water at low spring-tides, and in some parts not above one foot. About a mile and a half eastward of the W. extremity, there is a patch of sand and small stones only, about a cable's-length square, which dries at low spring-tide. About a mile south-eastward and south-westward of the W. end, where the largest rocks are seen, there is not above nine feet at low water.

[illegible]

Near the W. extremity of *Sarn-badrach*, *Bardsey Island* bears N. W. by W. *Penkilan Head*, in *Carnarvonshire*, N. W. by N. and *Sugar-loaf Hill*, near it, about a ship's-length out by *Penkilan Head*.

[illegible]

To avoid the W. end of this shoal, sailing southward or northward, keep *Penkilan Head* N. N. W. ½ W. or *Rywal Hill* N. by E. *Rywal* is a high tapering Hill in *Carnarvonshire*, which extends six or seven miles up the country, between two other hills, which are a little less than it.

Along the S. side.

To avoid the W. end of *Sarn-badrach*, along the S. side, sailing eastward toward *Barmouth*, keep *Sugar-loaf Hill* (which is near the W. corner of *Porthneigel Bay*) two ships-length out by *Penkilan Head*. To sail between the W. end of it and *Studwal's Road*, keep *Penkilan* N. N. W. till you are within two leagues of the Head, then steer for the Road.

[illegible]

To sail near the S. side of *Sarn-badrach*, eastwards toward *Barmouth Harbour*, keep *Cardervidrish Hill* S. E. ½ E. (*Cardervidrish* is the highest, and most remarkable hill above *Barmouth*): or keep *Mellvern Hill* (which is a round smooth Hill, above *Castlegwithal House*) E. by N. or covering, or just discovering, the N. end of an irregular, but level-topped hill behind it; which forms a remarkable gap, or valley, with another tapering and higher hill next northward of *Mellvern Hill*. When you are about the middle of the *Sarn*, then almost the whole of that flat-topped hill may be taken out by *Mellvern*, if necessary.

[illegible]

About a third of a mile S. W. from the largest stone, at the W. end of this *Sarn*, there is a small rock which just appears with very low springs. Also about a quarter of a mile from the N. side of the E. end, there is a bank of sand, on which there is not above four feet at low-water.

[illegible]

Within a cable's length of the shallow edge of *Sarn badrach*, the compass was affected all along, with magnetism; which made it sometimes stand many degrees wrong, and sometimes quite reversed the points. At the distance of two cables this was not sensible, the compass then pointing true. This was first discovered near the E. end, by the card turning suddenly quite round, when nothing extraordinary was near it, or nobody had touched the box. The experiment was frequently repeated along the shoal, and the compass always varied, when within a cable's-length of the edge of the shoal, but not at the distance of two cables-length from it.

The

From ABERISTWITH *to* BARDSEY ISLAND.

The S. bank of Bardsey.

The S. bank of *Bardsey* is an over-fall, or shallow sand-bank, which shews itself by a ripple in calms, and by a rough breaking sea in blowing weather. It begins about two and a half miles south from the S. end of *Bardsey Island*; and extends from thence above two miles southward, in three or four separate patches; none of which are above a quarter of a mile broad. The least water found on it, was at the N. end, where there was four fathoms at low-water: on other parts there are five for the most part, and six or eight near the edges of the over-falls, on each side. At the N. end of the S. bank, *Bardsey Hill* bears N. by E. and *Penrisian Point* E. by N. nearly. On this shoal the stream of tide, from low-water on the shore, till 4½ hours of flood, came from the W. side of *Bardsey* to the bank; and from thence ran S. E. by E. about two miles an hour, most of the time. This stream is called ebb, because it comes from the northward; as ebb in this neighbourhood commonly does; but it is really flood, for the water on the bank continued to rise all that time; perhaps it runs eastward with ebb tide likewise. At half-tide the largest ship cannot touch the bank; but to avoid the rough sea that may be on it, keep either within two miles of *Bardsey*, where there is nothing to be feared; or two leagues from it, on the south side of the shoal.

Morva-main, and Cefnmain, fictitious shoals.

Morva-main, and *Cefnmain*, are mentioned by *Lewis Morris*, and inserted in his draughts of *Wales*, as two shoals on the W. side of *Bardsey*: but the fishermen on *Bardsey* said, they had never heard of any shoal called *Morva-main*; and that *Cefnmain* was the edge of the eddy off the S. W. point of *Bardsey*, where there is a rough breaking sea in blowing weather; but no less water over it than twelve fathoms. However, the depth of the water along the W. side of *Bardsey*, was minutely examined two several fair days, but no shallows were found. The counter-tides along the edge of the eddy, making the sea often rough there, probably gave rise to *Morris's* mistake; as it is not likely that he ever sounded the depths, either on that side of the island, or on the S. side, on what he calls the *Triangle Bank*.

On the E. side of Cardigan Bay. ANCHORING-PLACES IN HARBOURS.

Along the east side of *Cardigan Bay*, the ground is all clean sand (the *Sarns* excepted) and the water of a moderate depth; so that when the wind is off the shore, or the weather moderate, vessels may stop a tide any where. If they are going into a harbour, it is most convenient to stop near the entry on three or four fathoms at low-water.

ABERDOVY *Harbour*.

Aberdovy Harbour, once a vessel has got into it, is very safe, and convenient for small vessels that draw not above eight or nine feet of water; for such may ride a-float off the town, about half a cable's-length from the shore. The bar and channel leading in are liable to shift. Some years ago the channel lay in straight to the anchorage at the town: now the entry is shifted toward the S. and lies in N. N. E. for about half a mile, and then runs E. by S. along the coast to the town. The least water on the bar, in the best of the channel, this winter 1769 (for the depth varies, when the channel varies), was four feet; but no vessel, above high-water, should rely on more than the ordinary rise of the tide (thirteen feet at high-water spring-tides, and ten with neaps), because of the difficulty of keeping in the deepest; for there are neither buoys, perches, nor distant land-marks, to lead a stranger through it. Commonly vessels lie a-ground on smooth sand near the houses, to avoid the inconveniency of riding in a tide-way, which, in this anchorage, is very strong; the stream of ebb, when strongest, running about four miles an hour, the stream of flood about two miles.

Stream of Tide in the anchorage. To sail over the Bar.

To sail over *Dovy Bar*, as it is at present, up to the anchorage of the town; take three quarters of flood, and keep some part of *Dinas Hill* (at *Aberistwith*) in sight, till you bring the N. side of the river, which lies eastward of *Aberdovy*, to bear E. by N.; keep that course, and you will see a hill about three miles from the shore of *Aberdovy*, with two sharp tops near each other, on the highest of which there is a small turret built, take that top N. E. by E. sail in that direction, till you perceive by the smoothness of the water where the bar and channel lies; continue sailing N. E. by E. in the smoothest water, till *Penrhingwerh Point* (the eastmost of two Points above *Aberdovy*), appears in a line with the south end of a regular hillock, at the narrow part of the river, eastward of *Aberdovy*, at the fetching-house; then steer E. by S. for *Aberdovy*, and anchor off the town about a cable's-length from the shore, on nine feet the least water: moor so as to ride E. or W. with the stream.

There is a small turret of turf, built on the top of the banks, westward of *Aberdovy*, which when taken in a line with the turret, on the two-topped hill before mentioned, leads in over the bar; but the turret on the banks is so small, and appears on land behind it, that a stranger will seldom be able to see it. Two moveable conspicuous signals, one on the shore, the other above the banks, to be shifted as the channel shifts, would make it very safe sailing over this bar into sufficient shelter, when with fresh westerly winds a vessel could not keep the sea. The sand on the N. side of the channel breaks off the sea and smooths it.

Aberdovy distinguished at a distance.

Aberdovy may be distinguished at a distance, by its position from *Cadernidris Hills*, being the first remarkable opening in the land southward of *Cadernidris*.

BARMOUTH *Harbour*.

Barmouth Harbour is fit for small vessels only, such as draw not above nine or ten feet water; and these must sail over the bar, about high-water, with spring-tide, and when the sea is not very rough there.

The North Bar.

There are two Bars and channels that lead into *Barmouth*, the *North Bar* and the *South Bar*; of which the South is the safest, and the easiest found, though the other is broadest, and has a foot of more water on it. The *South Bar* has only one foot on it at low spring-tide, the other two; but the last is so liable to vary, that the people of *Barmouth* that have been a week from home, seldom venture to sail over it, till a pilot comes off from the town to carry them in; except at spring-tide, and when the vessel draws not above seven feet of water. Besides, on the *North Bar*, in blowing weather, there are more breakers to be sailed through than on the *South Bar*. At present (1769) the best channel over the *North Bar*, is when the point of the *Black Rock* at the town bears E. ½ S. Ten feet is all the depth on the Bar that ought to be relied on at high-water, with spring-tide, allowing four feet for the fall, or hollow, of the sea; this Bar being very rarely without a great swell, or breakers on it.

The South Bar.

On the *South Bar*, there are never more than one great wave or two, till you are over it, and in smooth water. To sail over this Bar, take the last quarter of flood, and keep the perch (which may be seen near half a mile within the Bar) on the beachy point of *Penrhin*, till you are over the Bar: take the perch on the larboard hand going up, about ½ of a cable's-length, and steer between *Penrhin Point*, and the small island near it, but nearest the Point: turn round the E. end of that island for the town of *Barmouth*, and anchor close under the houses, where you will lie a-ground on clean sand out of the stream of tide.

Anchorage near Barmouth.

When a vessel gets within the bar, she can receive no damage, though she touches the ground: but if a vessel cannot sail up to the town, for want of wind or tide, there are two or three fathoms water in the channels, near each side of the island, where she may ride; though here the stream of tide is pretty strong.

Tide at Barmouth.

It is high water at *Barmouth* at eight, full and change days.

From BARDSEY ISLAND *to* PULCHELI.

Ordinary spring-tides rise thirteen feet perpendicular; neap-tides six or seven.

Barmouth distinguished at sea. The *Bay of Barmouth* may be distinguished at a distance, by *Caderidris Hill*, which is the highest, and most remarkable mountain in that neighbourhood, and appears with two tops; the southernmost of which is highest; and, when seen from the westward, is in a line with the north side of the entry of *Barmouth*.

MOCHRIS *Creek.*

Mochris is a small creek, two miles northward of *Sarn-badrick Shoal*, where small vessels that draw six or seven feet water may go in when the sea is smooth on the bar, and lie aground safe. The bar, at entry, is commonly rough and breaking, very narrow, and has about one foot of water on it at low spring-tide.

TRATH-MAUR, *and* TRATH-BACH *Harbours.*

These two places lie within one entry, and are fit for small vessels only, and these can go in only when the weather is moderate; for the channel is crooked and variable; the bar lies far from the land, and commonly has a great breaking sea on it. On the bar, where the channel begins, there are two or three feet of water at low spring-tide; but, a little above that, a sand-bank rises in the middle of the channel, which dries at low water with spring-tide. As the channel is uncertain, no vessel, that draws above seven feet, should go into this Bay; and when they go, should have three-quarters of flood, and smooth water; except the channel has been examined immediately before, and perches set up along it, or land-marks taken at the several turnings.

Tides, Races, Overfalls, and Rocks, near BARDSEY ISLAND.

Tides near Bardsey Island. On the shore of *Bardsey*, it is high-water at eight, on full and change days.

Spring-tides rise thirteen or fourteen feet perpendicular; neap six or seven.

Streams of tide. The stream of flood, near the W. side of *Bardsey*, runs northward; near the N. side, eastward; along the E. side, north-westward; near the S. end, scarce sensible; and on the south bank E. S. E.; the stream, through the middle of the Sound of *Bardsey*, runs north-westward, till it has past the Island, then turns more westerly; and continues so, probably, until it meets the main stream of flood between *Ireland* and *Wales*, which runs N. N. E. The stream, in the middle of *Bardsey Sound*, does not begin to run N. W. till three hours after low-water on the shore: it begins at the same time on the W. side: the stream of ebb does the contrary. This stream, when strongest, runs about seven miles an hour; therefore the Sound ought not to be attempted with a contrary spring-tide before the stream begins to slacken. Near the land, on the N. side of the Sound, there is a counter-tide, which begins to run contrary to the principal stream of flood, about two hours before the stream in the middle turns. One who is acquainted with this, may get through the Sound eastward to a harbour, when another is carried out to sea westward.

That part of the stream of flood, which runs near the N. side of *Bardsey*, within *Maen bigel Rock*, turns south-westward at the N. W. point of the Island, and runs so till it meets *Cafnewnan*, or the stream that comes along the S. W. point of the Island, off the middle of the west side, about a mile and a half from the shore; and, by that junction, forms a large eddy, within which there is little stream. The limits of this eddy is easily distinguished by a curved line of rough breaking sea along it. The stream without this eddy, may run about four miles an hour when strongest.

Overfall off Braichypulch Head, Off *Braichypulch Head*, the stream of ebb runs south-eastward through *Bardsey Sound*, and makes a rough breaking sea there like an overfall, though there is no shallow. Off that Head the stream is rough likewise in blowing weather, but not so rough as the ebb.

and one near Aberdaron Bay. There is also an over-fall, or race, on the N. side of the Sound, near the rock which is always above water, that lies about half a mile from *Aberdaron Bay*; but the water is sufficiently deep there.

Rocks near Bardsey Island. Maen-bigel. Carreg-ddu. Shoal near Maen-bigel. *Maen-bigel* is a small rock, which lies about a quarter of a mile from the N. W. point of *Bardsey*, and is covered with spring-tide only; as is also *Carreggaranw Rock*, which lies off the middle of the W. side of the Island. About a cable's-length N. W. from *Maen-bigel*, there is a small shoal, which commonly shews itself by the breakers about half ebb.

Anchoring-places from BARDSEY *to* PULCHELI.

Aberdaron Bay. In *Aberdaron Bay* a ship may stop any where in moderate weather but it is not safe to ride long there in winter, or in blowing weather, especially with S. or S. W. winds; for the ground is, for the most part, gravel, or gravel and sand, which does not hold well in hard gales. The best part to anchor in, is about half a mile from the head of the Bay, when *Aberdaron* church bears N. near the middle of the Bay, on four fathoms water. If it begins to blow from the S. or S. W. run for *Studwal's Road* in time. In this Bay, it is high-water on full and change days at 8¼. Spring-tides rise thirteen feet perpendicular.

Porth-nevil Bay. In the mouth of *Porth-nevil Bay* (by some called *Hell's Mouth*), a ship may stop any where in moderate weather, but should not go far up the Bay, nor lie long in it, any time of the year; for a great sea sets into it with W. and S. W. winds, and the ground does not hold well in blowing weather. When it begins to blow from the S. or S. W. run for *Studwal's Road*.

STUDWAL'S *Road.*

Studwal's Road. *Studwal's Road* is a good place of anchorage, of easy access, and fit for ships or vessels of any size: it is sufficiently sheltered from all winds, but the E. and S. E. which are seldom so violent as winds from the opposite quarter; and the anchor-ground is very good, being sand with strong clay a little below it. When ships from the westward, or between *Ireland* and *Wales*, are overtaken with hard gales from the western quarter, this is the safest place to run for, when they are not sure of getting into *Milford Haven* with day-light.

Rock in Studwal's Road. There is nothing to be feared in sailing into *Studwal's*, but one small rock, which dries at half ebb, and lies about a quarter of a mile eastward from *Studwal's Islands*. This rock is about half a cable's length long from S. to N.; and when there is any wind, is always to be seen either dry, or by a swell on it, or by the breakers. It bears S. E. by E. from the south end of the eastmost *Studwal's Island*, and is avoided on the W. side, by keeping within a cable's-length and a half, or within one cable-length of that Island; it is avoided along the S. end, while *Penkilan Head* is two ships-length out by the westmost of the two Islands: when past it, on the N. side, when the S. end of the E. Island bears W. and may steer straight in for the Road.

[illegible] In sailing between the westmost of these two Islands and the main, keep at least half a cable's length from the main side. In sailing between the two Islands, keep the middle, or nearest the E. Island, to avoid a narrow ledge of rocks, which runs N. E. near half a cable's-length from the N. end of the W. Island.

In *Studwal's Road*, the best anchorage for large ships is, when the west Island bears S. by W. and the black point of *Penrhyn-du* W. S. W.; or off the middle of the *Sandy Bay*, between *Black Point* and *Aber-soch River*, on four, or 4½ fathoms. Very large ships may ride farther eastward, on five, or 5½ fathoms; and small vessels may ride nearer the shore, on three, or 3½ fathoms at low-water. Anchorage.

In *Studwal's*, it is high-water on full and change days at eight. Spring-tides rise thirteen feet; neap-tides six or seven. The stream of tide in the Road is scarce sensible; between the Islands it runs about a mile and a half when strongest. Tides.

Studwal's Road may be distinguished at sea, by its position from *Bardsey Island*, and from *Penkilan Head*; and, when near it, by the two *Studwal's Islands*. Studwal's Road how distinguished.

POLCHELI *Harbour*.

This harbour is fit for small vessels only. It lies about five miles north-eastward from *Studwal's Road*. The entry to it may be distinguished from thence by the *Gimblet* (a rocky peninsula that forms the S. side of the entry). To sail into this Harbour; take three-quarters of flood, keep the *Gimblet* on your larboard-hand, about half a cable's-length off, and anchor in the bight of the *Gimblet*, making fast to a ring in the rock, or laying one anchor on the shore. Two feet is the least water on the bar at the point of the *Gimblet*. Spring-tides rise about thirteen feet perpendicular; neap tides six or seven. Spring-tides, when strongest, run about four miles an hour near the anchorage at the *Gimblet*; so that vessels must lie as near the *Gimblet* as they can, to be the less in the stream. Polcheli Harbour. Tides.

When small vessels, or such as draw not above ten or twelve feet, find it hard riding in *Studwal's Road*, they may run up to *Polcheli* after half-flood, where they will lie safe and easy, on clean sand, either near the *Gimblet*, or farther up the Harbour.

NAUTICAL DESCRIPTIONS

OF THE

COAST of NORTH WALES.

AND FROM THENCE TO

St. BEE'S HEAD *in* CUMBERLAND.

A Description of the Tides, Rocks, Shoals, Channels, Anchoring-places, and Harbours, in CAERNARVON BAY, *from* BARDSEY *to* HOLY-HEAD.

CHART VII.

Tides between BARDSEY *and* HOLY-HEAD. TIDES.

IT is high-water on the shore, opposite to *Bardsey*, at 8½ on the full and change days; at *Nevin* and *Caernarvon Bay*, at nine; in *Holy-head Bay*, at 9½. Time of High-water.

On this part of the coast, ordinary spring-tides rise thirteen feet perpendicular, extraordinary fifteen feet. Rise of the Tides.

The flood-tide comes from the S. W. and ebb from the N. E. and, within a league of the shore, does not run above a mile and a half an hour, when strongest, except in the rivers and narrow channels. Direction and Velocity of the Stream.

On the coast between *Bardsey* and *Holy-head Island*, there are several ledges, or shelving rocks that extend about a quarter of a mile from the shore; but no rocks or shoals that lie at a greater distance, except those near the bar of *Caernarvon*, which will be described with that river; two or three rocks in *Craig-[illegible] Bay*, near *Holy-head Island*, *Carrig-holad Rocks*, near the S. end of *Holy-head Island*, and *Maenpifcar Rock*, near a mile from the shore of *Rhoscolyn* in that Island, which dries about three-quarters of ebb, and bears from *Rhoscolyn Hill* (on which there is a [illegible]) N. W. by N. These Rocks being out of the track of shipping, and exhibited in the draft, a further description is unnecessary. ROCKS and SHOALS. Rocks near Holy-head Island.

The *Bay of Caernarvon* has, in most parts, a clean sandy bottom, and little stream of tide; so that vessels may stop almost any where a mile or two from the shore, in moderate weather, and the wind off the land; but the ground is not strong enough to hold sufficiently in blowing weather, especially with westerly winds, which raise a great sea in this Bay. ANCHORING-PLACES and HARBOURS. Bay of Caernarvon.

PORTHDIN-

From BARDSEY *to* HOLY-HEAD.

PORTHDINLLAYN *Harbour and Road.*

Porthdinllayn Harbour is fit for small vessels only, that draw not above ten feet water, and can lie a-ground easy; such may get within shelter of the pier at high-water, with neap-tides; with spring-tide there are two feet more within the pier head. The *Dublin* packets, when overtaken with strong N. W. winds, have sometimes run for this Harbour, and found shelter in it when they could not get into *Holy-head.*

Wheafter Rock. About a quarter of a mile eastward of *Porthdinllayn Point*, there is a small rock, called *Wheafter*, which dries at three-quarters of ebb. To avoid it coming in towards the harbour, keep above a quarter of a mile from the Point, till you bring *Bodeilias Road* in a line with the top of *Carnmadryn Hill* (which is a remarkable Hill, three miles south-westward of *Porthdinllayn*), then steer for the pier-head. The Road may be easily perceived, beginning near a small stored house, which stands below the banks about half a mile south-eastward of the pier.

Anchorage in the Bay. You may stop a tide in the Bay of *Porthdinllayn*, where the forementioned high-road is in a line with *Carnmadryn Hill*, about two cables-length from the shore, on 3½ or four fathoms, at low-water: the ground is clean, but does not hold well in blowing weather.

NEVYN *Harbour and Road.*

Nevyn Harbour is fit for very small vessels only, which draw not above six or seven feet water; for the pier-head dries about half-ebb. You may stop about half a mile from the shore, on three fathoms, nearly off the middle of the Bay; or nearer the pier, on two fathoms, when *Nevyn Point* bears on the banks of *Porthdinllayn*. The ground in this anchorage does not hold well in hard gales of wind.

CAERNARVON *Harbour and Bar.*

Vessels, that draw twelve feet of water, may sail into *Carnarvon Harbour* about high-water, with neap-tides, if they keep the channel; and may ride safe within the river, about one-third of a mile above *Abermenay Point*, on four or five fathoms, good ground.

The Bar. The *Bar of Caernarvon* is never quite dry, but there is not above a foot, or two, of water on it at low spring-tide. To sail over it along the N. or east-side, in order to spread the tide; keep *Holy-head Hill* without the little island at *Chlanegwithan Point.*

Rocks near Chlanchain Point. Shoal near it. About a cable's-length and a half S. S. W. from the extremity of *Chlan-chain Point*, there is a small blind rock, on which the least water is 2½ feet: to avoid this shoal along the S. or east-side, keep *Holy-head Hill* a ship's-length on the *Point of Abirfra*; or the small island at that Point, on the E. side of a saddle, or gap, which may be seen near the W. point of *Holy-head*, near two hillocks.

And near the South Bank. About half between *Chlan-chain Point* and the W. extremity of the *South Bank* (or *Middle Patch*, as it is commonly called), there is a small rocky shoal, on which the least water is four feet: to avoid it, do not sail in till after half-flood; for it lies right in the way to the channel.

North Bank. The *North Bank* extends from the bar eastward, almost to *Abermenay Point*, and forms the north side of the channel; it dries with low spring-tide only: the eastmost point of it is called the *Mussle-bank*, and is composed of stones, like paving stones.

South Bank. The west half of the *South Bank* is never dry, excepting a small part at the N. E. end, which dries with spring-tide only, and commonly has a breaking sea on it; the *E. half* of it dries gradually till low-water, and is divided from the other by a narrow variable channel, where there is two feet of water at low spring-tide. The N. or inner-side of the *South Bank*, is steep too, and always to be perceived by a ripple, or over-fall on it: the flood-tide sets southward over it, and ebb northward on it; which should be attended to in sailing out or in with little wind, or in turning against the wind.

To sail over Caernarvon Bar to anchorage. To sail over *Carnarvon Bar* to anchorage within *Abermenay Point*, take half-flood, or three-quarters; or, with ebb-tide, a brisk leading wind; keep two cables-length from *Chlan-chain Point* (to avoid the two fore-mentioned blind rocks), till you are just past it, then steer S. S. E. till you take the E. end of *Holy-head Hill* just on *Chlan-chain Point*, and keep that mark so, till you bring the *Lime-house* to be one-third from *Abermenay Point*, and two-thirds from *Bellan Point*; then steer N. N. E. bringing the *Lime-house* nearer, by degrees, to *Bellan Point*, till it is hid by it; then sail on the extremity of *Bellan Point*; and, to avoid the *Mussle Bank*, keep *Abermenay Point* open of the eastmost house of *Carnarvon*, or of the hill over it. You are a-breast of the *Mussle Bank*, when *Dinas-dinlle*, and the sand-hillocks of *Dwrlewyn* are in a line. Anchor where the *Lime-house* bears S. E. or E. S. E. on four fathoms water, two cables-length from the Point; or below the *Ferry-house* of *Abermenay*, on the E. side of the Point, with one anchor on shore. *Dinas-dinlle* is an old fort on the shore, about three miles southward, and appears like a small hillock, with a clay cliff below it.

Appearance of Dinas-dinlle. The *Point of Abermenay*, and the *Lime-house*, can scarce be perceived at the Bar, even in clear weather, and should be made more remarkable.

Anchorage off Chlan-chain Point. A vessel may stop a tide, especially with W. or N. W. winds, on the S. E. side of *Chlan-chain Point*, off a small sandy cove, which is a little westward of the old church, about 1½ cable's-length from the shore, on three fathoms water. There is a small rock north-eastward of this anchorage, which dries with spring-tide only, about two cables-length from the shore; this rock should be avoided with westerly winds.

Maltraeth Anchorage. In moderate weather a vessel may stop any where in the mouth of *Maltraeth Bay*, without going within the Points. Small vessels may sail up the channel about high-water, and lie safe all weathers on clean sand. The channel is almost dry at low-water, and lies close to the rocks on the N. side of the Bay.

Abirfra Anchorage. In moderate weather a vessel may stop a tide in *Abirfra Bay*, on four or five fathoms, clean sand, above two cables-length from the N. side of the Bay. Very small vessels may go up the channel of the rivulet, about high-water, and lie a-ground safe on clean sand. The channel is close to the N. side of the Bay, and not a ship's-length broad.

A Description of the Tides, Rocks, Shoals, Channels, Anchoring-places, and Harbours, between Holy-head *and* Orme's Head.

CHART VIII.

Tides between Holy-head *and* Orme's Head.

TIDES.

It is high-water in the harbour of *Holy-head* at 9½, on the full and change days of the moon; at *Lynas Point* at ten; in *Beaumaris* at 10½. — Time of high-water in Holy-head Harbour, at Lynas Point, at Beaumaris [illegible]

In *Holy-head Harbour*, spring-tide rises eighteen feet perpendicular, neap-tide twelve; in *Beaumaris Harbour* twenty-seven feet with spring-tide, eighteen with neaps. — [illegible] of the Tide, in Holy-head [illegible]

On the W. side of *Holy-head Island*, the stream of flood comes from the southward; and the stream of ebb from the northward; and each turns sooner near the land than at a distance from it. — Direction of the Streams.

Within a league of the shore off *Holy-head Bay*, spring-tide, when strongest, runs about six miles an hour, and neap-tide two; near the *Point of Lynas*, in *Anglesey*, spring-tide runs five miles an hour, and neap-tide about two. — Velocity of the Streams.

The only rocks or shoals between *Holy-head* and *Orme's Head*, that are above half a mile from the shore, are the *Platters* near the *Skerries Island*, and *Carreg-lidan* (or the *Cale Rock*), two miles east of the *Skerries*. — ROCKS and SHOALS.

The *Platters* rock lies about one third from the *Skerries*, and two-thirds from *Carmel's Point*, opposite to the *Skerries* and dries with spring-tide only. To avoid it in sailing along the S. side, keep mid-channel, or keep the *High-Mary's Rock* (which is always above water, and remarkable) on *Rubon Head*, in *Cibarwir* parish: when it is between *Halve Head*, and the *Middle-Mary's Island*, you are above a cable's-length S. of the *Platters*. — The Platters Rock.

Carreg-lidan (or the *Cale Rock*) bears E. from the *Skerries* light-house about two miles, and dries with extraordinary low spring-tide only: with ordinary spring-tide therefore, there may be two or three feet of water over it. To avoid it sailing within, or on the N. side of it, keep the light-house W. by S. To sail along the E. side of it, at a sufficient distance, keep *Land Holas* (the Hill above *Carmel's Point*) S. by W. — Carreg-lidan Rock.

In moderate weather, a ship may stop in *Holy-head Bay*, about the middle, on from three to 4½ fathoms water, and clean sand. If the wind begins to freshen from the N. or N. W. either weigh anchor, and work out in time, or wait the tide to sail into the harbour; for if it blows fresh from that quarter, a great sea sets into the Bay, and it is thought the ground will not hold sufficiently. — ANCHORING-PLACES. Holy-head Bay.

A vessel may stop a tide in *Kemes Bay*, in *Anglesey*, when the wind is off shore, on five or six fathoms, clean sand, near the middle, or towards the W. side, if the wind is between the S. and W. If the wind is between the E. northward to N. W. this place is not to be trusted. — Kemes Bay.

A vessel may stop in any part of *Red-wharf Bay* about a mile from the shore, when the wind is off the land. When the wind is from the westward, the best part is on the S. side of *Moelvre Island*, on three or 3½ fathoms, about two cables length from the island. — Red-wharf Bay.

With S. or E. winds, a ship may stop between *Orme's Head* and *Priestholm* in the mouth of *Conway Bay*, about a mile from the land, on from four to seven fathoms water. — Conway Bay.

Holy-Head *Harbour*.

HARBOURS.

Holy-head is a dry Harbour, well sheltered, and soft ground to lie on; and which has the benefit of a good light kept on the *Skerries* Island near the mouth of the bay, to shew vessels up in the night. Ships that draw fifteen or sixteen feet water, may go into this Harbour about high-water with spring-tide; and vessels that draw eleven feet, may go in about high-water with neap-tide.

The stream of Tide near the W. side of *Holy-head* bay, from the *North-Stack* to *Inisgyhi* Island, runs eastward the first three hours of flood, and then nine hours westward, within half a mile of the shore. Near the E. side of the bay it runs southward, or up the bay, from half flood on the shore to half ebb; and from half ebb to half flood it runs northward, or out of the bay. — Stream of Tide in the Bay.

In sailing for *Holy-head* Harbour there are two rocks to be avoided near *Inisgyhi* Island; the first is the *Platters*, which lies a quarter of a mile N. ½ E. from *Inisgyhi*, and is always below water; the least water over it is four feet; the *North Stack* head out by the low point of *Infeath*, clears it on the N. side; an old wind-mill, or turret, in a line with the eastmost part of *Inisgyhi*, clears it along the E. side. The other rock is a small one about half a cable's length northward from the middle of *Inisgyhi*, and dries with spring-tide only. — Rocks near the Harbour.

When there is not water enough to sail into this Harbour, stop off the mouth of it, about two cables-length from the entry on five fathoms water, when the mouth of the Harbour is a little open. — Anchoring-place near the entry.

The *Dublin* packets make fast to rings on the S. end of *Inisgyhi*, and are longer afloat than other vessels; by which means they sail in or out sooner than others that must lie farther up the Harbour. — Packets fall fast in and out.

Kemlys *Creek*.

Kemlys is a Creek fit for very small vessels only; the entry is very narrow, but within it is well sheltered, and the ground clean. At high-water, with spring-tide, there is eight feet water in it, and five with neap-tide.

Amlogh *Creek*.

Amlogh is a narrow Creek, in the mouth of which vessels may stop, when the wind is not on shore, on five or six fathoms water; or small vessels may run up to the head of the Creek about high-water.

Dillas *Creek*.

Dillas Creek is capable of very small vessels only, there being but eight or nine feet of water in it at high-water with spring-tide, and five or six with neap-tide. The channel is close along the W. side of the little Island which lies in the entry, near the house of *Dillas*.

PORTHLONGDY *Harbour.*

Porthlongdy is a bay where small vessels may lie aground in pretty good shelter. At high water with spring-tide there is thirteen feet of water in the channel, and nine with neap-tides. The channel is close along the W. side of the bay, and may be distinguished by the ripple or other peculiar appearance of the water there. The part where vessels commonly lie in is near the houses of *Porthlongdy*, which is sheltered most of the tide by the outer part of the sand, which dries at two hours of ebb.

BEAUMARIS *Harbour.*

Beaumaris is a large and safe harbour, commodious on many occasions for ships that sail in the *Irish* channel; because when it is expedient to run for a Harbour, they may sail into it at any time of the tide with a moderate breeze of wind. The ground is all clean, and the depth in most parts sufficient for large merchant ships. The entry is easily distinguished at sea, by its position with respect to *Great-Orme's Head*, *Penmanmawr* mountain, and *Priest-holm*.

[illegible] Before you enter the Harbour of *Beaumaris*, there is a foul sandy shoal which lies about half a mile northward of the W. end of *Priest-holm*; the least water on it is ten feet. A leading mark to it is, the W. end of *Priest-holm* in a line with the lowest part of the E. side of *Penmanmawr* mountain; therefore open the E. end of *Penmanmawr* with the W. end of *Priest-holm*, and you clear this shoal on the W. side; shut in the E. end of *Penmanmawr* to the top with the E. end of *Priest-holm*, and you clear it on the E. side.

Causeway rocks. In the entry of this Harbour, there is a ledge of rocks called the *Causeway*, extending from the W. end of *Priest-holm* about two cables-length south-westward, which dries every ebb tide, and from thence near as far south-eastward, which part dries with spring-tide only: on the extremity of the first part, there is a conspicuous perch kept; take the perch on the larboard hand going in, a cable's-length, or half a cable's-length, and at the perch steer south-westward, to avoid that part of the causeway which dries only with spring-tide. At the extremity of the causeway, the steeple of *Beaumaris* is in a line with the shoulder of *Lodge Hill*.

[illegible] The point of *Trwyn-du*, over against the perch, requires a birth of near a cable's-length at low-water; for it shallows so far eastward from that point, and on it there is but three feet at low spring tide.

[illegible] Near the S. side of *Trwyn-du* point, a sand-bank begins called *[illegible]*, which extends south-eastward along the bay of *Penmon* above a mile; it is about a quarter of a mile from the shore of *Penmon*, and dries with spring-tide only. Off the W. end of this bank a vessel may stop in moderate weather on 4½ fathoms water, about half a mile from the shore of *Penmon*: this stopping-place is called *Crafwood*.

[illegible] *Friars head*, about two miles farther up the bay, is [illegible]. To sail to *Friars* from the perch about low-water, keep the steeple of *Beaumaris* in a line with the shoulder of *Lodge-hill* (where it begins to slope downward) till you are past *Penmon* bay; then keep the steeple above the middle of the shoulder (or half down the slope) of *Lodge-hill*: it is convenient likewise to keep the lead going, to avoid shallow water on each side.

Anchorage. Anchor off the *Friars*, where there is a small opening between the low-water mark of *Priest-holm* and the point of *Trwyn-du* at *Penmon*, when *Friars* house bears N. by W. or N. N. W. on five or six fathoms water. Or anchor nearer to *Friars* (where you will ride more out of the tideway) on two fathoms at low-water, when *Friars* bears N. by W. and a little of the *[illegible]* is open; then *Trwyn-du* point will be open a sail's-breadth with the high-water mark of *Priest-holm*, and *Beaumaris* point in a line with the town of *Bangor*.

[illegible] In the anchorage off *Friars*, the stream of flood runs near two hours up, or south-eastward, after it is high-water on the shore; and the stream of ebb north-eastward two hours after low-water on the shore.

Time of high-water. It is high-water in *Beaumaris* bay, on the shore, at 10½ full and change days.

The anchorage off the town of *Beaumaris* is a cable's-length and a half from the high-water mark, on four or five fathoms at low-water, when *Priest-holm* is just covered by the point at the castle of *Beaumaris*.

CONWAY *Harbour.*

Conway is fit for small vessels only: they must lie aground below the bridge of the town. The channel is difficult, and almost dry near the entry at low spring-tide. The best time to enter it is at four hours of flood, when small vessels will have water over all, near the channel. Such as are under any necessity of going in sooner, may observe the following directions: Keep the S. end of *Priest-holm* N. W. ½ W.; or the northmost and lowest of two hummocks, which are above the point of *Lynas* in *Anglesey*, in the middle of the sound of *Priest-holm*; keep that mark on, sailing eastward till you are about a cable's length from the high-water mark at the W. end of *Penmaenbach Hill*, or till *Majlas* house (a farm-house with its gavel towards you in *Llandudno* parish) appears half between the top of *Little Orme's-head* and the north side of that head; then keeping *Majlas* house on some part of the head, steer E. by N. till *Majlas* bears on the valley near the E. end of the head; then steer E. for the perch which stands on the edge of the channel on the W. side; give it a birth of two ships-length on the starboard hand, and steer close along *[illegible]* point; from thence keep mid-channel for the town of *Conway*.

High-water and rise of the tides. It is high-water at *Conway* bar at 10½ on full and change days. Spring-tides rise 4½ fathoms perpendicular; neap ⅓ [illegible].

A Description of the Tides, Rocks, Shoals, Sand-banks, Channels, Anchoring-places, and Harbours, between ORME'S HEAD *and* FORMBY POINT.

CHART IX.

TIDES.

Tides between ORMES HEAD *and* FORMBY POINT.

Time of high-water. From *Great-Orme's Head* to *Formby Point* in *Lancashire*, it is high-water on the days of full and change of the Moon, about eleven o'clock.

Rise of the Tides. Spring-tides rise 4½ fathoms; neap-tides 2½.

The

From ORME'S HEAD *to* FORMBY POINT.

Velocity. The stream of tide from *Orme's Head* to *Chester* bar, runs about one mile an hour when strongest; from *Chester* bar eastward to *Parkgate*, about 3½; along the N. side of *Hoyle sand*, about two miles an hour when strongest.

Direction of the Stream. Flood-tide sets in from the westward along *Orme's Head*, but turns southward toward the rivers, and ebb-tide comes from the E. along *Mud-wharf* and *Hoyle* sand-banks, turning a little northerly off the mouths of the rivers: so that the flood leads toward *Hoyle* and *Burbo* sands, and ebb from them; for which allowance should be made in setting the course along these sands.

SANDBANKS. The most considerable sands and sand-banks between *Great Orme's Head* and the point of *Formby*, are *Hoyle* sand, *Chester* bar, *Burbo*, and *Mud-wharf*.

Hoyle sand. *Hoyle* sand extends about four leagues westward from *Hoyle* lake near *Hilbury* island, and terminates about two leagues N. from *Vorid* river in *Wales*. The W. end of it is dries at low-water with spring-tide only; the middle or broadest part about half ebb, and that part which is next *Hoyle* lake, making the north side of the lake or channel, is dry always except about high-water with spring-tide, and breaks off the sea from the anchorage there. *Buoys in the channel.* Along the E. side of *Hoyle* sand, there are three buoys placed to direct ships in the day through the channel to the entry of *Hoyle* lake; North-west Buoy, the Swash Buoy, and the E. Buoy. *Light-houses.* There are also two light-houses on shore to direct ships through the channel in the night, and called the sea-lights; one of which is moveable, and stands on the shore near *Mock-beggar-hall*, the other stands two miles from the shore on the top of *Bidston Hill*, a little eastward of a wind-mill. There are likewise two lights called the lake-lights, kept on the S. side of *Hoyle lake*, to lead ships in there in the night time.

Chester bar. *Chester* bar is a narrow sand-bank, about three miles long from S. E. to N. W.; it extends in a curve from *New House* in *Gelanesied* parish, near the W. end of *Hoyle* sand. The south end of it next *New House*, called *Middle Patch*, dries with extraordinary low spring-tides; the middle of it, called the *E* [illegible], dries at low-water with ordinary spring-tide; but the greatest part is never dry, and has from three to six feet of water over it at any time.

To sail over CHESTER *Bar to the Point of* AIR.

To sail over Chester bar to the point of Air. To sail over *Chester* bar from the W. in a ship that draws twelve feet water, take half flood at least; and when *Cragdeparr* hill bears S. S. E. and with *Moelfre Hill*, and *Comb Hill* forms an equilateral triangle, keep the two *Orme Heads* shut below, and a little open above; keep them so, and you avoid all danger on the main or S. side. To avoid the banks and shallows on the N. or *Hoyle* side, open the *Orme Heads* below near a ship's-length, but not more. If a vessel comes to *Chester* bar before half flood, and is in apprehension of being pinched for water, she may sail between the *Middle patch* and the *E*[illegible], by keeping the *Orme Heads* a little open below; and when *Crag-deparr Hill* and *Moelfre Hill* are in a line, then steer N. E. till you deepen the water to four fathoms at low-water, and then sail along *Hoyle* to the point of *Air*, giving that point a berth of two cables-length. To avoid that point of *Hoyle* which is opposite to *Air*, keep *Bidston* wind-mill out to the S. by *Leasby* sea-mark.

Burbo sand. *Burbo* sand-banks extend from the rock near *Liverpool* to *Formby* Point, and consist of several lesser banks or patches of spongy sand, with narrow guts or channels between them; these patches and channels frequently vary in their dimensions, and new patches and swashes are formed near them. Some of the lesser banks dry at low spring-tide only, some about low-water with neap-tide, and *Jerry* [illegible], about the middle of *Burbo*, dries at two hours of ebb. The channel to *Liverpool* lies along the E. side of *Burbo*, and the entry, as far up as *Crosby*, is pointed out by four buoys, two on each side. The flats of shallow water extend along all the W. side of *Burbo* a mile or two westward, on which there is from nine to three feet at low spring-tide.

Mud-wharf. *Mud-wharf* is a large sand-bank, which lies N. W. from *Formby Point*: it extends about five miles from the land, and dries at four hours of ebb. This bank shifts gradually westward, which makes the channel along the W. side of it vary likewise; so that the two conspicuous land-marks built on *Formby Point*, which, some years ago, when taken in a line, led through the middle of the channel, now lead over the end of *Burbo*, at the north-end buoy. Near the westmost point of *Mud-wharf*, there is a cask buoy, placed on 3½ fathoms, at low-water, which is to be taken on the larboard-hand going in.

ANCHORING-PLACES. *Between the Ormes Heads.* In the Bay between *Great Orme's Head*, and *Little Orme's Head*, a ship may stop a tide, in moderate weather, when the wind is W. or off the land, on six fathoms water, clean ground, about a mile from the shore; or half a mile from it on four fathoms.

Between Little Orme's Head, and Vorid River, or off Gelanesied parish. Or any where between *Little Orme's Head* and *Vorid River*, on 3½, or three fathoms the least water, a mile and a half, or two miles from the shore; or off *Gelanesied* parish, on two, or 2½ fathoms, near a mile from the shore. *Or W. of the Point of Air.* Or a mile westward of the *Point of Air*, on two or three fathoms, half a mile from the shore.

Or in Wild Road. Or, a mile eastward of the *Point of Air*, on five or six fathoms, in *Wild Road*. Here the stream of tide, when strongest, runs about 3½ miles an hour; and makes a rough sea, when the tide runs against the wind. In passing the *Point of Air*, give it a berth of two cables-length.

Or off Dalpool. Or, off *Dalpool* on 3½ fathoms, especially from half-ebb to half-flood; for, during that time, the banks without are dry, and break off the sea. When the sand-banks are all covered, a great sea sets in here, with westerly winds, which makes hard riding there. *To sail from Wild Road to Dalpool.* To sail from *Wild-road* to *Dalpool*, keep the southmost house of *Dalpool*, which stands below the *Clay-cliff*, E. by S. ½ S. or exactly in a line with a small barn, with a white end, which stands on the top of the Cliff. This is not a sharp mark, and therefore the barn must not be taken out on either side of the house. Anchor about two cables-length from high-water mark, when the houses below the Cliff bear E. by N. on 3½, or four fathoms, at low-water. The stream here runs about five miles an hour, when strongest.

Anchorage at Park gate. At *Park-gate*, vessels must lie a-ground on the beach, below the houses, to lie safe; for though there is 2½ fathoms in the channel off the town, and three fathoms a little above the town, yet the stream of tide is so strong, and the anchor-ground so bad, that the strength of the stream would make a vessel drag her anchor. Take the ground about two hours before high-water, below the houses of *Park-gate*.

To sail from DALPOOL *into* HOYLE LAKE.

To sail from *Dalpool* into *Hoyle Lake*, through the *Hilbury Deep*, or between the *Oalfast Bank* and *Hilbury Islands*, keep *Hefwal* church S. E. ½ S. or on the S. end of the *Cliff of Dalpool* (but not on the least open of it), till you see an opening between the S. end of *Great Hilbury Island*, and a rock near it; then steer N. or parallel to these islands, till the sea-mark on *Hilbury Island* bears E. N. E. then steer for the N. end of that Island, giving it a birth, and steer E. for *Hoyle Lake*.

VOYAGE

HARBOURS.

VORID *Creek.*

Vorid is a small River, dividing *Flint-shire* and *Denbigh-shire*, near the mouth of which small vessels may lie aground on clean sand, sheltered from the violence of the sea. There are two perches on the W. side of the channel, that point out its direction. To sail in with these perches, about one hour before high water, take the church of *Rudland* in a line, with the church of St. *Asaph*, and sail in that direction till you see the perches, keep them just open on the starboard-side, and give each a birth of a ship's-length. Anchor near *Lodge*, on the W. side of the River, just within the first point.

It is high-water at *Vorid River* at [illegible], full and change days.

In the channel there are fifteen feet at high-water, with spring-tide, and ten with neap tide.

HOYLE LAKE *Road.*

Hoyle Lake is a convenient place for all ships, or vessels, bound to *Liverpool*, to sail into at night, or to wait the tide for sailing through the *Rock-channel*, and also for vessels bound up the *River Dee*, when toward evening they have not tide sufficient to go over *Chester Bar*. The two sea-lights, and two lake-lights, make it as safe sailing into *Hoyle Lake* in the night as the day; and it is sheltered from the sea by *Hoyle Sand*, that part of it, which is next the anchorage, being always dry, except about high water with spring-tide. The channel to it, along *Hoyle*, has three buoys to it carefully placed, and often inspected, viz. the *North-west Buoy*, the *South-buoy*, and the *North-east buoy*, all of which are to be taken on the larboard-hand going in.

To sail into *Hoyle Lake* from the West; keep *Great Orme's Head* W. or W. ½ S. and that will bring you up with the north-west buoy of *Hoyle*, where the sea light-houses will appear in a line; bearing S. E. ½ E. and the summer-house on *Hilbry Island*, bearing S. S. E. ½ S. and open two ship's-length to the W. of the *Eye Island*; and a wind-mill which stands on the top of a hill, above *Parkgate*, bearing S. S. E. ½ E. and a handspike's-length out to the W. of *Dalpool Point*. From the *North-west Buoy*, steer S. E. ½ E. or keep the sea-lights in a line through the channel along *Hoyle*, passing the *South Buoy* on your starboard hand, till you come up with the *North-east Buoy*, or till the two lake-lights are in a line; in that direction, steer into *Hoyle Lake*, and anchor on three fathoms, at low-water: or, to ride safer, sail farther up the Lake, till the great light bears S. S. E. and anchor on three, four, or five fathoms.

Flood tide, in *Hoyle Lake*, when strongest, runs about 2½ miles an hour.

Shoal-riding with N. W. winds, and high spring-tide. This anchorage is safe, except about high-water, with spring-tide, when *Hoyle Sand* is quite covered, and the wind blows strong from the N. W. In such circumstances, there is a great sea, and hard riding in the Lake; and ships that have not a great deal of cable out, will be apt to drag their anchor.

LIVERPOOL *Harbour.*

That part of the *River Mersey*, which is near *Liverpool*, is well sheltered, the anchor-ground good in most parts, and the depth of water sufficient for the largest ships: the channels towards it are well pointed out by lights in the night-time, or by buoys or perches in the day. *Liverpool* has likewise the advantage of a considerable *rise* of tide in its wet docks, where the largest merchant ships may lie a-float, and take in, or unload their cargoes.

To sail from Hoyle Lake to Liverpool. To sail from *Hoyle Lake* to the anchorage off *Liverpool*; a-right anchor about half-flood; take the north-east buoy of *Hoyle*, and *Beggars'-patch* buoy (a cask) on your larboard-hand, *Mockbeggar* buoy (conical) on the starboard, *Brazil* buoy (a cask) on the larboard-hand: then, to sail through the *Rock Channel*, keep Beach land-marks in a line, and the rock-perch half a cable's-length on the starboard hand. Anchor off the *Magazines*, about three quarters of a mile above the *Rock Point*, and at least two cables-length from the high-water mark on the shore, when the houses bear W. by S. and the town of *Wallasie* are in sight by *Seacomb Point*, on from seven to thirteen fathoms at low-water. Or sail up to *Sloyne*, where there is little stream of tide, and the ground all clean, and anchor above two cables-length from the shore, on eight or nine fathoms at low-water. *Sloyne* is the best place of anchorage in this river. It is there where ships commonly lie to wait spring-tide for going into the docks. Right off the town of *Liverpool*, near the middle of the river, the bottom is rocky, and the tide very rapid; and therefore not a fit place to anchor in, though ships often stop there, and sometimes are obliged to leave their anchors behind them: spring tides, in that part, run about five miles an hour when strongest.

Anchorage off the Magazines.

Anchorage at Sloyne.

High-water, and rise of the tide. It is high-water in the *Mersey*, near *Liverpool*, at eleven, on full and change days.

Ordinary spring-tides rise twenty-seven feet perpendicular; extraordinary thirty-three feet: neap-tides rise fifteen or sixteen. Spring-tide, at the two old dock-gates, rise eighteen or nineteen feet perpendicular; neap-tide eleven or twelve: at the new dock-gates, probably, the tides rise higher.

To sail through FORMBY CHANNEL *to* LIVERPOOL.

Formby Channel. This Channel is not so safe as that along *Hoyle* and the *Rock Channel*; because *Mad-wharf* and *Potle Sands* frequently vary near the entry; and flood-tide setting in, and ebb-tide out through the *Swash* of *Bootle*, makes it difficult to keep the channel when there is little wind. The entry of *Formby Channel* is distinguishable at sea by two conspicuous land-marks erected on *Formby Point*, and the most dangerous parts of the banks are pointed out by cask-buoys, which are to be taken on the larboard-hand going in, and by conical, or can-buoys, which are to be taken on the starboard-hand.

To sail up the channel. To sail into *Formby Channel*, first get sight of *Formby* land-marks, and take them in a line, continuing that direction till you see *Mad-wharf Sand*, which has commonly a rough breaking sea on it; near the extremity of which you will see a cask-buoy, which must be taken on the larboard-hand. Keep the land-marks in a line, or nearly so, till you bring the beacon, that stands between them, a sail's breadth open to the E. of the [illegible], or west land-mark; which will lead to the N. E. buoy of *Burbo*, that of the N. [illegible]; and then *Liverpool* will be open with the land at the *Rock Point*. Take the [illegible] (a conical buoy) on your starboard hand, and steer S. by W. for *Taylor's Bank*, passing a cask-buoy on your larboard-hand, and *Taylor's Bank* buoy on your starboard-hand; then steer S. about two miles, till you see a cask buoy near *Crosby Point*; take it on the larboard hand, and steer about S. by E. ½ E. for the *Rock Perch*; give it a birth on the starboard-hand, of at least two ships-length, and anchor off the *Magazines*, or in *Sloyne Road*, as in the preceding article.

7

In

From FORMBY POINT *to* WALNEY.

In sailing through *Formby Channel*, with little wind, guard against being carried too much eastward, toward the land, with the stream of flood which sets in through the *Swashes of Burbo*; and against being carried on *Burbo* by the ebb-tide setting through them outward. — Caution in sailing in Formby Channel.

The above buoys and directions, are agreeable to a survey taken in 1771; but may not answer exactly now, as *Mad-wharf* and *Burbo* are found to vary a little every year. — Buoys not always exactly.

A Description of the Tides, Rocks, Shoals, Sand-banks, Channels, Anchoring-places, and Harbours, between FORMBY POINT, *and* WALNEY ISLAND.

CHART X.

From *Formby*, to St. *Bee's Head*, it is high water on the shore about eleven o'clock, on the full and change days of the moon. — TIDES. Time of high-water.

Spring-tide, on this part of the coast, rises 4½, or five fathoms perpendicular; neap-tide three. In the anchorage at *Piel-of-Foudrey*, spring-tide, the second day after the change, rose six fathoms perpendicular. — Rise of the Tide.

The stream of flood along the coast, from *Formby* to *Walney*, runs northward; and, off the middle of that island, meets the stream which comes round the north coast of *Ireland*, and from thence runs southward through the *Irish* channel. The opposition of these two streams destroy each other's force, and renders their currents scarce sensible in that neighbourhood; but, by accumulating the water in *Piel-of-Foudrey* anchorage, occasions a greater rise of the tide there than in other parts. — Direction of the Stream.

There are no rocks along this part of the coast. *Mad-wharf*, off *Formby*, which dries at four hours of ebb, is the only sand-bank that does not lie within the mouths of the bays or rivers. But the coast from *Formby*, to the *Point of Rossal*, near *Wyre Water*, is all shallow for above two miles from the shore; the depth being not above three fathoms at that distance off. The banks, in the bays and rivers, will be so well understood, by inspecting the draft, as by any description; and such as are near anchorage and harbours, will be described with them. — SHOALS and SAND-BANKS.

RIBBLE *River*.

Small vessels only, after four hours of flood, are safe to sail up *Ribble*; at which time they have water over most of the banks. The channels in this River being crooked, and without buoys, perches, and distinct land-marks, no directions will be sufficient for a stranger. — STOPPING-PLACES.

The ground, along this coast, is all clean sand; and the depth, for two or three leagues from the land, not above five or six fathoms at low-water: ships, in moderate weather, or when the wind is off the shore, may stop a tide any where from three miles to six miles from the land. — From shore to the edge of soundings.

WYRE-WATER *Harbour*. — HARBOURS.

Wyre-water is a river, in the mouth of which small vessels are sheltered by lying a-ground, within half a cable's-length of the high-water mark. At high-water, with spring-tide, there are four, or 4½ fathoms, in the channel leading to the entry of the Harbour; and at least twelve feet at high-water with neap-tide.

In sailing into *Wyre-water*, *North-wharf Bank* must be avoided. It extends about two miles northward of *Rossal Point*; is partly dry at half-ebb, with neap-tides, partly at four hours, and the W. and E. ends dry with spring-tide only. To avoid this Bank along the W. side, keep *Black-comb Hill* (in *Cumberland*), out to the W. of *Piel Castle* (in *Piel-of-Foudrey* in *Walney Island*), or keep *Red-bank's Cliff* south. To sail along the N. side of it, keep the steeple of *Lancaster* E. by N. or a little open to the S. of *High-field Fell*, or Hill; or stand no nearer that shore than in six or eight fathoms water. To sail through the channel into *Wyre River*; about half flood with spring-tide, or three-quarters with neap-tide, take the perch, which is near the entry, in a line with the summer-house at the W. point of the entry, till you are a-breast of the perch; give it a birth of two ships-length, on the starboard-hand; then steer S. or half a point westward of the summer-house, right on a perch which stands on the land, a musket-shot west of the summer-house, till you are within half a cable's-length of the shore, then steer in for the E. side of the entry, and drop anchor a quarter of a mile above the watch-house, and anchor so as to ride half a cable's-length from the high-water mark, that you may be the more out of the tide-way. Or run up to the *Neckins*, and lie in the bight, on the N. side of that peninsula, where there is very little stream. — North-wharf Bank. — Tide in Wyre-water.

In the mouth of this river, spring-tide, when strongest, runs four, or 4½ miles an hour. — Velocity of the Stream in Wyre.

SUNDERLAND *Harbour*.

a quarter of a cable's-length; and anchor off the westmost houses of the town, or run a-ground below the houses.

Channel to Lancaster.

At the key of *Lancaster*, large vessels may lie a-float all times of the tide, but the channel is irregular, variable, and shallow; the shallowest part of it having no more than five feet water on it, at high-water with neap-tide, and ten or eleven at high-water with spring-tide.

Kent *River*.

The *River Kent*, between *Sunderland* and the *Piel-of-Foudray*, is very dangerous, and not to be attempted by any stranger, except in necessity; as there are neither buoys, perches, or distinct land-marks to point out the channels to one that is not particularly acquainted. When a vessel is forced into this Bay, the only channels to be pursued are, either *Furness*, or *Grange*; the former on the west side of *Cartmel-wharfs Bank*, which dries about low-water only, the other on the E. side of it: at four hours of flood, a vessel, that draws ten or twelve feet, will have sufficient water over *Cartmel-wharfs*, near the channel. These channels often discover themselves, by the appearance of the water on them; a good look-out is therefore necessary here.

Piel-of-Foudray *Harbour*.

Piel-of-Foudray is a Harbour, near the S. end of *Walney Island*, where large merchant-ships may ride in good shelter, near the W. or S. W. side of *Ro Island*, on from three to five fathoms water. Small vessels commonly lie a-ground in the bight, on the E. side of *Piel-of-Foudray Island*, about a cable's-length from the high-water mark, when the house bears S. by W. In the anchorage, near *Ro Island*, the two streams of flood meet; one from the N. the other from the S. and make it troublesome to keep the anchor clear. The stream here runs about three miles an hour when strongest.

Channel to How's-end.

In the channel, near *How's-end*, in *Walney*, there are only two or three feet of water at low spring-tide; but the tide in it rises about five fathoms perpendicular, so that a large vessel may go in at half-tide.

Foula Tongue.

On the south side of this channel, there is a rock called *Foula Tongue*, which dries at low spring-tide only, and extends south-westward from *Foula Island*, about a mile. To avoid this rock, keep the outermost sand-hillocks, on *How's-end*, north, till you are about a cable's-length from the shore, or half a cable from the edge of the sea; or keep the extremity of the *How's Point* on the old castle, till you are within a cable's-length of the shore, then steer N. E. or on the *Old Garth Point* in *Foula*, giving the Point at the old castle a birth of a cable's-length, and steer for *Ro Island* anchorage.

To sail into Piel-of-Foudray from the S.

To sail into *Piel-of-Foudray* from the S.; first make the old castle on that Island (which is remarkable, and easily seen, at three leagues distance), keep the castle N. by E. or N. by E. ½ E. and after half-flood steer for the *How's-point of Walney*; give it a small birth, and steer for the E. side of *Piel-of-Foudray Island*, giving the S. end of it a birth of a cable's-length; anchor in the bight of the Island, on four fathoms at high-water, a cable's-length from the high-water mark, when the house bears S. by W. where you will ground before low-water: or come to an anchor farther up, on the W. or N. W. side of *Ro Island*, about half a cable's-length from the high-water mark, and ride, or moor, with no more than half a cable out.

To sail into Piel-of-Foudray from the N.

To sail into *Piel-of-Foudray* from the N.; take half-flood, and keep *Black-comb Hill* out by *Walney* (to avoid *Helpsford Sand*) till you take out a small remarkable knole on *Foula Island* by *How's-end*; then sail for the *How's-end*, giving it a small birth; from thence for the E. side of *Piel-of-Foudray*, giving the S. end of it a birth of near a cable's-length, and anchor in the bight, or near *Ro Island*, as directed in the preceding paragraph.

The stream of tide, near the W. side of *Walney*, begins to run S. E. at the last quarter of flood on the shore, and continues till it is one quarter flowed, then runs nine hours N. E.

A Description of the Tides, Rocks, Shoals, Channels, Anchoring-places, and Harbours, between Piel-of-Foudray *and St.* Bee's Head.

CHART XI.

Tides between Piel-of-Foudray *and St.* Bee's Head.

TIDES.

Time of High-water.

Between *Piel-of-Foudray*, and St. *Bee's Head* in *Cumberland*, it is high-water on the shore at eleven, on full and change days.

Rise of the Tides.

Spring-tide rises twenty feet perpendicular; neap-tide six or seven.

Direction and Velocity of the Streams.

Flood comes from the northward, and ebb from the S.; and, when strongest, run about one mile an hour along the coast.

ROCKS and SHOALS. Helpsford Sand. Shoal of Walney. Selker Rock. Drig Rock.

The rocks and shoals to be avoided between *Piel-of-Foudray* and St. *Bee's Head*, are *Helpsford Sand*, which extends above a mile W. from the S. end of *Walney*; a shoal off the N. end of *Walney*, in the entry of *Duddon Bay*, with several patches of sand, near a league from the shore, that dry with spring-tide only: *Selker Rock*, a mile westward of *Selker Point*, the middle of which dries with very low spring-tide only; and *Drig Rock*, which is a small shoal, about three miles northward of *Ravenglass*, near a mile from the shore, on which there is the least water: as is N. St. *Bee's Head* is out near a handspike-length by the S. part of the Head. Keep above a league from the N. end of *Walney Island*, and above a mile from the rest of the coast, and these rocks and shoals will be avoided.

ANCHORAGE.

Along this coast vessels may stop a tide in moderate weather any where, if the last-mentioned shoals are avoided.

Duddon *Sands*.

Only small vessels can get into safety in this Bay; for I was informed that there was not above seven or eight feet of water over most of the banks at high-water with spring-tide; with neap-tide, therefore, there is but two or three feet on them at high-water.

RAVINGLASS *Harbour.*

Ravinglass is a dry Harbour in *Cumberland*, where three rivulets, *Esk*, *Mite*, and *Irt*, unite. There is a buoy placed a little within the mouth of the Channel, in the middle near a fish-weir, which marks the entry. At this buoy, and in most of the Channel, the depth is three fathoms at high-water with neap-tide. The best part for vessels to lie aground on, is half a cable's-length from the W. end of the town of *Ravinglass*, on the S. side of a perch, which stands on the point of the sand there. At this anchorage, in the mouth of the *River Esk*, and also at the confluence of the two other rivers, there are three fathoms at high-water with spring-tide, and are free with neaps.

To sail into *Ravinglass Harbour*; take four hours of flood, keep above a mile from the coast (to avoid *Selker* and *Drig Rocks*) till *Ravinglass* town bears E. N. E. steer in that course till you see the buoy bearing E. and then steer right for it, keeping within a ship's-length of it on either hand: when you are just past the buoy, steer E. N. E. or keep *Ravinglass* a sail's-breadth open to the N. of you then, till you are about half a mile from the E. end of the sandy hillocks; hook the small bay, which begins there; keep near a cable's-length from the point at the end of that small bay, and anchor half a cable's-length from the W. end of the town; or off the perch, in the meeting of the three rivers. When the buoy in the entry bears E. it is also in a line with the S. shoulder of *Newtown-bent Hill*, which is a small hill, half a mile S. of *Ravinglass*, on which some corn fields and furz-bushes may be seen. To sail into Ravinglass.

NAUTICAL DESCRIPTIONS

OF THE

ISLE of MAN,

And of the COAST

FROM

St. BEE's HEAD *in* CUMBERLAND, *to* CANTIRE *in* SCOTLAND.

A Description of the Tides, Rocks, Shoals, Channels, Sand-banks, Anchoring-places, and Harbours in the ISLE OF MAN.

CHART XII.

Tides round the ISLE OF MAN.

TIDES.

ON the full and change days it is high-water on the shore, at *Peel* in the *Isle of Man*, at 10¼; at the *Calf* at 10¼; at *Douglas* at 10¼; at *Ramsey* at 10¾, at the *Point of Ayre* at ten. Time of high-water at Peel, at the Calf, at Douglas, at Ramsey, at the Point of Ayre.

In the *Isle of Man* spring-tide rises eighteen or twenty feet perpendicular; neap-tide nine or ten. Rise of the Tide.

The stream of tide, near the *Chickens* and *Eye Rocks*, at the *Calf*, run about 5½ miles an hour with spring-tide, when it is strongest; neap-tide two miles. Flood, with spring-tide, runs more easterly from the *Eye Rock* than it doth with neap-tide. With spring-tide the stream of flood changes very suddenly at the *Chickens*, there being little or no slack-water; but ebb-tide there is slack above an hour before the stream of flood is sensible. Velocity of the Stream, at the Chickens and Eye Rocks, near the Calf.

In the Sound of the *Calf of Man*, spring-tide, when strongest, runs about four miles an hour. The stream here begins to run north-westward two hours before high-water on the shore, and continues so till two hours before low water. In the Sound of the Calf.

Near the extremity of *Scarlet Point*, the stream, when strongest, runs about three miles an hour. Near Scarlet Point.

Near the extremity of *Langness Point*, spring-tides, when strongest, run about five miles an hour; neap-tides one and a half. The stream along the E. side of *Langness*, when strongest, runs about three miles an hour. This stream runs ten hours southward, and only two hours northward. Near Langness.

Near *Douglas Head*, spring-tide, when strongest, runs about four miles an hour; neap-tide one and a half. Near Douglas Head.

Near the *Point of Ayre*, on the N. and E. sides, the stream runs about four miles an hour when strongest. Near the Point of Ayre.

Between

stop in moderate weather, on ten or eleven fathoms water: the fishermen say, there is clay below the gravel. This place of anchorage is, when the Castle bears N. and the South Head, or Scarlet Point, N. W. by N. Up this Bay there are several rocks that dry about low-water, or with spring-tide only; and a great sea sets into it with S. and S. W. winds.

Castleton Harbour is in the mouth of the river below the Castle, and is capable of very small vessels only. At the key there are only six or seven feet at high-water with neap tide; and ten or twelve feet with spring-tide.

DERBY *Haven.*

Derby Haven lies on the E. side of the isthmus of *Langness*: in the road, the ground is clean, the depth sufficient for large merchant-ships, and the anchorage sheltered from all winds, except the E. and S. E. which are seldom violent, so that this place is justly reckoned the best anchorage in the *Isle of Man*. If a key was built at the Point, on the N. side of the Bay (which might be done at little expence), that would render the harbour very safe and convenient for vessels to lie a-ground in occasionally, or when the wind was too hard for riding in the road. The best anchorage in the road, is on the N. side of the small Island, a little nearer that Island than to the N. side of the Bay, on three, or 3½ fathoms water, when the Castle on the little Island bears S. E. by S. Small vessels may ride farther up the Bay, on two fathoms the least water, where the ruinous chapel bears S. by E. which is a little before light is seen through the belfry. Give the small Island a birth going out and in; for it shallows about half a cable's-length from that part. In sailing along the S. side of *Langness Point*, give it a birth of at least a cable's-length, to avoid a rock near the S. W. point of it, and a rocky ledge from the S. E. part of it. Advert likewise, that the stream along the E. side of *Langness* runs about ten hours southward, viz. from two hours of flood till the last of ebb on the shore; and, when strongest, runs about five miles an hour. Spring-tide here rises about twenty feet perpendicular; neap-tide ten or eleven.

DOUGLAS *Harbour and Bay.*

A vessel that draws ten feet of water may go into *Douglas Harbour* about high water with neap tide; a ship that draws fourteen may have water to go in about high-water with spring-tide; but as the entry is narrow, and a shallow ledge extends from the shore right opposite to the pier-head, about one-third of a cable's-length; a ship that draws above eleven or twelve feet should not hazard to go into this harbour in blowing weather, except in necessity; when she must keep within a ship's length of the key-head. From *August* to *April* there is a light on the key head to direct vessels into the Harbour in the night-time. Ledge against the entry.

Douglas Bay is, for the most part, clean ground, but in blowing weather it does not hold sufficiently; and being exposed to the winds on one half of the compass, cannot be reckoned safe anchorage, except in moderate weather to stop a tide in. The best part to stop in is, off the entry of the Harbour, about two or three cables-length north-eastward of the *Point of Douglas Head*, when the brewery (which stands on a rising ground about half a mile above *Douglas*) is a little open to the E. of the old fort at the key-head. In sailing up *Douglas Bay*, avoid St. *Mary's Rock*, which lies about two cables-length eastward of the old fort at the key-head, and is covered with spring-tide only. Douglas Bay. St. Mary's Rock.

RAMSEY *Bay and Harbour.*

Ramsey Bay being open to the S. and E. there is a great sea, and hard riding in it, when the wind blows strong from these quarters. When the wind is any thing from the westward, there is very good riding in this Bay, especially on the S. side, in five or six fathoms water, the bottom being stiff clay. Anchor a mile, or a mile and half, eastward of the town of *Ramsey*, when the chapel at the S. end of the town bears W. by S. and *Maughold's Head* S. S. E. or S. by E. Large ships may anchor farther from the shore, on eight or nine fathoms the least water. Ramsey Bay. Anchorage.

Ramsey Harbour is capable of small vessels only, such as draw not above eight or nine feet of water; for the tide does not begin to come within the Harbour, till about two hours before high-water; and the channel along the key coming in, and the basin where vessels lie, are both narrow. At high-water, with spring-tide, there is sixteen or seventeen feet in the channel coming in along the key, and ten or eleven at high-water with neap-tide: but as it is much shallower within the Harbour, vessels should not attempt going in till about one hour before high water, except in such weather as they may take the ground near the entry, and be sheltered by the key, till the tide rises for going into the basin. Harbour.

In *Ramsey Harbour* it is high-water, full and change days, at 10½. High water full and change.

PEEL *Harbour and Bay.*

Peel Harbour is capable of very small vessels only, there being no more than eight feet water at the key-head at high-water with ordinary spring tide, and five or six within the Harbour.

In *Peel Bay* a vessel may ride, in moderate weather, on three or four fathoms in the middle of the Bay, the Castle bearing S. S. W. or S. W. by W. When the Castle bears S. W. about half a mile off, there is 5½ fathoms rocky ground, which is the only foul ground in this Bay. The best part for large ships to stop in is, when the Castle bears S. W. somewhat more than half a mile, on seven fathoms water, when Creg-willey's *Hough* is in a line with the N. end of *Slew-hallen Hill*; and a gap, or cove, in *Contrary Head*, just appears by *Pistol Head*, which is the N. part of *Contrary Head*. Foul ground.

A Description of the Tides, Rocks, Shoals, and Anchoring-places, in the MOUTH OF SOLWAY FIRTH.

CHART XIII.

Tides in the Mouth of SOLWAY FIRTH. TIDES.

In the mouth of *Solway Firth*, both on the *English* and *Scotch* side, it is high-water on the full and change days of the moon at eleven o'clock. Time of high-water.

SOLWAY FIRTH.

Rise of the Tide. Spring-tides rise twenty feet perpendicular; neap-tides eleven or twelve feet.

Velocity of the Stream. Spring-tides near *Burrow Head*, in *Scotland*, run about three miles an hour when strongest; neap-tides one. In other parts of the coast, included in this draft, the stream is not so strong.

Direction of the Stream. The principal stream of flood that fills *Solway Firth*, comes from the N. W. between the *Mule of Cantire* and *Ireland*; part of which runs along the *Mule of Galloway*, and from thence up *Solway Firth*.

ROCKS and SHOALS. There are no rocks or shoals in the mouth of *Solway Firth*, excepting such as lie within the bays or harbours, and will be described with them, or may be seen distinctly in the draft.

ANCHORING-PLACES and HARBOURS.

ISLE OF WHITEHORN *Harbour*.

This is a dry Harbour, at the N. end of the *Isle of Whitehorn*, where small vessels may lie safe along the key. Within the key there is ten feet of water, at high-water with neap-tide, and fifteen with spring-tide. There is a rocky ledge near the W. point of the entry into this bay, which extends eastward from the shore about a cable's-length, and dries at half-ebb.

[illegible] The stream of tide from *Burrow Head* to *Stone Head* (near the *Isle of Whitehorn*), within half a mile of the shore, runs three hours eastward, and nine hours westward: the stream begins to run westward at half-flood, and continues till low-water. One mile from the shore the stream is regular, six hours W. and six E. The westward stream near the shore, when strongest, runs about three miles an hour; the eastward stream is much slower.

BAY OF WIGTON.

In the *Bay of Wigton* there are several places, where vessels may stop in moderate weather, or when the wind blows off shore, but no proper harbour.

[illegible] In the Bay, a mile northward of *Stone Head*, a vessel may stop within half a mile of the shore, on seven or eight fathoms water, clean sand.

In Garlies-town Bay. Off the mouth of *Garlies-town Bay*, between *Edgerness* and *Galloway Heafe*, a vessel may stop on clean ground, the depth from two to six fathoms. Anchor about two cables-length from the shore on either side. In *Garlies-town Bay*, on the E. side, off *Edgerness*, there is fourteen feet of water at high-water with neap-tide, and twenty feet with spring-tide, within the stony ledge opposite to *Garlies-town*; but the sand there is full of large stones, and therefore not fit for vessels to ground on. This place might be easily cleared of the stones, and a good harbour made there.

In the water of Cree. To the water of *Cree* the channel lies along the E. side of the *Bay of Wigton*, about half a mile from the shore; but being crooked, and having no buoy nor perch in it, it is very difficult to keep in the channel. At high-water with spring-tide, there is from [illegible] to [illegible] fathoms water in it, as far up almost as to the ferry, and the ground all oozy, and soft for a vessel to lie on when she takes the ground: at high-water with neap-tide, there is from fifteen to ten feet in this channel. A vessel that draws nine or ten feet may go up the water of *Cree* about four hours of flood, provided the channel can be distinguished by the appearance of the water so as to keep near it; which commonly may be done; there will then be sufficient water to carry a vessel a mile above *Carsluth*, where when she grounds she will be pretty well sheltered by the banks without her.

At Wigton. The channel to *Wigton* is very crooked and shallow, and can admit only of small barks at any time.

KIRCUDBRIGHT *Bay and Harbour*.

The *Bay of Kircudbright* is a dry Harbour, where ships that draw ten or twelve feet water may get into shelter at high-water with neap-tide, and ground on soft mud. The channel in, is close along the *Torres Head*, on the E. side of the entry. The best parts to lie on are, the *Monks-Man's Lake*, about a quarter of a mile eastward of the first perch, which stands on the shore, on the N. side of *Torres Head*; or on the N. side of St. *Mary's Isle* (a peninsula), near the town of *Kircudbright*. Vessels may wait the tide, by dropping anchor between the *island Little Ross* and *Torres Head*, on [illegible], or four fathoms water.

To sail in. The deepest of the channel along *Torres Head*, is about half a cable's-length from the shore, until you have got about a cable's-length from the first perch, then stand nearer the shore, and take the perch on the starboard-hand, about a ship's-length, and sail north-eastward for the *Monks Man's-Lake*. If you intend to go farther up; when you have passed the perch, about a cable's length, steer northward for the second perch, which stands at the south-west end of St. *Mary's Isle*, take it on the starboard-hand about two ship's-length; from thence steer half a point westward of the third perch; take it on the larboard-hand about two ships-length, and a fish-yard, on the opposite side of the channel, on your starboard-hand, one ship's-length. Above this there are three more fish yards before you reach the town; the first of which is to be taken on the larboard-hand, and the other two on the starboard. Part of each of these fish-yards are to be seen about half-ebb; but there should be a perch at each of them so high as to be seen at high-water. Above the third perch, before the vessel grounds, take care to make her lean toward the bank, for it is pretty steep.

Shoal near the [illegible]. On the E. side of the *Ross*, at the mouth of the *Bay of Kircudbright*, there is a small shoal, near a quarter of a mile from the end of the rocky cliff, on which the least water is six feet: it lies about half a mile northward of the small island of *Ross*, but it is out of the way of vessels going up the Bay, except they are turning in.

A Description of the Tides, Rocks, Shoals, Sand-banks, Channels, Anchoring-places, and Harbours in SOLWAY FIRTH.

C H A R T XIV.

TIDES.

Tides in SOLWAY FIRTH.

Time of High-water on the English side, and on the Scotch side. It is high-water on the full and change days of the moon in *Whitehaven*, in *Cumberland*, at eleven o'clock; in *Mary-Port* at [illegible]; at *Bowness* and *Annan* at twelve; at *Satterness Point*, in *Scotland*, at [illegible]; in the harbour of *Kircudbright* at eleven.

SOLWAY FIRTH.

Spring-tides in *Solway Firth*, on both sides, rise about twenty feet perpendicular; neap-tides about twelve: off *Carsthorn*, near the mouth of the river *Nith*, spring-tide rises seventeen or eighteen feet perpendicular; near *Satterness Point* it rises twenty-four feet. — *Rise of the Tide.*

The stream of flood, which fills *Solway Firth*, comes from the north-west, between the *Mull of Cantire* in *Scotland* and *Rathlin Island* in *Ireland*, and from thence runs along the *Mull of Galloway* up *Solway Firth*. — *Direction of the Stream.*

The stream along the shore, on the *English* side, between *St. Bee's Head* and *Mary-Port*, runs about two miles an hour when strongest; from *Mary-Port* to *Skinburness*, three miles; from *Skinburness* to *Bowness*, five or six miles an hour: neap-tides have about one-third of that velocity. — *Velocity of the Stream on the English side.*

The stream on the *Scotch* side, between the *Bay of Kirkcudbright* and *Barnbourry Road*, when strongest, runs about three miles an hour; along the *Point of Satterness*, it runs five miles; and in the channel off *Annan* about six miles. — *Velocity on the Scotch side.*

Rocks, Banks, and Shoals on the ENGLISH *Side of* SOLWAY FIRTH. — ROCKS and SHOALS.

Workington Bank lies about four miles N. W. of *Workington*, is about three miles long from N. E. to S. W. and one mile broad; the least water on it is two fathoms at low water. On the W. end of this shoal, *St. Bee's Head* bears S. by W. ½ W. *Workington Hall* S. S. E. and in a line with *Wingill's* (which is the northwest of three small clumps of wood that may be seen on the top of a rising ground, about three miles S. of *Workington*), and *Mary-Port* E. by S. The shallowest part of it is on the E. end, next *Robin-rig Bank*. To sail along the E. side of this Bank, or between it and *Workington*, keep *St. Bee's Head* S. S. W. or *Mary-Port* E. ½ N. when it will be in a line with *Crosby*, which is a remarkable house on the top of a hill, two or three miles from *Mary-Port*. — *Workington Bank.*

Robin-rig Bank is a long curved sand-bank, that forms one side of what is called the *English Channel*. Only that part of it dries which is next *Workington Bank*, which it does with low spring-tide only: the rest has five or nine feet of water over it, and is always to be distinguished by the breakers, or by a ripple on it. Between *Robin-rig* and *Dumroof Bank* lies *Middle Bank*, part of which dries with spring-tide only. — *Robin-rig Bank.* — *Middle Bank.*

Dubmill Scarp is a broad sand between *Allonby* and *Beckfoot*, which extends about two miles from the shore; the outer end of it dries with spring-tide only; there are two rocks on it that dry about half ebb, one of which lies about a mile from *Dubmill Point*, the other half a mile. When *Hilton Castle* is on the E. end of *Allonby*, you are then near the S. side of *Dubmill Scarp*. There is a channel near the shore, in which there is a foot or two of water at low spring-tide. To avoid the extremity of this sand, keep *St. Bee's Head* a ship's length without *Harrington*, or keep *Silloth Point* and *Hawly Hill* in a line: *Hawly Hill* is a small top of a hill by itself, tapering regularly, and the farthest visible. When *Beckfoot* bears S. E. you are a little eastward of it; then, to avoid *Silloth Bank*, steer in nearer the shore. — *Dubmill Scarp.* — *Two cautions.*

Allonby's Scar is a rock almost a quarter of a mile long, which dries at low spring-tide only, and lies about mid-channel between *Dubmill-scarp* and *Robin-rig Bank*. — *Allonby's Scar.*

Silloth Bank lies near a mile and half from the nearest part of the shore at *Silloth*, and begins to dry on the W. end at half-ebb. Between the middle of it and *Skinburness*, there is a patch of sand that dries with spring-tide only. — *Silloth Bank.* — *Patch of Sand.*

No vessel should sail eastward in *Solway Firth*, on the *English* side, above *Dubmill-scarp*, except between half flood and high-water; for, if they happen to ground with ebb-tide on any Bank in the tide-way, the stream, particularly with spring-tide, will wash away the sand from the ship's side so as to overset her. If a vessel is under any necessity of running a-ground, it should be done, if possible, under shelter of some point, or bight on the shore, to break the strength of the stream; and not in a channel, or on a detached Bank. The like caution is necessary on the *Scotch* side above *Carsthorn*. — *Caution in sailing along the E. side of Solway Firth.*

WHITEHAVEN *Harbour.* — HARBOURS.

Whitehaven is a dry Harbour, divided into several basons, by strong keys that break off the sea, and shelter vessels within them: that within the second key as you enter, is the best for large vessels that draw above ten feet water. In this bason there are seventeen or eighteen feet at high-water with spring-tide, and nine or ten at high-water with neap-tide. There is a light kept on *St. Bee's Head* to shew vessels into *Solway Firth* at night: and when there are eight feet of water in the Harbour of *Whitehaven*, colours are hoisted in the day on one of the pier-ends, and a lanthorn light at night. — *On the English side of Solway Firth.*

In this Harbour it is high-water on full and change days at eleven hours. — *High-water full and change.*

Spring-tide off the Harbour rises twenty feet perpendicular; neap-tide ten. — *Rise of the Tide.*

PARTON *Harbour.*

Parton is a small dry Harbour, a mile and a half northward of *Whitehaven*, and is capable of small vessels only. There are thirteen feet of water in it at high-water with spring-tide, and seven or eight with neap-tide.

PORT-HARRINGTON.

Port Harrington lies about four miles northward of *Whitehaven*, and has twelve feet water in it at high-water with spring-tide, and seven or eight with neap-tide.

WORKINGTON *Harbour.*

In *Workington* Harbour there is thirteen feet at high-water with ordinary spring-tides, and seven or eight with neap-tides. When there are eight feet of water in this Harbour, colours are hoisted in the day, and a lighted lanthorn hung by a rope at night, on the starboard hand going in, about two ships-length from the channel. To sail into *Workington Harbour*, keep about one cables-length from the edge of the sea, until the lanthorn bears about S. E. then steer right for it, from thence steer E. into the Harbour.

Workington may be distinguished at sea by *Howraniched Hill*, which has a small tower on the top of it, and stands about half a mile south-eastward of the Harbour's-mouth. — *Workington distinguished at sea.*

There was a proposal some years ago for deepening the water in the entry of this harbour, and making it more commodious to sail out of it than it was with certain winds then; by extending the pier-head eastward, and the bulker-work on the E. side of the entry, north-eastward. I have not yet learned whether this has been carried into execution.

MARY-PORT *Harbour.*

In *Mary-Port* (formerly called *Allen-foot*) there are twelve feet of water, at high-water, with ordinary spring-tide, and eight with neap-tide. This place may be distinguished at sea by a glass-house on the Point near the W. end of the town.

The North Coast of MAN, *and* BAY OF LUCE.

Time of High-water. It is high-water here on full and change-days at 11½.

Banks and Shoals on the SCOTCH *Side of* SOLWAY FIRTH.

Barnbowry Bank. *Barnbowry Bank* extends from the *Point of Saturness* along the coast, about seven miles W. by S.: about two thirds of that part of it, which is next *Saturness*, dries at two hours of ebb, most of the rest of it at four hours of ebb; and the west extremity, which lies about two miles S. by E. from *Heston Island*, has six feet of water over it at low-water, with ordinary spring tide. This Bank may be distinguished, for the most part, by a ripple when it is little wind, and by the breakers in blowing weather.

Bank S. of Barnbowry. About a mile southward from the middle of *Barnbowry* there is a small Bank, which dries with spring-tide only.

Dowroof Bank. *Dowroof Bank* is about four miles long from S. W. to N. E. The eastmost extremity of it bears about three miles S. by W. from the *Point of Saturness*, on which there is a land-mark, or building like a light-house, and called the *Light house*, but no light is kept on it: the W. extremity bears S. W. ¼ S. from the *Point of Saturness*, and dries with spring-tide only: the E. end dries at four hours of ebb. This Bank may be distinguished by the breakers on it, except about slack water in extraordinary fine weather. There is a gut, or channel, near the middle of *Dowroof*, about half a mile wide, and two or three fathoms deep at low-water.

Blackshaw Bank. *Blackshaw Bank* begins about a mile eastward of *Dowroof*, and extends eastward across the mouth of the river *Nith*, in one continued sand, as far as *Annan*. The W. extremity of it bears S. ¾ W. about a mile and a half from the land-mark on *Saturness Point*: this end dries at four hours of ebb; a part of it next that dries only with spring-tide, and the rest about three quarters of ebb.

To sail through the Scotch channel. *Dowroof*, and the W. end of *Blackshaw Bank* on one side, and *Barnbowry* on the other, form what is called the *Scotch Channel*. These Banks, and their limits, are, for the most part, to be distinguished by the breakers, or appearance of the water on them; and therefore in sailing this way it is prudent to keep a good look-out. To sail through the *Scotch Channel* from the westward, take flood-tide, and keep within a league, or a league and a half of the *Scotch* coast, till you are a-breast of *Ard Hill*, near *Heston Island*; then keep the *Ross of Kirkcudbright* open of *Abby Head* a ship's-length or two, till the land-mark on *Saturness Point* bears N. E. and on *Arbigland House*, or nearly so, and keep that mark on till you are half a mile, or three-quarters, from the *Point of Saturness*; then steer E. N. E. past *Saturness Point*. If you want tide, or a pilot, to go farther up, anchor about half a mile E. S. E. from the Point, on six fathoms water; or sail to *Carsthorn*, and

Anchorage near Saturness Point, and in the river Nith. lie a-ground at the *Black Muscle-scap*; the southmost houses of *Carsthorn* bearing W. N. W. about two cables-length, where there is clean sand and pretty good shelter. Or you may lie on clean ground in the Channel, near *Carlaverock Castle*, where you will float before half flood. If you want to go farther up toward *Dumfries*, sail as soon with the flood-tide as you float, and keep as near the Channel as you can judge by the appearance of the water in it, which is commonly to be distinguished by the eye, and drop anchor a-breast of *Kelton*, about two miles below *Dumfries*.

Stream of tide. The stream above *Carsthorn* runs up only three hours, and down nine hours; the first three hours of the ebb, or downward stream, is weak. Spring-tide at *Carsthorn* rises seventeen or eighteen feet.

A Description of the Tides, Rocks, Shoals, and Anchoring-places, on the North Coast of the ISLE OF MAN, *and in the* BAY OF LUCE *in* SCOTLAND.

CHART XV.

TIDES.

Tides between the ISLE OF MAN *and the* BAY OF LUCE.

Time of high-water. It is high-water on the north of the *Isle of Man* at ten, and at the *Mule of Galloway* in *Scotland* at eleven o'clock; but the stream turns westward at six, on the full and change days of the moon; and at *Burrow Head* at eleven.

[illegible] In the *Isle of Man*, spring-tides rise eighteen or twenty feet perpendicular; neap-tides nine or ten: in the *Bay of Luce* spring-tides rise twelve or thirteen feet; neap-tides six or seven.

Velocity of the stream [illegible] Near the *Point of Ayre* in *Man*, spring-tides, when strongest, run about four miles an hour; and also in the middle between the *Isle of Man* and the *Mule of Galloway*; neap-tides run 1½. Near the *Mule Head of Galloway*, spring-tides run about six miles an hour when strongest; neap-tides two. In the *Bay of Luce* the stream of tide is scarce sensible.

Direction of the stream of flood. The principal stream of flood comes from the north-westward along the north coast of *Ireland*, and between *Ireland* and *Cantire*; from thence a branch of it sets south-eastward toward *Galloway* in *Scotland*, running up *Solway Firth*, and between *Galloway* and the *Isle of Man*. That part of the stream of flood which runs near the *Mule Head*, runs from thence two or three miles eastward, then turns northward up the *Bay of Luce*, but shifts gradually toward the south as the flood advances. Also, the first of flood, at the distance of a mile or two southward from the *Mule Head*, runs eastward along the coast, and toward *Solway Firth*, but shifts gradually southward toward the *Isle of Man*, so that near the end of flood the stream seems to run directly on it.

Stream of ebb. The stream of ebb takes the contrary direction, running at first about W. S. W. as if were on *Strangford* in *Ireland*, and turning gradually toward the north, as the ebb-tide advances, till at last it runs northward toward the *Mule of Cantire*. Ebb-tide, near the *Mule of Galloway*, is said to be stronger than the flood; and

Ebb stronger than flood. the first of the ebb stronger than the rest of it.

[illegible] From the *Mule Head* of *Galloway*, to *Crummel Point*, the stream within half a mile of the shore, runs northward during the first two hours of ebb, and then runs southward till the last of the flood.

BANKS and SHOALS. The rocks and shoals, near the *Isle of Man*, having been described already in page 20, thither we refer for such as fall within this chart.

In the Bay of Luce, Muckle and Little Scars. The only rocks or shoals in the *Bay of Luce*, are the *Muckle* and *Little Scars*, which lie in the mouth of the Bay, near the middle, and are always considerably above water, and easily seen. There are no shoals lying off them; there are two or three rocks near the *Little Scar*, which the sea sometimes washes over.

h In

The FIRTH OF CLYDE.

In moderate weather, especially with W. and S. W. winds, a vessel may stop on the W. side of the *Bay of Luce* any where on clean sandy ground, and a moderate depth of water. The best parts are, off the *E. Tarbet*, or the Kilbrews, about a quarter of a mile from the shore, on 3½, or four fathoms oozy ground. Also, — STOPPING-PLACES. Off E. Tarbet.

Off the islands called the *Mulls*, on 3½ fathoms, about a quarter of a mile from that shore. Also, — Off the Mull Heads.

Off *Mary-port* on two fathoms, sand. Also, — Off Mary Port.

In the bays of *Dunorre* and *Chapel-rossan*, a vessel that draws not above eight feet water may go in at high-water, and lie a-ground on the S. sides of these bays on clean sand, and pretty well sheltered; avoid a ledge on the S. point of both bays, which extend eastward a cable's-length from the shore. Or a vessel may anchor off the mouth of these bays on two fathoms clean ground, about half a mile from the shore. In the middle of *Chapel-rossan Bay*, there is a rocky shoal extending eastward from the low-water mark about a cable's-length, the least water on it is about six feet. — Dunorre and Chapel-rossan.

In the *Bay of Luce* spring-tides rise twelve or thirteen feet. — Rise of the Tide.

It is high-water in the *Bay of Luce*, on full and change-days, at eleven. — Time of high water.

PORT-NESSIK *Harbour*. — HARBOURS.

Port-Nessil, near *Logan House*, is capable of very small vessels only; for it dries within the key at half-ebb. A vessel that draws six or seven feet may lie sheltered from N. and N. W. winds, by running a-ground at high-water, close along the pier-head.

PORT-PATRICK *Harbour*.

Port-Patrick is a small dry Harbour, open to the westward, and without the conveniency of a key to shelter boats or vessels that come into it. Small vessels must go in at high-water, and run a-ground on the N. side of the creek, so as to be out of the reach of the sea in case the wind should blow from the W. or S. W. There are two rocks in the mouth of this bay; one on each side, and always above water; between these two rocks a vessel may stop a tide, in moderate weather, on two fathoms deep at low-water. The ferry-boats that cross between *Scotland* and *Ireland* sail from this place to *Donaghadee* near *Belfast Bay*.

In *Port-Patrick* Harbour it is high-water on the shore at 11½ on the full and change days; but the stream off the mouth of the Harbour turns northward about ten o'clock. — Time of High-water.

Along this part of the coast the stream of flood runs southward, and the ebb northward. — Direction of the Streams.

Spring-tides, within a mile of the shore, run about four miles an hour when strongest. — Velocity of the Streams.

A Description of the Tides, Rocks, Shoals, Anchoring-places, and Harbours in the FIRTH OF CLYDE, *from* LOCH RYAN *to* ARRAN ISLAND *and* CANTIRE.

CHART XVI.

Tides in the FIRTH OF CLYDE, *between* LOCH RYAN *and* ARRAN ISLAND, *and* CANTIRE. — TIDES.

In *Loch Ryan*, it is high-water on the full and change-days at 11½, on the shore of *Arran Island* at eleven; on the shore of *Sana Island*, and the adjacent shore of *Cantire*, at 11½; but the stream in the Sound of *Sana*, and along the coast westward to the *Mull of Cantire*, turns one hour, sometimes two hours sooner, being affected by the winds; and runs eastward only four or five hours, and westward seven or eight hours; beginning one, or two hours before low-water to run eastward, and continuing till the second or third hour of flood, then runs westward. — Time of High-water in Loch Ryan. Arran. Sana and Cantire. Stream runs stronger.

In *Loch Ryan*, ordinary spring-tides rise eight or nine feet perpendicular; neap-tides four or five; in *Arran* the same; on *Sana Island*, and the coast of *Cantire*, spring-tide rises five or six feet perpendicular, neap-tide two. The fall and rise of the tide in *Cantire* is much affected by the winds; W. and S. W. winds increase the rise, and N. and N. E. winds diminish it. — Rise of the Tide. Affected by Winds.

In the *Firth of Clyde*, the principal stream of flood comes from the N. W. between *Cantire* and *Ireland*, and sets up the *Clyde* between *Cantire* and *Arran*, and between *Arran* and *Ilsa*. The stream of flood, within a mile of the *Mull Head*, runs southward, and turns two hours sooner than at a greater distance from the Head; so that a vessel that keeps near the west coast of *Cantire* will have the benefit of the stream two hours before another that is above a mile from that land. — Direction of the Streams.

About a league westward of the *Mull of Cantire*, spring-tide, when strongest, runs about six miles an hour: within a mile of the Head the stream runs about two miles an hour when strongest; between *Cantire* and *Arran Island*, and between *Ilsa* and *Arran*, it runs about one mile an hour when strongest. Two or three miles eastward of *Sana Island*, the stream runs about three miles an hour when strongest. — Velocity of the Streams.

The *Firth of Clyde* makes a very fine entry to the safest and most commodious rivers for shipping that is either in *Britain* or *Ireland*: ships have neither rock nor shoal to fear on any part of the coast above a quarter of a mile from the shore, excepting *Paterson's Rock*, near *Sana Island*, and *Garroch Head*, eastward of *Campbelton Harbour*; and the *Crag of Ilsa* serves as a most remarkable and conspicuous beacon to direct ships up the channel to a number of very fine safe Harbours. — ROCKS and SHOALS.

Paterson's Rock lies about a mile east of the S. side of *Sana Island* near *Cantire*, and dries about low-water. — Paterson's Rock.

At this Rock, *Rosscraig's Head*, near *Campbelton*, bears N. E. by N. the *Mull Head of Cantire* is hid by *Sana*; and *Glenmore Rock*, near the E. end of *Sana*, and always above water, appears on the middle of *Hungerrock Island*. While the *Mull Head* is seen out to the S. of *Sana*, you are on the S. side of *Paterson's Rock*; while the *Mull Head* is out to the N. of *Sana*, you are on the N. side of it; while *Glenmore Rock* appears on the W. end of *Hungerrock*, you are on the E. side of *Paterson's Rock*; and while *Glenmore* appears on the E. end

W. N. W. and in a line with the top of the north-westmost black hill visible, close to which top there is a remarkable gap: also *Bone-ross Rock* is in a line with the *Point of Corwhil*, or with the E. end of the land at that bay. The bay being low land, the *Point of Corwhil* looks like an Island.

STOPPING-PLACES. In the *Firth of Clyde* the ground, above a mile from the shore, is, for the most part, clean sand, or mud; therefore when the weather is moderate, or the wind off shore, a ship may stop a tide almost any where eastward of *Loch Ryan* and *Campbelton*, a mile or more from the land, except where the water is too deep.

HARBOURS.

LOCH RYAN *Harbour*.

Loch Ryan is a capacious bay, of easy access, sufficiently sheltered, good holding ground, and the depth of water fit for large ships as well as small vessels.

Star Bank. The only shoal to be avoided in it is the *Star*, which is a tongue of sand, about three miles up the Harbour, on the W. side, which extends a mile and a half south-eastward from a small point at *Kirkbride*: a ridge along the middle of this bank dries at low spring-tide only, and is above a quarter of a mile broad; on the N. side of the *Star* the water is shallow, having not above two fathoms on it at low-water.

Anchorage. A large ship going in about low-water with spring-tide, should sail within a cable's-length of the *Kern Point*. The best anchorage for large ships is about half a mile southward of the *Kern Point*, on six or seven fathoms water; and must take care to ride no nearer the shore on the E. side than between two and three cables-length. Small vessels may ride any where farther up the bay, two or three cables-length from the shore; but the safest and most convenient part for them is, on the W. side of the *Star*, where there is no sensible stream of tide, and no great swell of the sea with any wind.

Stream of Tide near the Kern Point. Off the *Kern Point*, and for about a mile southward of it, spring-tides, when strongest, run about two miles an hour; wherefore ships ought to moor N. and S. so as to ride with the stream.

GARVIN *Harbour*.

Garvin Harbour is a little narrow creek, in the mouth of *Garvin Water*, where small vessels may go in about high-water, and lie aground on sand, sheltered from the sea. The channel is almost dry at low-water with spring-tide: at high-water with spring-tide there is nine or ten feet in it. Enter on the N. side of the perch, taking it about a ship's-length on the starboard hand.

ARRAN *Harbour*.

South-west Arran Ledge. On the south end of *Arran*, from *Bennan* westward to *Laggan Bay*, there is a continued ledge along shore, which extends above a quarter of a mile from it.

Bennan Rock. Off the N. end of the *Corsefield Cowderrel*, and a-breast of the hill near it, there is a Rock called *Bennan*, near half a mile from the shore, which dries at low spring-tide only. The rest of the coast of *Arran* has no rocks or ledges above a cable's-length from it.

Tide near Arran. It is high-water on the shore of *Arran*, on full and change days, at 11½.

Stream of Tide. The stream of flood along the E. and W. sides of *Arran* sets northward; along the S. and N. ends of it, sets eastward; but the stream is scarce sensible near any part of this Island, except near *Pladda Island*, where it runs about one mile an hour when strongest.

LAMLASH *Harbour in* ARRAN ISLAND.

In *Lamlash Harbour*, near the W. end of *Arran*, the ground is good, the depth of water sufficient for the largest ships, and the bay pretty well sheltered, but N. E. winds set in a great swelling sea into it. The N. side of the bay shallows about two cables-length from the shore. The best parts to ride in are, off the houses in *Lamlash Island*, on nine or ten fathoms water; or about two cables-length E. by N. or E. N. E. from the pier at the town of *Lamlash*.

LOCH RONSA IN ARRAN ISLAND.

In *Loch Ronsa* the ground is very good, and the water sufficient for large ships, but the place being narrow, it is fit for small vessels only.

Ledge. On the E. side of the entry, there is a rocky ledge dry at low-water, which extends near one-third over to the opposite side. To avoid this ledge, keep the middle. Anchor a-breast of the houses of *Balloon*, nearest the E. side of the bay, about a cable's-length N. of the peninsula on which the old castle stands, on five or six fathoms water.

Anchorage in Whiting Bay. In the summer-time, or with the wind off shore, a vessel may stop in *Whiting Bay*, southward of *Lamlash Island*, on clean ground, about two cable's-length from the shore, eastward of *Largymore*. Or in any part of *Brodick*

And in Brodick Bay. *Bay*, a league northward of *Lamlash*.

CAMPBELTON *Harbour*.

Campbelton Loch is large, well-sheltered, the ground good, the depth sufficient for the largest ships, and very little to be feared in sailing into it.

Ottard Shoal. *Ottard Shoal*, described before, lies near two miles E. N. E. from the entry of the Harbour, and has no less water on it than twelve feet.

Sandy Banks. Near the *Point of Smerby*, three-quarters of a mile northward of the entry, there are rocks above a quarter of a mile from the shore, that dry about low-water. To avoid them, keep the rock *Bone-ross*, which is near *Saddel*, open with the north end of *Arran*.

[illegible] On the north side of the entry of *Lough Campbelton*, a little above *Ben-drow*, there is a spit of sand which extends southward from the shore near *Trench*, more than half way to the middle of the sandy-beach between *Ben-drow* and *Cleveresfield Point*. A large ship, in sailing in or out, should keep about half a cable's-length from the southmost part of that sandy beach, which is always above water, except at the top of high spring-tide: a small vessel may keep the middle, and have water sufficient any time of the tide.

Any part of this bay is safe anchorage; only on the S. side of the bay, for about half a mile along the shore, the sand shoals about a cable's-length out.

Mouth of the CLYDE.

only about low-water. *Paterson's Rock*, described before, lies a mile E. of *Sanda*, and dries at low-water. The coast of *Cantire* over-against *Sanda*, from *Dunaverty* to *Macharioch*, is all bordered with rocks and ledges which dry at low spring-tide, and extend above a cable's length from the high-water mark. The ledge off [illegible] extends south-eastward above a quarter of a mile.

In sailing to the anchorage in *Sanda* from the W. keep above half a cable's length from the N. side of the island, particularly the head on the W. side of the anchorage. Anchor about half a cable's-length eastward of the head, on three or four fathoms at low-water; where the houses in the island bear S. by W. and *Fair-head* in *Ireland* is just shut in by the head in *Sanda*. Anchorage.

A Description of the Tides, Rocks, Shoals, Anchoring-places, and Harbours in the MOUTH *of the* CLYDE, *and in* LOCH FYNE.

CHART XVII.

Tides between the MOUTH *of* CLYDE *and* LOCH FYNE. TIDES.

In the Mouth of the *River Clyde*, from *Arran Island* to the *Old Kirk*, it is high-water on the shore about 11½ on full and change days. Time of high-water.

Spring-tide rises eight or nine feet perpendicular; neap-tide four or five. Rise of the Tide.

In the Mouth of the *Clyde*, spring-tides, when strongest, run not above one mile an hour, excepting in the *Kyles of Bute*, and a few other narrow channels, where they run about two miles an hour.

Rocks and Shoals along the Coast from GARVIN *to the* CUMRAY ISLANDS. ROCKS and SHOALS.

Brest Rock lies about three quarters of a mile S. S. W. from *Turnberry Point* in *Kirkoswald* parish; it dries at half-ebb, and extends about half a mile from the nearest shore. Brest Rock.

On the N. side of the *Bay of Ayr*, there is a rocky ledge which extends N. W. about two cables-length from the *Salt-pans*; and a quarter of a mile farther out lies *Salt-pan Rock*; the top of which dries with extraordinary spring-tides only. Salt-pan Rock.

The *Salt-pan Shoal* extends from *Salt-pan Rock*, near half way to *Lady Island*. It is composed partly of gravel, and partly of rocks; the least water on it is two fathoms. A leading-mark on this shoal is, when the *Lepers House* (a small ruinous House a little above the *Salt-pans*) is seen between the two *Salt-pans*; or when *Lady Isle* is in a line with the *Cock*, or northmost hill, of *Arran*. When the westmost of the two *Salt-pans* is in a line with the *Lepers House*, you are then a little eastward of this shoal; when the eastmost *Salt-pan* is in one with the *Lepers House*, you are then to the westward of it; when the *House of Troon* bears N. by E. or the Heads of *Ayr* S. W. you clear it along the N. E. end. Salt-pan Shoal.

Eastward from the extremity of *Salt-pan Shoal* there is a rock which extends from the shore near half a mile W. S. W. Rock eastward of Salt-pan Shoal.

There are two shoals that lie above a cable's-length from the S. W. side of the *Point of Troon*; one extends north-eastward from the extremity of the Point about two cables-length; and one lies E. N. E. from that Point three-quarters of a mile, which dries about half-ebb. Rocks near Point of Troon.

The water is shallow for about a quarter of a mile eastward and north-eastward of *Lady Isle*: the depth at low-water, with spring-tide, is from six to nine feet. Lady Isle Shoals.

Lappock Rock lies near half way between *Troon Point* and *Irvine*, and dries at four hours of ebb: the water is shallow a cable's-length from it on all sides except the north: it bears N. by E. from *Troon Point*, and N. E. from the little beacon on *Lady Island*, and W. N. W. from the *Castle of Dundonald*. The steeples of *Ayr*, seen by the *Point of Troon*, clears it along the W. side. Lappock Rock.

Horse Island has two rocks near the S. W. side, shallow water near the E. side, and several rocks that dry about half ebb between it and *Castle-craigs Point*. Horse Island Shoals.

Brigurd Sand lies along the coast from *Portincross Castle* to *Fairly Road*, and for the most part extends from the *Point of Ury*, half over to the *Great Cumray Island*. To avoid this Sand sailing along the E. side of the *Cumray Island*, keep nearer to the *Great Cumray* than to the *Point of Ury*; or keep the eastmost part of *Cumray* (a round point) on the top of *Knock Hill*, which is a sharp-topped hill, about a mile and a half northward of *Largs Kirk*. Brigurd Sand.

Skermorlie (or *Skelmorlie*) *Bank* lies about half way between the *Point of Toward* and *Skermorlie*; it is composed of shell sand and small gravel stones. On it the house of *Skermorlie* bears S. E. the *Point of Toward* W. N. W. and the *Point of Cloch* (in *Old Kirk* parish) N. E. ½ N. the least water on this Bank is 3½ fathoms, which is on the N. side of it, and not above a cable's-length in extent; so that none but the largest ships, about low-water, can touch this Bank; the depth being moderate, small merchant ships may stop at anchor on it, when it is not convenient to go into a better harbour. Leading marks to it are, the top of *Lamlash Island*, in *Arran*, appearing a very little nearer to the *Little Cumray* than to the S. end of *Bute* (called *Garroch Head*), and the house of *Kames* in *Bute*, just covered by the *Point of Toward*. Skermorlie Bank.

The few rocks and ledges near *Arran Isle* have been described in the preceding Chart, to which we refer, as none of them can be said to be dangerous. Arran Shoals described in Chart.

on four or five fathoms at low-water. In the summer-time, or in moderate weather, a vessel may stop in *Kerill Bay*: anchor towards the S. side, when *Lamlash Isle* is shut in by the S. side of the Bay. There is a ledge on the N. side of this Bay, which extends from the shore about a cable's-length.

HARBOURS.

AYR *Harbour.*

Ayr is a dry Harbour, and not capable of vessels that draw above eight feet of water, except when they have the advantage of extraordinary high spring-tides to raise the water on the bar. The bar lies a little without the perches, and has not above one foot of water over it at low spring-tides: with ordinary spring-tide there are nine feet on it at high-water; with ordinary neap-tides, about eight feet. With fresh southerly winds the water on the bar rises a foot or two higher than ordinary; for S. and S. W. winds raise the tides in the river *Clyde*, and N. and N. E. winds hinder their rise.

Nicholas Rock. About half a cable's-length south-westward from the perch, near the S. side of the bar, lies *Nicholas Rock*, which dries with spring-tides only. You avoid it along the W. side, when the outermost perch, on the S. side of the bar, is in a line with the outermost perch on the north side of the bar.

Not safe riding long here. A vessel may wait a tide off the mouth of this Harbour; but if the weather is not very promising, she ought not to anchor a whole night on this coast. If wind and tide do not serve to go in with, it will be prudent to run for *Lamlash* in *Arran*, or *Farly Road* opposite to the *Cumrays*, rather than to ride at anchor one night off the Harbour's mouth.

Rise of the Tides. Spring-tides here rise eight feet perpendicular; neap-tides four or five.

IRVIN *Harbour.*

Irvin is a dry Harbour, fit for small vessels only, that draw not above eight or nine feet water; and these must have high-water with spring-tide to go in with. With low-water, spring-tide, there is only a foot or two of water in the channel, except when high winds, or freshes in the river, increase it. There are perches placed along the S. side of the channel, from which you must keep about three ships-length, till you are within a half a cable's-length of a point on which there is some wooden work erected, like a pier; keep about two ships-length from this point and wooden work.

Rise of the Tide. Spring-tides here rise eight feet perpendicular; neap-tides four or five.

Southward from the mouth of this Harbour, the ground is in many places foul, and therefore not fit for anchoring on; northward of the mouth of the Harbour the ground is clearer and better. But if the wind and tide do not serve to carry a vessel in, it is better to run for *Lamlash*, or *Farly Road*, than to lie a night at anchor off the Harbour's mouth, except in summer when the weather is very moderate.

SALTCOATS *Harbour.*

This Harbour is dry at low-water, and fit for small vessels only, which draw not above eight feet of water, and these cannot get in but at high-water with spring-tide. In sailing in or out, keep within a quarter of a cable's-length of the *Rock Nebok*, which is always above water. The larboard-side, going in, is all foul and rocky; the rocks partly dry at half-ebb.

When the wind is not on shore, a vessel that draws not above eight feet may sail in about half-tide, and ground near the key-head, where she may lie pretty safe till the tide makes for going within it.

Stopping Place. The stopping-place off the mouth of this Harbour is near two cables-length from the key, on 3½ or four fathoms; where the key-head bears N. E. by N. or in a line with the kirk; which has no steeple, but is the largest building towards the N. end of the town.

FARLY *Road.*

Farly Road is pretty good anchorage in moderate weather; or when the wind does not blow hard from the W. or S. W. The place of anchorage is on the N. side of *Farly Bank*, somewhat more than a cable's-length from the shore, when the light-house on the *Little Cumray* is in a line with the southmost top of *Goatfell Hills* in *Arran*, on six fathoms water.

Sand-Bank. About two cables-length from the shore of *Farly*, a sand-bank begins and extends northward about a cable's-length; the least water on it is eight feet. At this bank the light-house bears about W. by S. the old castle above *Farly* S. E. by E. and the southmost house of *Farly* in a line with the old castle: the southmost house of *Farly* is a small house on the shore, with its end toward the sea. To avoid this bank on the N. side, going into *Farly Road*, keep the northmost point of *Little Cumray* in a line with the most tapering top (not the highest) of *Goatfell Hills* in *Arran*.

BUTE ISLAND.

The Bay of ROTHSEY.

The *Bay of Rothsey* (vulgo *Rosa*) is pretty well sheltered, and the ground very good and all clean. Anchor in any part on the E. side of the Bay; the most convenient is two cables-length N. of the pier-head.

KAMES *Bay.*

The *Bay of Kames* is good ground, and pretty well sheltered. Anchor about two cables-length from the head of the Bay.

KYLES OF BUTE.

The *Kyles of Bute* (or the channel on the N. and N. E. sides of the Island) are of easy access, well sheltered, the ground extraordinary good, and the depth of water sufficient for the greatest ships. Large ships in the E. Kyles, may anchor any where near the middle of the Sound: small vessels may anchor about a cable's-length from the shore on either side; or in the *Bay of Rubodach*, on the S. side of the small islands (the largest of which is *Hammore*), on three or four fathoms water.

In sailing between *Hammore* and *Bute*, keep nearest to *Hammore*.

Rock E. of Rude Point. About half a mile eastward of *Rude Point* (the N. W. point of *Bute*), there is a small rock dry at low-water, which lies half a cable's-length N. eastward of a small point.

Rock on the W. side of Inchmarnock. On the W. side of *Inchmarnock Island*, near the N. end, there is a rock near a cable's-length from the shore, which dries at half-ebb.

The Mouth of the CLYDE.

The stream of tide is scarce sensible on any part of the coast of *Bute*, except in the *Kyles*, near *Rudadach*, where, when strongest, it runs about two miles an hour. In the *Kyles* the stream of flood sets in from the S. W. and goes out S. E. through the E. *Kyle*. The stream in the *Kyles* turns half an hour before high or low-water on the shore. [Stream of Tide at the Kyles of Bute.]

Loch Riddin, or Loch Ruel.

Loch Riddin is a small arm of the sea, northward of the *Kyles of Bute*, which is well sheltered, has good ground, and depth sufficient for any ship. Take *Ilandirek*, the small island which is about a quarter of a mile up the Loch, on the starboard-hand going in, and anchor northward of that island, on ten or twelve fathoms. With spring-tides it ebbs dry from the head of the bay, till within three-quarters of a mile of *Ilandirek*.

Loch Strevin.

Loch Strevin is well sheltered, the ground all clean and good, and no rock nor shoal to be feared in it; but the water is deeper than merchant-ships chuse to ride on, except within a mile of the head of the Loch, where it is also best sheltered. The high land on each side of it, makes it subject to violent squalls of wind, when it blows fresh, either from the E. or W. quarter. The best anchorage in *Loch Strevin* is as high up as *Artari*, where the depth is twelve or fifteen fathoms. In coming in along the E. part of the *Point of Tewart*, give it a birth of about two cables length.

Loch Fyne.

Loch Fyne begins about six miles north of the *Island Arran*, and is an extensive and extraordinary fine place for shipping; particularly for large ships that may anchor on deep water, without being obliged to shelter in coves. The mouth, as far up as *Otter*, is five or six miles wide; and neither rock nor shoal in any part of it that lies two cables length from the land. Above *Otter* the width is contracted to about a mile, or three-quarters, for the most part; but without causing any considerable increase in the velocity of the stream of tide. The only danger, almost, to be avoided in going up this Loch, is *Rainaboterach Bank*; which is a Bank of gravel and sand that extends westward from *Otter*, about two-thirds over to *Gighan Island*. The top, or N. side of it, is dry at two hours of ebb; the south side, and the westmost extremity, dry only at low-water. To avoid the extremity of *Rainaboterach*, keep within half a mile, or above a cable's-length from *Gighan*: or keep *Castle Lachlin* in sight by the coast on the S. or starboard-side of the Loch going up. [Sand that dries?]

Rocks and shoals near the land, above *Rainaboterach*, to be avoided, are a ledge that extends half a cable southward from the E. point of *Loch Gare*; a rock two cables-length N. E. from *Ken-yune*, which dries about half-ebb; a sand-bank a cable's-length eastward of the *Point of Minart*, near a rock which is always above water. [Ledge near Loch Gare.] [Rock near Ken-yune.] [Sand-bank near Minart.]

The ground in *Loch Fyne* is all clean and good, but the water in the middle rather too deep for anchorage; between *Rainaboterach Spit*, and *Ken-yune*, it is from twenty to thirty fathoms; from *Castle Lachlin* to *Inveraray*, it is from thirty to seventy fathoms. Near one side therefore, about a cable's-length or two from the shore, is the best anchorage for large ships, and the N. side better than the south. Along the N. side the best parts are, a little above *Ken-yune*, between *Achagyle* and *Tychlaldach*: in the *French Farland* at *Kilbride*, anchor a cable's-length eastward from the point, on six or eight fathoms, taking care to avoid a spit of sand on the E. side of the rivulet, which dries above a cable's-length from the shore; in the mouth of the bay of *Inveraray*, off the castle, on fifteen fathoms; or about a cable's-length eastward of the west point of this bay, on six or seven fathoms water; about half a cable's-length N. E. of this anchorage, there is a small rocky shoal, on which the least water is eighteen feet, which should be avoided in dropping anchor. A pretty high sea sets along the bay of *Inveraray*, when it blows hard from the S. W. which makes the shelter of the fore-mentioned point the more convenient for vessels that are not well provided with anchors and cables: off the mouth of that rivulet, it dries about two cables-length from the high-water mark, but there is a perch placed on the extremity of this spit. [Anchorage in Loch-Fyne.] [Along the N. side, Tychlaldach, French Farland.] [Inveraray Bay.]

On the S. side, *Ilanvoran* is the best anchorage; anchor on the E. side of the island, about a cable's-length from the shore, on fourteen fathoms. [South side Ilanvoran?]

On the W. side of the mouth of *Loch Fyne*, the bay of *East Tarbit* is well sheltered, and the ground good; small vessels may ride very safe and smooth here all weathers, on four or five fathoms water; but the entry being narrow, it requires a leading-wind. On the S. side of this creek, over-against *Ilanaskiach* (or *Card Island*), there is a ledge that extends a ship's-length from the shore, on which there is a perch; the channel is between this perch and the small island opposite it. Anchor as soon as you have past the old castle. A small vessel, if necessary, may anchor on the N. side of *Ilanaskiach*, but keep the middle going in, or nearest to the island, to avoid a small rock near the point on the main, on which the least water is three or four feet. [Coves in Loch Fyne for small vessels. E. Tarbit.]

Loch Gilp, being open to the south, is only fit for vessels to ride in, in the summer-time. There are rocks, always above water, on the E. side of this bay that shelter it a little. Anchor within two cables-length northward of *Duncan Rock*, on two or three fathoms, where that rock covers the entry of the narrow part of *Loch Fyne*. [Loch Gilp.]

Loch Gare is the safest and best creek in *Loch Fyne* for a vessel that draws not above ten or twelve feet of water. In the narrowest part of the entry, it shoals a little way from the shore on each side; therefore keep near the middle, or somewhat toward the west side. Anchor near the middle of the bay, but rather nearer the W. than to the E. side; for there the water is deepest. [Loch Gare.]

In the bay of *Minart*, two miles above *Loch Gare*, a vessel may ride pretty well sheltered, when one anchor is laid on shore, and another north-eastward. In going in, keep about half a cable's-length from the point opposite to a sand-bank, which lies about a cable's-length eastward from the point, and as mentioned above. [Minart Bay.]

It is high-water at *Inveraray*, in *Loch Fyne*, at 12½, on the full and change-days. Spring-tides rise eight or ten feet perpendicular. The stream of tide is scarce sensible in this Loch any where, except near the point of *Rainaboterach Bank*, where it runs about two miles an hour when strongest. [Tides in Loch Fyne.]

A Description of the Tides, Rocks, Shoals, Sand-banks, Anchoring-places, and Harbours in the CLYDE, *from the* CUMRAY ISLANDS *to* GLASGOW.

CHART XVIII.

TIDES. *Tides in the* CLYDE, *between the* CUMRAY ISLANDS *and* GLASGOW.

Clyde in General. No River whatever can be safer, or is better provided with spacious well-sheltered arms of the sea, all easy of access, and capable of numerous fleets, than the *Clyde* is. In approaching it there are neither rocks nor shoals, nor rapid tides to be feared. *Ailsa* is a high mountain in the mouth of it, conspicuous at more than ten leagues distance, and serves as a remarkable beacon to direct ships towards it; there is a light-house on the *Little Cumray* to direct them farther up, and to good shelter in the night; and there is hardly one opening to be seen, but what a stranger, without draft or pilot, might venture safely to run for in the day-time, and find good anchorage within it. This river is provided by nature with every conveniency for navigation, excepting a sufficient rise of the tide for wet and dry docks for great ships; the ordinary rise of spring-tide, as far up as *Greenock*, being no more than ten feet perpendicular.

Time of High-water. In the *River Clyde*, from the *Cumrays* to *Port Glasgow*, it is high-water on the shore, on full and change-days of the moon, about 11½.

Rise of the Tide. Ordinary spring-tides rise ten feet perpendicular; extraordinary eleven or twelve; neap-tides six or seven.

Velocity of the Stream. The stream of tide, between the *Cumrays* and *Greenock*, where strongest, does not run above a mile and a half an hour; except in the narrow part of *Garloch*, where it runs four or five miles.

ROCKS and SHOALS. The rocks and shoals in this part of the *Clyde*, and in or near the harbours, are, a sandy shoal, extending near a quarter of a mile S. W. from *Portachur*, the S. W. point of *Cumray Island*, on which the least water is twelve feet.

Skelmorlie Bank. *Skelmorlie Bank*, described in the preceding Chart, on which the least water is 3½ fathoms.

Bridge Rock. *Bridge Rock* lies about a mile north-eastward of the *Point of Toward*, and about a quarter of a mile from the shore: it dries at two hours of ebb; to avoid it, keep the *Point of Toward* on the westmost of the *Goatfell Hills* in *Arran Island*. The *Goatfell Hills* all taper to the top.

The Gantocks Rock. The *Gantocks Rock* lies about a quarter of a mile S. from the old castle of *Dunoon*; the top of it is covered only with high spring-tides, and has a sufficient depth half a cable's-length from it quite round.

Roseneath Shoal. *Roseneath Shoal* lies near half way between *Mickle Rosk* in *Roseneath*, and the *White-farland Point* on the opposite side; is composed of sand and large stones, and the least water on it is five feet; there is a buoy sometimes kept on it. Leading marks to the shoal are, the *White-farland Point* in a line with the top of a remarkable hill over it, and bearing S. S. W. ½ W.; the castle of *Ardmorgan* just appearing eastward of a small rising on *Roseneath*, about a quarter of a mile from the Point; and the barn of *Greenock House* (a single house in the middle of the wood) a ship's-length W. of the wind-mill at *Greenock*. To avoid this shoal sailing E. or W. keep nearer to the *White-farland* than to *Roseneath*; or within half a mile of *Roseneath* shore.

STOPPING PLACES. Between the *Cumrays* and *Greenock*, the ground is almost all clean and good, so that, avoiding the rocks described, a ship may stop any where if the depth is moderate, and the weather not very bad. The usual and most convenient places for stopping are,

Cumray, Bute, Skelmorlie Bank. On the E. side of the *Cumray Island*, and of *Bute*, as before mentioned: on *Skelmorlie Bank*, when the weather is moderate. Also,

In *Old Kirk Bay*, off the middle of it, on twelve or fourteen fathoms, about a quarter of a mile from the shore.

In Holy Loch. In the mouth of *Holy Loch*, which is all good ground, and of a moderate depth; or a cable's-length or two westward of the *White Beachy Point*, which is about the middle of the S. side of the bay, on fourteen fathoms. This is a good place for waiting a wind to sail farther up the *Clyde*, or out of it to the southward.

Gourock Bay. In *Gourock Bay*, off the middle of it, and about two cables-length from the shore, on eight or ten fathoms, when the E. end of the bay bears W. by S.

Tail of the Greenock Bank. At the W. end, or tail, of *Greenock Bank*, on ten or eleven fathoms water, anchor when the wind-mill bears S. W. and the point of the *White-farland* N. W. by W. Or anchor two or three cables-length from the shore, but before you are so far E. as to have the rope-work, or westmost house of *Greenock* bearing S. W. or in a line with the west end of a bush of fir trees, which may be seen above *Greenock House*. This is the common place to wait the tide for going into *Greenock* harbour, or up to *Port Glasgow*; here moor N. and S. if it blows fresh, or if you stay a whole winter's night; for in hard gales ships have dragged their anchors here; but perhaps it has been owing to negligence in mooring, or in sparing out cable.

HARBOURS. The harbours in and near *Bute* are described in the fore-going Chart.

LOCH LONG.

Loch Long is all clean and good-holding ground, but the S. end, or widest part of it, is too deep for ordinary merchant ships to ride in. The best part of this Loch is about a mile from the head of it, between *Ardgartan* and *New-tarbet*, where the water is of a moderate depth, and not so liable to violent squalls of wind from the hills as other parts. When N. and N. W. winds blow fresh, the squalls, sudden calms, and variable winds, are very troublesome in the Loch. Above the house of *New-tarbet*, about two or three cables-length from the head of the Loch, on eight or nine fathoms water is good anchorage, and very little subject to these squalls and sudden calms.

LOCH GOIL.

Loch Goil is all clean good ground, but in blowing weather is subject to the same squalls and varying winds as *Loch-long* is, which makes it troublesome sailing in or out, and sometimes hard riding. The best places of anchorage are, off the old castle of *Carrik*, on fourteen or fifteen fathoms; or at the head of the Loch, about two cables-length from the shore.

The RIVER CLYDE.

GERLOCH.

Gerloch is a very safe place to ride in, being well sheltered, and the ground sufficiently good over it all. In sailing towards the mouth of this Loch, avoid *Rosneath* shoal described before; and *Madalva*) *Rock*, which lies above a cable's-length eastward of *Roherrash*, on the W. side of the entry, and dries at half-ebb. The water is shallow near a cable's-length from that rock on all sides; so that to avoid it and the shallows, it is necessary to keep two cables-length from the *Point of Roherrash*. A leading-mark to that rock is, when the castle of *Rosneath* appears through a narrow avenue in the trees, which extends south-eastward from the *Castle*. [illegible]

The usual anchorage is in *Rosneath Bay*, near two cables-length from the shore, on seven fathoms water, where the castle bears S. E. by S. and the mill stands W. by S. The stream of ebb in this anchorage runs about two miles an hour when strongest; but the stream of flood is scarce sensible, being reflected northward by the beachy point below the castle of *Rosneath*. [illegible]

All that part of *Gerloch*, which is northward of the *Corran*, or *Narrow*, at *Clachan*, is good and safe anchorage. On the E. side of the *Corran* there is a spit, or ridge, of small stones, called *Ramsewell*, which extends eastward about two-thirds over toward the *Point of Clachan*; one half of which is dry at half-ebb, and the whole about low-water. To sail through the *Corran* northward; take flood-tide, and keep within half a cable's-length from the high-water mark of the *Point of Clachan* on the larboard-side, till you are just past that Point, then steer a little eastward of N. to avoid a rock which lies on the N. side of the Point, about half a cable's-length from the high-water mark. [illegible]

Spring-tides in the *Corran*, when strongest, run about five miles an hour. [illegible]

GREENOCK *Harbour*.

Greenock Harbour is dry at low-water, except between the pier-heads, where there are two feet at the lowest tides. Within the Harbour the ground is soft and easy for vessels to lie on. There is a firm and convenient graving-bank on the E. side of *Mid key*. Ships that draw eleven feet water may go into this Harbour with spring-tide. To sail into *Greenock Harbour*, about high-water keep one half, or one-fourth, of a cable's-length from the *Rope-work Key*, and about half a cable's-length from the key of *Greenock*, to avoid *Greenock Bank*, till you open the entrance of the Harbour, then sail in.

Cockle Bank (the W. end of which is sometimes called *Greenock Bank*) reaches from the W. end of the town of *Greenock* to the old castle of *Newark*, at *Port Glasgow*. Part of the W. end of it, or *Greenock Bank*, dries with spring-tide only; the rest dries at low-water commonly.

Near the W. end of *Greenock Bank* is good anchorage for ships of any burthen; and is the place where vessels usually wait the tide to sail into *Greenock Harbour*, or up to *Port Glasgow*. Anchor on ten or eleven fathoms water, when the wind-mill, near *Greenock*, bears S. W. and the point of the *White-forland* N. W. by W.

PORT GLASGOW.

Port Glasgow harbour is dry at low-water, and, with spring-tide, is capable of vessels that draw ten or eleven feet of water: the ground is soft and easy to lie on; and a good place for graving ships hath been made there since this survey was taken. The channel from *Greenock* to *Port Glasgow* is narrow and intricate, as far as *Garvil Point*; there being neither beacon, nor buoy, to direct vessels through it; therefore this part of the channel requires a pilot. About a quarter of a mile N. from the *Garvil Point*, there is a buoy on the south edge of the *Cockle Bank*; keep that buoy on the larboard-hand, and if it is low-water, keep about a cable's-length from it. Near the E. side of *Garvil Point* there is a beacon, which take on the starboard-hand, keeping not less than two ship's-length from it, nor more than half a cable to avoid the *Cockle Bank*. Between this last beacon and *Port-glasgow*, there is first a buoy, and then a beacon; keep both these on the starboard hand, sailing no nearer to them than two ships-length, and no farther than half a cable. There is also a beacon near the key of *Port Glasgow*, to be taken on the starboard-hand, above two ships-length. Enter the harbour about high-water.

DUMBARTON *Harbour*.

Dumbarton Harbour is a creek in the mouth of the river, where vessels that draw not above nine or ten feet water may go in at high water, and lie a-ground on soft mud; but it is not thought that any directions will be sufficient to direct a stranger into it. If a pilot cannot be got, or if he happens not to be well acquainted with this Harbour, the following directions may be found serviceable. Sail to *Port Glasgow* by the directions for that Harbour; and at half-flood weigh anchor and sail, keeping a cable's-length from the shore at the old castle of *Newark*; from thence steer eastward between *Ardoch* and *Dumbarton Castle* about two miles, till you are a-breast of *Finlayston*, when you will steer somewhat nearer the S. than to the N. side of the *Clyde*; then steer south-eastward for the westmost buoy off *Dumbarton Castle*, where stop at anchor till it is near high-water: then take that buoy on the larboard-hand, about a quarter of a cable's-length, and the other buoy, a little eastward of it, on the starboard-hand about a ship's-length, and stand in for the E. side of the entry, and keep that side close till you are past the Castle.

Only lighters, or very small vessels, have water up to the key of *Glasgow*.

NAUTICAL DESCRIPTIONS

OF THE

WEST COAST and WESTERN ISLANDS

OF

S C O T L A N D,

FROM

CANTIRE *to* CAPE-WRATH, *and the* BUTT *of the* LEWIS.

A Description of the Tides, Rocks, Shoals, Channels, Anchoring-places, and Harbours in the South Part of ARGYLESHIRE, *from the Mull of* CANTIRE *to the Islands of* GIA, JURA, *and* ILA.

C H A R T XX.

Tides from CANTIRE *to* GIA, JURA, *and* ILA.

TIDES. [illegible]

ALONG the W. side of the *Mull of Cantire* it is high-water on the shore at eleven o'clock, on full and change-days, and the stream above a mile from the coast turns at that time; but within a mile of the shore the stream turns two hours sooner; near *Gia Island* it is high-water on full and change-days at ... on the coast of *Knapdale*, and on the S. end of *Jura Island*, and E. side of *Ila Island*, at 7½; but the stream in the sound of *Ila* turns half an hour, sometimes an hour sooner. At *Kilchoman*, at 4½; at the point of the *Rove of Ila*, and *Ilan-nan-ron*, at eleven. On this part of the coast, spring-tides rise about five feet perpendicular, and neap-tides ... or ...; excepting with strong gales of W. or S. W. winds, when they rise a foot or two higher; N. and N. E. winds prevent their usual rise.

Off the W. side of the *Mull of Cantire*, spring-tide, when strongest, runs about six miles an hour; neap-tide two.

Between the *Mull of Cantire* and *Gia Island*, spring-tide runs about one mile an hour, when strongest.

Off *Knapdale*, near the *Macormack Islands*, spring-tide, when strongest, runs about three miles an hour; near the S. E. coast of *Jura*, off the small islands, it runs about one mile an hour.

In the sound of *Ila*, spring-tide, when strongest, runs five miles an hour and neap-tide ...

Along the south coast of *Ila* the stream of tide is scarce sensible, till you come to the *Mull of Kinhowth* (or *Machrihanish*), where spring-tides, when strongest, run about four miles an hour; and neap-tides one, or ... From the *Mull of Kinhowth* to the *Rove*, the stream is not above ... mile an hour: at the E. side of the *Rove*, it runs about five miles an hour when strongest; and near *Oversay Island* runs six or eight, and makes a rough breaking sea, and whirlpools, in which boats have been lost. This rough sea is called *Corryvreckan*.

Corryvreckan Whirlpool. [illegible]

From the *Rove of Ila*, till within two miles of *Tarver Head*, the stream is scarce sensible; near *Tarver* it runs four miles an hour when strongest.

The stream of flood between the *Mull of Cantire* and the *Islands Gia* and *Jura*, sets northward. The flood on the S. side of *Ila* comes from the south-westward, along the N. W. coast of *Ireland*, and divides on the S. E. part of *Ila*, near *Ardmore Island*; one branch of which runs through the sound of *Ila* northward; the other runs westward along the coast of *Ila* to the *Mull of Kinhowth* and the *Rove*, and from thence northeastward along the N. coast of *Ila* to the *Gulph of Corryvreckan*.

Rocks and Shoals between the MULL OF CANTIRE *and* GIA, JURA, *and* ILA.

ROCKS and SHOALS.

The only rocks or shoals near the *Mull of Cantire* are, a rock off the N. point of the head at *Dunaverty*, which lies about half a cable's length from the shore, and dries about half-ebb; and a rocky shoal off the *Point Ufale*, at the fale-pans, which lies about a quarter of a mile from the shore, on which the least water is thought to be three or four feet. On this shoal the sea swells and breaks in the calmest weather.

K

About

From CANTIRE *to* GIA, KNAPDALE, JURA, *and* ILA.

About half a mile westward from the *Point of Barrbeure*, in *Kilean* parish, there is a small rock which dries at half-ebb. Leading-marks to it are, the southernmost hill of *Gee* on the smallest, or northmost, of the four *Paps of Jura*; and the *Head of Kara* in *Gia*, in a line with the highest hill of *Ila*, which appears with an arched top southward of the sound of *Ila*. This rock is avoided along the W. side, when a small rock, always above water, near the *Point of Rabintorduch*, in *Kilean* parish on the main, is in a line with the highest hill near the *Mule of Cantire*.

About one-third from *Cara Island*, and two-thirds from the *Point of Barrbeure*, there is a blind rock, on which the least water is six feet. Leading-marks to it are, the S. head of *Cara Island*, bearing W. by N. and the W. end of *Ila*, quite shut in by *Cara Island*; and the *House of Cara*, in a line with the northmost, and most tapering hill in *Ila*, near the sound.

Skervigigalam Rock lies above a quarter of a mile E. S. E. from the northmost point of *Ilan Gigilum*. The middle of it dries two hours after high-water, the N. end at half-ebb, and the S. end with spring-tides only. To avoid it, keep above a cable's-length from the middle part of the Rock.

There is a rocky shoal which lies E. S. E. from *Skervigigalam* about a quarter of a mile, on which nine feet is the least water. A leading mark to it is, the northmost point of *Cara Island*, on the *Mule of Kenlarvik* (or *Mule-naben*) in *Ila*: *Skervigigalam Rock*, on the N. end of *Island Gigilum*, clears it along the N. side.

E. S. E. from the *House of Cara*, above a quarter of a mile, there is a rocky shoal, on which the least water is twelve feet. A leading-mark to it is, the upper westmost small house of *Cara*, a very little open to the S. of the principal house, and the lowermost house just shut on it: also *Skerforlach House* in *Gia*, in a line with the rock near the south end of *Gigilum*, which is always above water.

The N. side of *Cara Island*, and from thence to the anchorage at *Gigilum*, is full of scattered rocks, some of which are always above water, and some dry about half-ebb, or lower; these rocks shelter the anchorage.

Eastward from *Ilan Garvilan*, on the E. side of *Gia*, and almost half-way between *Ardaverish* in *Gia*, and *Balachoyarran* on the main, there is a rock that dries about half-ebb. A leading-mark to it is, the southmost *Pap* of *Jura*, a little open to the S. of the highest hill of *Gia*. That hill and Pap, in a line, clears it along the N. side.

About half a mile north-eastward from E. *Garvilan Island*, and S. S. E. from F[illegible] (which is always above water), there is a small rock, which dries about half-ebb. At the [illegible] of the *Mule of Cantire* is a little more than one-third from the southermost visible point of the *Mule of Cantire*, and about two-thirds from *Cara Island*. To avoid this rock on the E. side, keep nearer to the *Ranaharn* side, on the main, than to *Gia*; or keep *Garvanlan Rock* (which is always above water) on the sharp top of the low hill below *Kilberry House* in S. *Knapdale*; the E. side of that top looks as if it was a precipice.

S. by E. from the N. E. end of *Gia*, and near half way between that and *Ranaharin* on the Main, there is a rocky shoal, on which the least water is three feet. Leading-marks to it are, the highest hill in *Gia*, bearing about W.; *Garvanlan Rock*, bearing N. N. E. and on the *House of Kilberry* in S. *Knapdale*; and the N. point of *Gia* a little northward of the northmost of the four *Paps*, or high hills, of *Jura*.

About half a mile northward of the N. end of *Gia* there is a cluster of rocks always above water, of which *Dusker* is the largest. Eastward of *Dusker*, near a quarter of a mile, there is a rock which dries at low-water; this rock is avoided on the E. side, near half a mile, when the *Mule of Cantire* is in the least open of, or only a little shut in by, any part of the E. side of *Gia*. It is avoided along the N. side by steering E. or E. by S. from the northmost, or smallest, of the cluster of rocks always above water; or while that northmost rock is in a line with any of the hills of *Ila* southward of *Macarter's Head* in the sound of *Ila*.

On the N. W. side of *Gia*, there is a rock which lies two cables-length from the shore, abreast of the largest hill, and dries about low-water. To sail along the W. side of this rock, keep the sharp top of the hill, next northward of *Kilberry* in S. *Knapdale*, fairly in sight by W. *Garvilan Island*.

ANCHORING-PLACES.

GIGILUM *Anchorage in* GIA ISLAND.

Gigilum Road is the most common and convenient anchorage in *Gia*: the ground is good, the water a sufficient depth, and the anchorage pretty well sheltered by *Gigilum Islands* and *Rocks* on the S. and W. sides, and by *Gia* and a sand-bank on the N. and E. sides. This harbour may be entered from the S. and W. either along the West side of *Gigilum Islands*, or along the E. side; but the E. side is the safest channel. To sail in at the E. entry, the surest way is to keep within a quarter of a mile from the S. E. side of *Cara Island*, and from two to half a cable's-length of the E. side of *Ilan Gigilum*. Anchor about a cable, or half a cable's-length W. or north-westward of the N. E. point of *Gigilum*; or about half between a rock always above water (which lies near a small sandy cove in *Gia*), and the N. end of *Gigilum*, on three or four fathoms water.

It is high-water on the shore of *Gia*, about two o'clock, on full and change-days; and spring-tides rise five or six feet; but both are liable to some variation by the winds.

A vessel that draws not above eight or ten feet water, may ride very safe on the N. side of E. *Garvilan Island* (on the E. side of *Garvilan*), off *Drymachra*; the Ground is good, and the bay pretty well sheltered. A vessel from the N. must sail in along the W. side of *Fladale Rock*; a vessel from the southward must avoid the several rocks and shoals in the way to *Garvilan*, as before directed, and enter between the E. point of *Garvilan* and the rock near it, which is always above water; but must keep somewhat nearer to *Garvilan* than to the rock.

The *Bay of Tarbit* is very safe in the summer-time. In sailing in avoid a shoal on the N. side of the Bay, on which there is only six feet at low-water, and lies half a cable's-length from the shore. Anchor on the S. side of the Bay, two cables-length from the shore, if the vessel is large; a small vessel may anchor nearer it.

WEST LOCH-TARBIT *Harbour*.

W. Loch Tarbit.

The bay of *West Loch-Tarbit* is well-sheltered; the depth of water, for above a mile up, sufficient for the largest ships; but the ground, being a soft mud, and not of the stiff kind, does not hold well in hard gales, except there is a full cable out. A vessel may anchor in any part of it in moderate weather, if the shoals, to be described hereafter, are avoided: the two most common places of anchorage are, for large ships, off *Ardpatrick*, in the mouth of the Loch; and, for small vessels, on the E. side of *Eleanagallagan*.

On the S. side of *Elan-Traya*, there are several rocks that lie above half a cable's-length off, partly dry about half-ebb, and partly at low-water. These are avoided, by keeping a cable's-length from the Island, or one-third from it, and two-thirds from the S. or starboard-side of the entry.

There.

From CANTIRE *to* GIA, KNAPDALE, JURA, *and* ILA.

There is a sand-bank that extends from the E. point of *Corran*, near one-third over to the N. side of the Loch. To avoid it, keep toward the N. side; or sail no nearer the S. side, than till the eastmost extremity of *Ilen-traya* is in a line with the west end of the highest hill in *Gia Island*.

Off *Dunstaid*, on the N. side of the Loch, about one-third from that side, and two-thirds from the opposite side, there is a small blind rock, on which the least water is five feet. A leading mark to this shoal is, the westmost point visible on the N. side of the Loch, appearing in one with a sink, or hollow, in the rising ground at the S. end of *Gia*: keep that rising ground out by the point, or keep the middle of the Loch, and you avoid this shoal.

At the head of W. *Loch Tarbet*, the tide falls and rises very little; rarely above two feet perpendicular with spring-tide, and often not once; and the fall and rise are very irregular; falling and rising alternately two or three times in an hour, or six or seven times in twelve hours time, sometimes falling as much in one or two hours, as it rises in six or eight. The inhabitants observe, that with strong westerly and S. W. winds the fall of the tide is scarce sensible any time of the day; and that with strong northerly winds the water hardly rises at all for a whole day, but continues about the low-water height.

LOCH KYLISPORT.

Loch Kylisport (sometimes called *Loch Kylifad*, or *Kylifad*) being open to the south, and the ground a soft kind of ooze, which does not hold well in blowing weather, is not reckoned safe anchorage, except in the summer-time. The safest part to ride in is near the head of the bay, about a cable's-length or two eastward of a rock, which lies in the middle, and is always above water.

Brackrypp Rock lies about half a mile W. by S. from *Kerckrypp*, at the mouth of *Loch-kylisport*, and dries at low-water only.

LOCH-ACHAITIL.

Loch-Achaitil is a very fine harbour, fit for ships or vessels of any size. The ground is good, the depth from six to thirteen fathoms, and only one rock in the way up, which is quite covered only with spring-tide. Ships may anchor in any part of this Loch, above *Castle Sween*; but the N. side is to be preferred, as it is best sheltered against N. and westerly winds, which are commonly the most violent on this coast. At the head, in *Kilmichael Bay*, a vessel may ride in any weather with only one anchor out.

The rocks and shoals to be avoided in sailing toward this Loch, are a small rock on the N. side of the two *Machermore Islands*; the north end of which dries with spring-tide only; the south end has from six to twelve feet water on it; it lies a little nearer *Ilen-machermore* than to *Dunmore-machermore*.

Off the mouth of *Loch-nakill*, about a mile southward, and half a mile westward of the point of *Danna Island*, there is a small shoal, on which the least water is four feet. It is avoided along the W. side, while the highest hill of *Gia* (which is near the middle of the Island) is seen without, or westward of, *Ilen-machermore*: it is avoided along the E. side, when the westmost hill of *Gia* appears a little westward of *Ilen-machermore*.

LOCH-NAKILL.

Loch-Nakill is very good anchorage in the summer-time; or a ship may stop a tide, or a night, in it at any time, except when the wind blows hard from the S. W. to which quarter it is open. Anchor on the west side of the bay, before you are a-breast of an old chapel, which stands near the shore, on four or five fathoms water. The shoal off the mouth of this Loch is described with the preceding Loch; it lies about a mile southward of the mouth of the Loch, and has four feet the least water on it.

LOCH DALGAÜL in JURA ISLAND.

Loch Dalgaül is a small cove, but the anchor-ground good, the water sufficiently deep for any merchant-ship, and pretty well sheltered: it is convenient for vessels bound to the southward. Anchor near the middle of the bay, when *Gia Island* is just shut in by the N. point of the entry, and the northmost Pap of *Jura* bears N. W. ¼ W.

On the N. N. E. and N. W. sides of this bay, it shoals near two cables-length from the shore; therefore in turning in or out, a vessel must not stand too near these sides. On the S. W. sides it is sufficiently deep half a cable's-length from the shore.

Harbour of the small Isles of JURA ISLAND.

This Harbour is sufficiently sheltered in the anchorage on the W. side of *Gore Island*; but the ground there being only gravel, or sand, covered with long grass, and the depth not above 4½ fathoms, it is only fit for small vessels; and these in the winter should always moor, in case one anchor should drag. Anchor off the middle of *Island Gore*, a-breast of the *Kern*, about half way to the west side of the bay, on 3½ fathoms. You may sail into this anchorage, either along the S. or the N. end of *Island Gore*. To sail along the south end of it, keep about a quarter of a cable's-length from the point of the Island, to avoid a rock which dries at half-ebb, and lies near mid-way between the *Island Gore* and the point of a rock always above water, on the larboard-hand going in. To sail to the anchorage along the N. side of *Island Gore*, between it and *Island Cromin*, avoid a small rock on the E. side of *Island Gore*, about a cable's-length S. E. from the *Kern*, which dries with spring-tide only; and stand half over to the W. side of the bay, before you turn southward; to avoid a shoal partly rocky, and partly gravel, that extends westward from *Island Gore*, near half over to the W. side of the bay. S. Entry. N. Entry.

In the summer-time there is good anchorage on the N. and W. sides of *Ilen-Pladda*: and along the S. side of *Ilen-Fraoch*.

Skervaill Rock lies about two miles E. S. E. from *Loch Nagail* in *Jura*, and is never quite covered with the tide; but is not three feet above the surface at high-water with spring-tide. It is sufficiently deep above half a cable's-length from it on all sides.

Colbern Rock lies about a mile south-south-eastward from *Island Gore*, and is always a little above water. A leading mark to it is, the S. end of *Island Gore*, S. by E. and in a line with *Benmore Hill* in *Jura*. Keep above half a cable's-length from the N. and S. sides of it.

ILA

ILA ISLAND.

Rocks and Shoals near ILA ISLAND.

Rocks along the S. coast.

Along the S. coast of *Ila* there are a great number of rocks, many of them always above water; some of them dry about half-ebb, and at low-water, and some with *spring-tide* only; but, excepting the *Shoal Ottersmouth*, there is none of them that lies above a mile and a quarter from the nearest shore. The two outermost are *Taylor* westward, and a rock off *Ardmorsky* eastward, which are large remarkable rocks always above water; all the other rocks lie nearer to *Ila* than these two; and ships along this side of *Ila* must keep without them to avoid the rest.

Taylor Rock.

Ottersmouth Shoal.

Ottersmouth is a small rocky shoal that lies near a league southward of *Ila*-*Tone*, on which the least water is twelve feet. There is always a sensible stream of tide running over this shoal, but none perceptible near it. At this shoal, *Beanaharie*, at the S. E. point of *Ila*, bears N. E. ¼ E. and *Taylor Rock* N. ¾ W. and on the gap at the top of the *Hill Knockanirard* is near *Loch Lanlamis*, and a small black point, which is just perceptible, near *Mulmule* (or the *Mule of Knockanirard*), is exactly on that head; when this small point is without, or southward of the *Mule*, you are half a mile northward of *Ottersmouth*.

No dangerous rocks along the W. side of Ila.

There are no rocks or shoals that lie above a third part of a mile from the shore on the W. side of *Ila*, except near *Lochindaal* harbour.

Rocks along the N. side of Ila. Ballach Rocks.

The only rocks to be avoided along the N. side of *Ila*, are *Ballach Rocks*, the rocks and ledges near *Ila*-*Nove*, and *Pessaghan Rock*, near *Ruveal*, the E. point. *Ballach Rocks* are covered with spring-tide, and lie near a mile E. N. E. from *Ila-Nove*. To sail along the N. side of them, keep the hill of *Torrore Head* out to the N. by *Ila-Nove*.

Pessaghan Rock.

Pessaghan Rock is always above water, and no shoal near it, except a rock about a cable's-length northward of it, which is covered alternately by the tide.

The rocks in the sound of *Ila* will be described with that sound.

The Sound of ILA *Anchorage.*

Anchorage in Ila.

The Sound of *Ila* lies in the common tract of shipping to and from the north; and on that account is pretty much frequented by them, but it cannot be recommended as a safe place to ride in, in the winter, or in blowing weather; for the stream of tide is rapid, and the ground, for the most part, gravel, which does not hold well. A tide, or a night, is all the time any vessel should stop here in harvest or winter, except in *Mudegal's Bay*, when one cable is made fast to a ring, or rock, on the shore.

Mudegal's Bay.

Mudegal's Bay is that cove, or bight, which is on the E. side of the Sound, near the houses of *Folin*. Here, by making fast on shore, a vessel that draws twelve feet water may stop out of the stream of tide. A large vessel must avoid a shoal at the N. point of the bay, which extends about a cable's-length from the shore, and on which there is but nine feet at low spring-tide. No vessels should lie so far out as this shoal, because she will then ride more in the stream.

Whitefarland Anchorage.

The *White farland* is another part of the Sound of *Ila*, where vessels may stop out of the strength of the stream; but the ground is hard sand, with a mixture of gravel, and long weeds, which entangle the anchor, and make it drag in blowing weather. The best part here to anchor in, is at the S. end of a small bush of wood, and abreast of a small white stone, which may be perceived at the top of the banks, near which there is a dike built of turf and stones that goes down to the sea. Drop anchor in three or four fathoms, when the point of the *White farland* is a little shut on the northmost part of *Ila*.

Rocks in the Sound of Ila. Skervoir Rock.

Skervoir is a rock westward of *Fruchdan Island*, about half a mile; the west end of it is not quite covered, except at high-water with spring-tide, the rest dries only with spring-tide, or at low-water. The westmost end of this rock bears S. ¾ E. from *Glashdan Island*; so that *Glashdan* bearing N. clears it on the west side. A leading mark to it is, the point of the low *Glashdan Island*, just shut on the point of *Ila*, next S. of *Ardmore*; these two points open, clears it on the W. side. In sailing this way, when the rocks, or marks, cannot be distinctly seen, the safest course is, to keep within a cable's-length, or two, from the *Ila* side.

Skerrivey Rock.

Skerrivey Rock lies in the N. entry of the Sound of *Ila*, within half a mile of the *Jura* side, and is covered with spring-tide only.

About a mile eastward of *Skerrivey*, and off the mouth of a deep-channeled rivulet, that appears to run down in two branches from *Breanore Hill* in *Jura*, there is a rock which is said to dry with extraordinary low tides only. All that part of the coast of *Jura*, which lies eastward of *Skerrivey*, to the mouth of *Loch Tarbit*, is shallow for about a quarter of a mile from the shore.

ANCHORING-PLACES in Ila. On the S. coast of Ila-Tone.

There are two places on the S. coast of *Ila*, where a vessel may stop at anchor in the summer-time. One is on the N. side of *Ila-Tone*, off a small cove, where there is a ruinous chapel, on four fathoms sandy ground.

Mouth of Loch Lanlamis.

The next stopping-place, on the S. coast of *Ila*, is near the mouth of the *Bay Lanlamis*, on the E. side, within a ledge of rocks that are always above water, on from three to five fathoms, clean sand.

LOCHINDAAL *Harbour.*

Lochindaal is the only part in *Ila* where vessels may ride in safety in the winter-time. Small vessels that draw not above nine or ten feet water may ride quite well sheltered; larger ships, that draw fifteen feet, must ride with the mouth of the Loch open, and therefore not in so great safety when the wind is W. or S. W. The best anchorage is in *Kilarow Bay*, when the house of *Bowmore* bears S. S. E. and somewhat nearer to the S. than to the N. side of the Harbour, on three fathoms at low-water. Ships that draw fourteen feet water, must anchor more to the eastward, when *Bowmore House* bears S. E. by E. on four fathoms clean ground.

Spits of sand in the Lochindaal.

In the entry of this Harbour, there are two spits of sand; one on the S. side, which never dries, extending from the *Point of Ardrarb* northward; the other extending southward from the corner of the opposite bay, which dries gradually from high-water to low; these two spits of sand almost inclose the entry of this Harbour, and serve to break off the violence of the sea. In the channel between them, there is only two, or 2½ fathoms, at low spring-tide.

To sail in.

To sail into *Kilarow Bay* keep nearest the N. or *Rowe* side, till you are about half a mile eastward of the mill (which stands on the W. side of a small *Cove*, with a rivulet running through it), when you will be abreast of two small patches of sand on the shore; or till *Beanarioid Hill* (at the W. end of the *Rinns*) bears W. by S. then steer E. right through the middle of the bay, till *Bowmore House* (a little westward of which there is a small kero on a hillock) bears S. E. or S. S. E. there drop anchor. Give a good scope of cable at first, that the anchor may fasten well in the ground, for a great many parts of the bottom are covered with grass, which hinder the anchor to catch hold once it stirs.

LOCH TARBERT *in* JURA ISLAND.

Loch Tarbert, especially on the S. side, is full of small rocks; some of which are always above water, some dry about low-water, and some with spring-tide only; which will be better understood by inspecting the draft, than by a description. The safest anchorage is a quarter of a mile above Cumbery, or the narrow part, on the south side of the Loch; but it is hazardous going up so far, except one is well acquainted, or perches were placed on some of the rocks by the way. The best rule is to keep half a cable from what is seen on the N. side of the Loch; for no shoals lie farther off than that. The best anchorage near the mouth of this Loch, which is likewise of easy access, is in the *Bay Glenbatrig*, on the W. side of that Bay, on three or four fathoms; when the point on the larboard-hand coming in, is just closed with the land on the S. side of the entry. Keep about a cable's-length from the point going past it, and anchor above a cable's length eastward of it. Anchorage in Glenbatrig.

About half a mile eastward of the last-mentioned anchorage, there are a cluster of small rocks always above water; on the E. side of these rocks a ship may ride safe on five fathoms water: keep half a cable's-length from these rocks going up to this anchorage. Anchorage E. of Glenbatrig.

In moderate weather a vessel may stop in the bay of *Rumsdale*, near the E. side of the point, on three, or $3\frac{1}{2}$, fathoms water.

A Description of the Tides, Rocks, Shoals, Channels, Anchoring-places, and Harbours on the West Coast of SCOTLAND, *from the N. of* JURA *and* ILA, *to the Sound of* MULL, *and the adjacent Main.*

C H A R T XXI.

Tides from JURA *and* ILA *to the Sound of* MULL.

TIDES.

In the Sound of *Ila*, and on the shore of *Colonsa Island*, it is high-water on full and change-days at $5\frac{1}{2}$; in the *Gulf of Corywrekan*, at $4\frac{1}{2}$; along the S. side of *Mull*, at five; in *Lismore Island*, at $5\frac{1}{2}$. Time of high-water at Ila, Colonsa, Corywrekan, Mull, Lismore. [illegible]

Between the N. coast of *Jura Island*, and the Sound of *Mull*, ordinary spring-tide rises ten or eleven feet perpendicular; ordinary neap-tides five or six.

Near the N. E. point of *Jura*, off *Kraignurach*, spring-tides, when strongest, run about five miles an hour; neap-tides $1\frac{1}{2}$; in the *Gulf of Corywrekan*, between *Jura* and *Scarba Islands*, sixteen, as is thought; between *Long Island* and *Garveloch* five; between the N. coasts of *Jura* and *Ila*, and the S. coast of *Mull*, the stream is scarce sensible; between *Garveloch Island*, and *Loch Don*, on the S. E. side of *Mull*, it is scarce sensible; between *Loch Don*, and *Lismore Island*, the stream runs about three miles an hour when strongest. Velocity of the Stream near the N. E. Point of Jura, in Corywrekan; [illegible]

On this part of the coast, the stream of flood comes from the southward; at the N. E. point of *Jura*, between *Rissanro Island* and *Kraignurach*, the strength of the flood sets through the Sound of *Scarba*, westward to the *Whirlpool*, or *Gulf of Corywrekan*: part of the stream of flood, which runs along the E. side of *Rissanro Island*, continues its course northward, on the E. sides of *Scarba* and *Lunga Islands*, towards the Sound of *Mull*, and the inlets on the main. [illegible]

The stream of flood, near *Colonsa Island*, comes from the S. W. divides off the shoals, near *Ilanoronsa*, and runs along both sides of *Colonsa* northward; but with very great velocity, except along the E. side of *Oronsa Island*, where it runs about one mile an hour when strongest.

The GULF OF CORYVRECHAN.

Corywrekan is a violent breaking sea, and whirlpool, formed between the *Islands Jura* and *Scarba*, which will wash over any ship's deck, and be apt to sink her if the hatches are open. The whirlpool is occasioned chiefly by an excessive rapid tide, which runs over a high steep rock, which lies on the N. side of the Sound, near the W. point of *Scarba*. The rock tapers almost to a point at the top; over which the least water found was fifteen fathoms: about twenty-five fathoms from it, on the E. and W. sides, the water is thirty-five fathoms deep; and fifty fathoms from it, the depth is forty-seven and fifty fathoms; fifty fathoms from it north-westward, the water is eighty-three fathoms deep; and two hundred fathoms from it south-westward, the depth is ninety-one fathoms; so that this rock must be near one hundred fathoms perpendicular, and its top fifteen fathoms below the surface of the sea. As this rock the stream is so excessively rapid, and the sea swells and breaks so violently, even in the calmest weather, that it is impossible to measure the greatest celerity of the stream; but it does not seem to be less than twelve or fourteen miles an hour. The principal stream of flood enters this Sound from the eastward, and runs out towards the N. W. forming an eddy about two miles long on the W. end of *Scarba*. During the time that the stream of flood runs westward through the middle of this Sound, there is a counter-stream that runs eastward, close along the shore of *Scarba*; and at a small point of that Island, opposite to the whirlpools, is reflected southward toward them; and by its oblique direction, contributes to increase their gyration, and the rage of the waves. This counter-stream seemed to run about five or six miles an hour; for a boat with six oars, in a calm day, could not stem it. The sea here continues to break, during ebb-tide, as well as with flood, but not so violently as with the flood. The sea rages, and forms itself into whirlpools on the *Jura* side of the Sound likewise, both with ebb and flood; but the waves do not swell to such a height as in the part called the Gulf on the *Scarba* side. During slack water, which continues about half an hour with spring-tide, and a whole hour with neap-tide, the sea in this Sound is as smooth as in other neighbouring parts. The stream of flood and ebb sets in on the *Jura* side half an hour sooner than on the *Scarba* side.

If a vessel happens to be becalmed near the E. entry of this Sound, with flood and spring-tide, if there is not a brisk breeze of wind, it will be in vain to attempt to get past Corywrekan, either by sailing or towing; the To ... a vessel near Corywrekan.

the most prudent way seems to be, to secure the hatches, and every thing that is loose on deck, and to endeavour, by the sails and helm, to steer the vessel right through the middle of the Sound, so as the tide may carry her between the most violent breakers, which lie on each side. If the tide shall happen to carry her very near the *Jura* side, it will be best not to attempt to get clear of it altogether, but to keep so near to it so that the tide may carry her between the eastmost small island and *Jura*; by which means, if the wind is any thing favourable, she may be brought into a small bay in *Jura*, opposite to the little island, where she may ride on clean ground, and pretty well sheltered, till the tide becomes favourable. To avoid being carried through *Corywrekan*, when coming from the south with flood-tide; keep near *Rifsantra Island*, and then a moderate breeze of wind will be sufficient to carry the vessel past the Sound of *Scarba*: or the tide alone will do it, except when it is about an hour before high-water.

ROCKS and SHOALS.

Rocks and Shoals between KNAPDALE *and the Sound of* MULL.

[illegible] About a cable's-length N. E. by E. from *Ruisker Island*, there is a blind rock, on which there are but two feet of water at low spring-tide. *Jura* open of *Ruisker*; or the W. end of *Ruisker* on *Corrabradyne*, clears it along the W. side: any of the *Paps of Jura*, southward of *Ruisker*, clears it on the N. side.

[illegible] Near a cable's-length southward from the S. W. point of *Rifsantra Island*, there is a rock that dries about half-ebb.

[illegible] About two cables-length north-westward from the N. end of *Rifsan tiebfadra Island*, there is a small rock that dries about half-ebb. It is avoided along the W. side, when the opening between *Rifsantra Island* and the main appears smaller than between *Rifsantra* and *Jura*. It is avoided along the E. side, sailing between it and *Rifsantraifadra*, when *Rifsantra* bears on any part of *Jura*.

[illegible] About a cable's-length southward of the S. end of *Ilanabrau*, on the W. side of *Luing Island*, there is a rock which dries with spring-tide only.

[illegible] The rock, or small island, *Dubber*, which lies N. of *Reastirum*, and about half a mile westward of *Bis-tubrar*, has a ledge that extends southward half a cable's-length from the S. end of it, and one that extends as far northward from the N. side of it.

[illegible] On the N. side of *Balnahua Island*, there is a ledge of rocks that extend near a quarter of a mile north-eastward; the extremity of which dries with spring-tide only. To avoid this ledge along the E. side; keep the *House of Balnahua* a little westward of the top of the highest hill of *Scarba Island*, or the *Point of Duart* shut in by *Inch Island*.

Bent Shoal. *Bent* is a rocky shoal, always below water, which lies about a mile N. N. E. from *Balnahua Island*, and S. W. ½ W. from the highest part of *Eysdal Island*. The least water on it is four feet. Near the shallowest part of this shoal, the smallest of the two *Tony Rocks* is in a line with the westmost high head of *Mull*, called *Ealmore-charsfa*; the *House of Balnahua* is in one with the highest part of *Scarba Hill*, and the west point of *Inch Island*, just closing with the *Point of Duart* in *Mull*. To avoid *Bent* on the E. side; keep the S. extremity of *Blada Island* on, or a little W. of the eastmost point of *Scarba*: or the low point of *Duart* shut in a ship's-length by *Inch Island*: or the *House of Balnahua* a little westward of the highest hill of *Scarba*. To avoid it on the W. side; take the N. extremity of *Blada Island* on, or open with, the eastmost point of *Scarba*: or the greatest *Tony Rock* on the westmost high head of *Mull*: or the *House of Balnahua* S. by W.: or the *Point of Duart* open a ship's-length of *Inch Island*. To avoid it on the N. side, keep the greatest *Tony Rock* in a line with the *Point of Ross* in *Mull*.

Rock near Garvilarb-[illegible] Island. About a mile W. S. W. from the middle of *Garvilachan-meanu Island*, there is a small rock that dries with spring-tide only. A leading mark to it is, the westmost high head of *Mull*, seen between *Ilarbann Island* and the small low island near E. of it. *Dubarn*, on the W. head of *Mull*, clears it along the W. side: and the small low island on that head, clears it along the E. side.

A rock on the E. side of it. On the E. side of *Garvilarbua-meanu*, there is a rock about a cable's-length from the shore, which dries about half-ebb.

Rock E. of Garvilarb-[illegible] On the E. side of *Garvilarbua-meanu*, there is a rock about a cable's-length from the shore, which dries about half-ebb.

[illegible] About a quarter of a mile E. S. E. from the N. end of *Garvalarb-na-naon Island*, there is a small rock, which dries at half-ebb.

[illegible] There is a rock that extends near a mile W. S. W. from *Ben Garbred*, on the E. side of *Oransa*, which dries about half-ebb; and a shoal which lies about a quarter of a mile southward from the middle of the rock, on which there are six feet at low-water.

[illegible] About a mile south-westward from *Dana-warn*, there are two or three rocks that dry with spring-tide only; and some shoals on which the sea frequently breaks, even in moderate weather. A leading-mark to the southmost of these shoals, is *Rewaal Point* in *Ila*, on the S. end of *Brainore Hill* in *Jura*. To avoid these shoals along the S. side, sail no nearer *Colonsa* than till *Rewaal* bears on the middle of *Brainore Hill*.

[illegible] There are several rocks and shoals that lie westward of *Ard-sginsh Point* in *Colonsa*; several of which are always above water, some always below it, and some dry only at low-water: those that are always below water break often in moderate weather, and therefore must have but little water over them. To avoid these rocks and shoals, keep two miles from that part of *Colonsa*; or one mile without the rocks that are always above water.

[illegible] *Brenachorya* is a rocky shoal, near the N. end of *Insh Island*, westward of *Seil Island*, on which the least water is twelve feet: it lies near a quarter of a mile N. W. from the *Rock Dubber*, which is always above water. Leading-marks to it are, *Garvelach* (by some called the *Mare Island*), about a ship's-length open with the W. end of *Insh Island*; and the east end of *Insh Island*, on *Dunmore Head*, near *Eysdal Island*. To avoid this shoal along the N. side; keep the *Rock Tony* open of the W. end of *Insh*: to sail between it and *Dubber*, keep *Eysdal* open of *Insh Island*.

[illegible] There is a ledge of rocks that extends above a cable's-length eastward of *Dubber*: to avoid it sailing along the E. side of *Dubber*, keep *Garvelach Island* open of *Insh Island*.

[illegible] The *Rock Dubber*, near *Kerrera*, lies above a mile W. from the S. end of that island, and is always above water. About a quarter of a mile W. by S. from *Dubber*, there is a small rock, called *Bo-nis*, which is always below water, but the weeds are seen on the surface at low spring-tide. To sail near this shoal, along the W. side of it, keep the W. end of *Insh Island* (which is N. of *Eysdal*) on, or E. of the *Paps of Jura*: or the E. end of *Insh*, upon the middle of the hill in *Jura*, which appears next W. of *Scarba*. This hill in *Jura* appears with two tops, and a level part between them; the middle of this level part is the middle of the hill meant.

[illegible] *Carrigadra Rock* lies off the W. end of *Lysmore Island*, about three-quarters of a mile S. W. by W. from *Lismore*, and S. E. from *Duart Castle* in *Mull*: it is always dry, except about high-water with spring-tide. A leading-mark to it is, the westmost head visible in *Mull*, in a line with the S. end of the westmost of the

S *Mare*

From JURA *and* ILA, *to the Sound of* MULL *and* ICOLMKIEL.

Mare Islands. The *Mare Isles* open of that head of *Mull*, clears it along the S. side: that head seen in a line with the largest *Mare Island*, clears *Carrigindra* along the W. and N. sides.

Dubhartach is a remarkable rock, always above water, and may be seen from a ship's deck three or four leagues off. It bears S. W. ½ W. from the highest hill of *Icolmkiel*, about five leagues. There is a ledge of rocks that extends about half a mile westward from *Dubhartach*; the extremity of which, and a part in the middle, are not covered till about high-water. At *Dubhartach*, *Braimore* in *Jura* bears about S. E. by S. the W. end of *Ila* S. by E. *Benymore Hill* in *Mull* about N. by W. [illegible]

The *Torrin Rocks* are a numerous cluster, that extend about four miles S. W. from the W. end of *Ross* in *Mull*; the greatest part of which are always above water; but some dry at half-ebb, and some with spring-tide only. The breakers may be seen on all of them when there is but little wind, and often when it is calm. About a mile westward of the highest *Torrin Rocks*, there are three small rocks, the westmost of which dries at two hours of ebb: to avoid these three along the W. side, keep both the *Reloe Isles*, or rocks, in sight by the W. side of *Soay Island*. [illegible]

Skerybale Rock is always above water, and lies about a mile S. W. from *Ilanmore Island*. Half way between this Rock and the S. entrance of *Loch Tuelkiel*, lies *Bonaimarver Rock*, which dries about half-ebb. The common channel, along this side of *Ross*, is near *Bonaimarver*, either between it and *Ross*, or between it and *Skerybale*. To sail between it and *Ross*, take *Iarnamule* in a line with the S. end of *Icolmkiel* (*Iarnamule* appears like a uniform hill about two miles N. W.): to sail between *Bonaimarver* and *Skerybale*, keep the S. end of *Icolmkiel* southward of *Iarnamule*; not regarding the rocks, or small islands, that lie near *Icolmkiel*. [illegible] [illegible]

About half a mile northward from *Soay Island*, there is a rock, which dries at half-ebb; and another rock about half a mile S of it. [illegible]

About one-third from *Icolmkiel*, and two-thirds from *Soay*, there are two rocks that are either dry at low spring-tide, or have very little water over them. [illegible]

There are two small islands, or rocks, that lie above a mile westward from the N. end of *Icolmkiel*, called *Reloe*: about one-fourth from *Reloe*, and three-fourths from *Icolmkiel*, there are two small rocks; that next *Reloe* dries about half-ebb. To sail between these rocks and *Icolmkiel*, keep mid-channel; or keep the W. point of *Icolmkiel* in a line with, or shut in by, the E. point of *Soay*. [illegible]

Harbours and Anchoring-places from JURA, *along the Main, to the Sound of* MULL; *and from thence westward to* ICOLMKIEL ISLAND. HARBOURS and ANCHORING-PLACES.

CARSEG *Harbour.*

Carseg is a small creek in *Ilan-carseg*; but it is sufficiently sheltered, the ground good, and the depth sufficient for the largest ships. Anchor in nine fathoms in the mouth of the bay, near the middle, when the S. point of *Ilan-carseg* bears W. ½ S. There are two rocks half way between this anchorage and the narrow sound at the N. end of the Island; the southernmost of which is covered about high-water only, and the other dries about half ebb, and reaches to about a ship's-length of the main. The west side of these rocks is shallow, but the E. side is deep enough for ordinary vessels. A good pilot may carry a vessel this way through the N. entry.

LOCH CRINAN.

Loch Crinan, being open to the W. is not sufficiently sheltered for vessels in the winter-time; nor is it safe to ride long in it at any time of the year. The ground, however, is clean, and in some parts very good; and it may be convenient on some occasions to run for this bay, when the wind, or tide, is contrary, and a vessel, bound to the northward, cannot get to *Carseg*, or to the small islands of *Jura*, where there is better shelter. The best anchorage is between *Ilan-droya*, and the rock which is always above water that lies about a quarter of a mile eastward of it. In moderate weather a ship may stop any where northward of *Ilan-droya*, about two cables-length from the Island.

LOCH CRAGNISH.

Loch Cragnish is pretty well sheltered, the ground all good, and the water of sufficient depth for large ships. In the summer-time a ship may ride safe in any part of it: in the season when hard gales of wind should be guarded against, the best anchorage is at the E. end of *Ilan-ree*, between the point of that Island and Ormzy. In coming to this place of anchorage, avoid a small rock, which lies about a cable's-length S. W. from the S. W. point of *Ilan-malerson*.

The flood-tide comes in along the E. side of *Garrivisa Island*, and goes out through the sound along the N. side of that Island. On the E. side of *Garrivisa*, the stream does not run above one mile an hour when strongest; in the Sound, between the Island and the *Point of Cragnish*, it runs about five miles an hour; therefore, to sail in through the Sound, a vessel must have ebb-tide. [illegible]

Little Loch Cragnish is the cove at *Castle Cragnish*, on the N. side of the Point. A vessel may stop a tide in the mouth of this cove, in five or six fathoms water, but she must not go within the cove; for the water shallows fast after you are half a cable's-length within it. [illegible]

LOCH MELFORT.

Loch Melfort (comprehending the whole bay between *Luing Island* and the main) is a spacious well-sheltered harbour, capable of fleets of the largest ships: the ground is all good, the depth in sheltered places moderate, and little or nothing to fear failing in from the south, but the stream of flood which runs toward *Corywrekan*, between *Jura* and *Scarba*. A ship may stop any where along the E. side of *Luing*, a little more than a cable's-length from the shore, on from four to eight fathoms water; avoid a rock that lies about half a mile northward of *Kilchattan*, about a cable's-length from the shore, and dries about half-ebb; or, on the N. and E. sides of *Shuna*, on from four to twelve fathoms. Ships in winter will ride easier and smoother in the *Bay of Melfort* any where, but especially eastward of the *Point of Ardefure*, on ten or twelve fathoms water; give the point of the island, between *Kilchoan* and *Ardefure*, a birth of above a cable's-length, to avoid a ledge which extends southward from it. Or in *Loch Ardinuddy*, off the sandy cove at *Ardinuddy House*, on from six to thirteen fathoms. Coming into this harbour from the S. with little wind and flood-tide, take *Risanore*, and *Risan-nak-sean Island* on the larboard-hand, to avoid being carried by the stream into *Corywrekan*. [illegible] [illegible]

Scarba

SCARBA *Anchorage.*

In the bay, on the E. side of *Scarba Island*, a vessel may stop a tide on clean sand below the wood, near the northmost houses, about two cables-length from the shore. Near the point, on the S. side of this bay, there is a rocky shoal extending above a cable's-length from the shore, on which the least water is six feet; to avoid it, keep *Balnahua Island* (distinguishable by a white house on it) open of the N. point of *Scarba*.

Rock.

BLACKMILL *Bay.*

Blackmill Bay, in *Luing Island*, is sometimes a convenient place to stop a tide in, whether a vessel is bound northward or southward; because the tides in the neighbourhood of it are very rapid, and spring-tide not to be stemmed, without a fresh breeze of following wind. Anchor in the mouth of the bay, on six or seven fathoms water. It shoals pretty fast as you go up to the bay. Drop anchor when the northmost point of *Luing Island* is just shut with the N. point of this Bay.

BLACK *Harbour.*

Black Harbour is a small creek on the W. side of *Luing*, and eastward of *Blada Island* and *Dubh-sgeir Rock*. It is sheltered by rocks, to which small vessels may make fast, and ride safe on three fathoms water. The rock that shelters it most on the N. side, lies E. from *Dubh-sgeir*, is the largest on the N. side of the anchorage, and has a ledge that extends about half a cable's-length south-westward from it: on the starboard-hand going in, and above a cable's-length south-westward from the anchorage, there is a rock that dries with spring-tide only. To avoid these two rocks, keep the middle between the rocks that are always above water; or keep the N. end of the hill of *Balnahua Island* just shut on the westmost high land of *Mull*. This mark will lead between the ledge and spring-tide rock.

A ledge and Rock.

EYSDIL *Harbour.*

Eysdil Harbour is of difficult access, and only fit for small vessels that draw not above eight feet of water. The creek is not frequented by any vessels, but such as go to take in slate at the island; and these vessels, by throwing out their ballast in the anchorage, have made it shallower than it used to be formerly; and in time will render it incapable of floating the smallest vessels at low-water.

The best place of anchorage is a little northward of a small point to the middle of the Harbour, about half a cable's-length from the shore. There are two entries to the Harbour; one from the N. and another from the S. There are rocks in each that dry at low-water with spring-tide. A vessel that draws not above eight feet of water, may sail in through the N. entry at half-tide, by keeping the middle, or nearest to *Eysdil*. In the S. entry the channel is about one-third from the *Point of Eysdil*, till you are just past that Point; then steer N. or N.N.W. to the middle of the N. entry, about half a cable's-length; then steer for the anchorage off the Point in the middle of the bay. On this Point it is necessary to have a land-fast, because the ground does not hold well when it blows hard from the W.

N. Entry.
S. Entry.

LOCH FUCHAN.

Loch Feuchan is almost dry in the entry at low spring-tide, and the stream of tide runs pretty strong through it. A small vessel, with a pilot, may go into this Harbour at half-flood, by keeping near the E. side: anchor off *Ardincaple House*, where the ground is very good, but the soundings unequal.

Sound of KERRERA.

In the *Sound of Kerrera* (by some called the *Horse Shoe*, from a small creek in *Kerrera*, which is so named), there is very good anchorage for ships and vessels of any size; and it is a convenient place for vessels that are bound either northward or southward. The best parts to ride in are, in the bay of *Oban*; and opposite to *Oban*, near *Kerrera*; and between the ferry-house of *Kerrera* and *Ardantrive*, nearest the latter, on eight or ten fathoms, without going within the bay; for it shallows fast near the shore.

Horse-shoe Creek.

The *Horse-shoe* is a small creek in *Kerrera*, about half a mile westward of *Ardantrive*, in the mouth of which a vessel may ride very safe with an anchor on each side. Or a vessel may lie a-ground within this creek, on a soft oozy bottom.

Rocks in the Sound of Kerrera.
Rock off Glenshellach.

Off *Glenshellach*, almost over-against the ferry-house of *Kerrera*, there is a rock that dries with spring-tide only; it lies about one-third from *Glenshellach*, and two-thirds from the ferry-house of *Kerrera*. To avoid this rock, keep the middle of the Sound; or keep the westmost visible part of *Kerrera* a ship's-length on the westmost visible part of *Seil Island*. A leading mark to this point is, these two points just shut.

Off Oban.

On the S. W. side of the *Bay of Oban*, there is a rock which dries with spring-tide only, that lies about a cable's-length northward from the land. To sail along the N. side of this rock, keep about mid-channel, or keep *Kerrera* open of the main. To sail between it and the main, keep the main close on *Kerrera*.

Between Oban and Dunolly.

Between *Dunolly Castle* and *Oban*, there is a narrow ledge that dries with spring-tide, and extends about half a cable's-length westward from the point.

Anchorage in Gânarb Bay.

In the *Bay of Gânarb*, at the N. E. end of *Kerrera*, a vessel may stop a tide on good ground on any side of the rock, which is always above water; or on either side of *Eilean-ans*.

LOCH ETIVE.

Loch Etive is an excellent harbour, once a vessel has got within it; but the entrance of it is shallow, the canal (or channel into it) narrow and rocky, and the tide there extending rapid; so that it is fit only for small vessels. The entrance between *Lidard Point* and *Ean-beach* dries almost half over at low spring-tide, and from thence to near *Ean-beach* there is but six feet there. There are two rocks in the entry, the southmost of which dries at low-water, and the northmost at half ebb: the channel into *Loch Etive* is on the S. side of these rocks, about a ship's-length from the shore. The stream of tide in the *Narrow* runs eight or ten miles an hour when strongest, and commonly breaks from side to side; so that it is not safe for vessels to sail through that channel, except with the very first of the flood going up; or with slack water flood, or first of the ebb, going out.

Anchorage near Dunstaffnage.

There is pretty good anchorage on the S. side of the Point on which the castle of *Dunstaffnage* stands. Sail to this anchorage with flood-tide, and between the *Point of Ean-beach*, turn the Point and anchor

directly

directly below the castle, within a cable's-length of the shore. This is a convenient place to wait the proper time of tide for failing up the Sound.

Along the E. side of *Ilan-kearb* spring-tides run about four miles an hour in the Sound, between *Ilan-kearb* and *Dunstaffnage*, they run about three miles when strongest.

In the summer-time a vessel may stop a little eastward of the obelisk that stands on the top of a hill, near the house of *Ardmakreish*; or off the house *Ardenkeogh*, about half a mile from the shore. Half way between *Ardenkeogh* and the obelisk, the water is too shallow to anchor on at a cable's-length distance from the shore; therefore anchor two cables-length from it. Half way between the obelisk and the house, there is a small point, within which a vessel may lie a-ground on soft mud without any damage. Anchorage of Ardentrive. [illegible]

About a quarter of a mile westward of *Rainagarden* there is a small rock, which dries with spring-tide only, which must be avoided in failing from the N. for *Ardmakreish* anchorage. [illegible]

LOCH CRERIN.

Loch Crerin is well sheltered, good ground, and safe anchorage all over; but is shallow in the entry about low-water, and the stream rapid. A vessel that draws ten feet water should not go in till half-flood; one that draws thirteen, not till the last quarter of flood.

Off the N. point of the entry, there is a ledge of rocks that extend near a quarter of mile S. W. from the high-water mark, the extremity of which is covered at high-water only. Over-against the extremity of this ledge there is a rocky shoal, reaching from *Urifle* about half way over, on which there is but four feet of water at low spring-tide. To shun this shoal going into *Loch Crerin*, before half-flood (for at half-tide there are ten or twelve feet in the middle), keep about one-fourth from the rock, which is covered at high-water only, mentioned before, and three-fourths from the *Urifle* side. The stream of tide in the narrowest part of this entry runs about three miles an hour when strongest. Ledge and Shoal in the entry. Stream of Tide.

The most convenient anchorage in *Loch Crerin* seems to be on the N. or S. side of *Rannacaileach*, any where above a cable's-length from the shore. Anchorage.

LISMORE ISLAND.

Ramfay Bay, near the E. end of *Lismore*, is the only safe anchorage in this island; the ground is good, the harbour pretty well sheltered, and the depth sufficient for any ship. Take the island that shelters the harbour on the larboard-hand going in, and anchor nearest the N. side. [illegible]

Carrigindra Rock lies ½ of a mile from *Lady Island*, and is covered with spring-tide only. [illegible]

Half between *Cragg Island*, and *Ramminish Island*, there is a small rock that dries about half-ebb. [illegible]

There is a ledge that extends northward from *Bandarriffore* about a cable's-length; and a rock that lies north-eastward from it above half a mile. [illegible]

Near *Portnakeapan Point*, there is a rock always above water; and a rock a cable's-length westward from it that dries about half-ebb. [illegible]

About two cables-length E. N. E. from *Glasheilan*, there is a rock that dries at low-water only. To avoid it on the E. side, keep *Castle Stalker*, or the small island close by it, on the *Kirk of Appin*. [illegible]

About a cable's-length S. W. from *Bernaduin*, there is a small rock that dries about half-ebb. [illegible]

Between *Lady Island* and *Bernarey Island*, about half way, there is a rock that dries about half-ebb; and a shoal about a cable's-length westward from it, on which the least water is twelve feet. [illegible]

LOCH DON *in* MULL ISLAND.

A vessel may stop a tide in the mouth of this creek; but there is no water for riding within it, for it shoals soon after you enter it. Anchor nearest the W. side, on four or five fathoms at low-water, when a small high island, at the E. end of the *Mare Islands*, is in a line with the W. point of this bay.

LOCH SPELIV.

This Loch has exceeding good ground, and is well-sheltered, but it is shallow in the entry; having not above three feet of water at low spring-tide; so that a vessel that draws seven or eight feet must have half tide at least to go in with; larger vessels must go in with the last quarter of flood. The N. side of the entry is a little deeper than the S. side, but yet requires a moderate birth. Some regard must also be had to the stream of tide in the narrowest part, where it runs about a mile an hour when strongest. Anchor any where between *Gauleshuls* and *Ardura*.

LOCH BŪY.

Loch Būy being open to the S. W. is exposed to a great sea when it blows from that quarter, especially in winter; and also to violent squalls of wind from the neighbouring mountains; but in summer a ship may ride pretty safe near the head of the bay, on the E. side. Anchor off *Loggan*, about half between *Hangarry* and the head of the Loch.

Anchorage in COLINSA ISLAND.

In *Colinsa* there is no place sufficiently sheltered for vessels to ride in blowing weather. In moderate weather they may ride in clean ground in the bay on the E. side of *Oronsa*, about a cable's-length westward of the rocky point of *Ilan-worarb*, on three fathoms water. Avoid that ledge coming in; and take care not to ride near a ledge that runs south-eastward above a cable's-length from *Oronsa*. [illegible]

In the summer-time a ship may stop in any part along the E. side of *Colinsa*, within half a mile of the shore; for the ground all along is clean, of a moderate depth, and there is no sensible stream of tide there. On E. [illegible] of Colinsa.

Anchorage near the W. Side of ROSS *in* MULL.

LOCH TIERKIEL.

Loch Tierkiel, in the S. W. point of *Mull*, is pretty good anchorage in the summer-time; the swell of the sea being broke by *Ilan-Aulanain*, and a number of small rocks on the S. and N. sides of it. In the S. entry there is a rock which dries with spring-tide only, that lies about a cable's-length eastward of the *Point of Ilan-Aulanain*. To sail on the E. side of that rock, and avoid two other small rocks that lie eastward of it, and dry at half ebb, keep the rock *Skerrichandaw* (which is always above water on the E. side of the entry) Rocks in the S. Entry.

on the westmost of the three *Paps of Jura*. Avoid *Runarvaer Rock*, which dries at half-ebb. Anchor about the middle, between *Ilean-buinan* and *Ivarogen*, on three or four fathoms of water.

ICOLMKILL *Island.*

Anchorage. In *Icolmkill* there is no harbour; but a vessel may stop a tide in moderate weather on the E. side of it, off the middle of the Island, about two cables-length from the shore, on from four to six fathoms water.

Sand-bank in the Sound. In the Sound of *Icolmkill*, about the middle, there is a sand-bank which extends about three-quarters of a mile westward and southward from *Runnahaun*; a spit on the west end reaches within a cable's-length of *Icolmkill*. The east part of this bank dries with very low spring-tides only; other parts have one or two fathoms over them. You are near the S. end of the bank, when the steeple of the old abbey of *Icolmkill* is in a line with the highest hill of that Island: you are near the N. end of the bank, when you are a-breast of the S. end of *Runnahaun*. About high-water, a vessel that draws ten or eleven feet may sail over any part of it: a vessel that draws eight or nine may sail over it any where at half-tide. At low-water it is best to keep about a cable's-length from *Icolmkill*: or to take the extreme point of *Ross*, in *Runnahaun*, on the highest top of *Torris Rock*, which, in this channel, appears with two tops. To sail between this bank and *Runnahaun*, keep half a cable's-length from that Island.

POLTERRIV *Creek.*

Polterriv is a Creek on the E. side of *Runnahaun*, where small vessels may ride safe with one anchor a-shore, on eight or nine feet water. Enter at the S. end of the Island, and give it a moderate birth as you go in; and anchor on the N. side of a small Island, that lies about two cables-length up.

Stream of Tide. The stream of flood in the Sound of *Icolmkill* comes from the southward, and runs not above one mile an hour when strongest. Between *Icolmkill* and *Dubartach Rock*, the stream was not sensible with neap-tide.

A Description of the Tides, Rocks, Shoals, Channels, Anchoring-places, and Harbours in the Sound of MULL, *and the adjacent Main.*

CHART XXII.

TIDES. *Tides in the Sound of* MULL *and adjacent Lochs.*

Time of High-water. On this part of the coast it is high-water on full and change days at 5½.

Rise of the Tide. Ordinary spring-tides rise eleven feet perpendicular; neap-tides six or seven.

Direction of the Stream and Velocity. The stream of flood comes from the southward, and sets northward through the Sound of *Mull* past *Ardnamurchan*, and into the several arms of the sea by the way; but has very little velocity in them, except in narrow channels. In the Sound of *Mull* spring-tides, when strongest, run two miles an hour.

ROCKS. *Rocks in the Sound of* MULL.

Carrigindre Rock. The rocks in and near the Sound of *Mull* are; *Carrigindre Rock* (described before), which lies about a mile S. W. by W. from the W. point of *Lismore Island*, and is covered with spring-tide only.

Glasbdan Shoal. About a cable's-length northward of the *Glasbdan Rocks* (which lie half a mile westward of *Rue-na-Gall*), there is a small rocky shoal, on which the least water is six feet. A leading-mark to this shoal is, the E. extremity of *Lady Island*, near *Lismore*, seen in the opening between the two *Glasbdan Rocks*. *Lady Island*, either eastward or westward of *Glasbdan*, clears this shoal. To avoid it along the north side, keep two cables-length from *Glasbdan*.

Shoal near the small islands. Between the small green islands (near the middle of the Sound) and *Mull*, about mid-way, there is a shoal, partly rocks and partly sand: near the W. end of it, the weeds are seen in the surface of the water with low spring-tide, where it may be four feet deep; the rest has from six to twelve feet over it. To sail between this shoal and the small islands, keep about one-third from the small islands, and two-thirds from *Mull*: or sail as near the islands as you please. To sail along the N. side of this shoal, keep the northmost part of these islands E. by S. or E. ½ S.

Stirks of Morven. The *Stirks of Morven* are two rocks that lie about half a mile W. by N. from the extremity of the *Point of Ardtornish*; the northmost of them is covered with spring-tide only, the southmost dries at half-ebb. To sail between the *Stirks* and the Point of *Ardtornish* keep within two cables-length of the Point. To sail along the N. side of them, if necessary, keep about half a cable's-length from the northmost *Stirk*.

Red-rocks. The *Red-rocks* lie about a mile N. W. ½ N. from the *Point of Ardtornish*, and dry about half-ebb. To sail close along the W. side of the *Red-rocks* and of the *Stirks*, keep the *Point of Drumnin* in *Morven* (near which there is a remarkable ruinous house) S. by E. To sail along the E. side of the *Red-rocks* and *Stirks*, keep the ruinous house, which is on *Drumnin Point*, on *Bengallo Hill* in *Torsay* near the S. E. end of *Mull*.

Rock between the Red-rocks and the Stirks. About one-third from the *Red-rocks*, and two-thirds from the *Stirks*, there is a small rock, the weeds on which appear in the surface of the water at low spring-tide, when there may be three or four feet over it.

New Rock. The *New Rock* lies about a mile N. N. E. of the harbour of *Tobermorry*. It is not above ten fathoms long, and is never above water; but with ordinary spring-tide the weeds on it may be seen in the surface, when there are four feet of water over it. Leading-marks to it are, *Rudhaver Point* in *Mull* in one with the highest hill of *Coll Island*, which appears with two tops, the southmost of which is highest; and the *Red-rocks* (which dry at half-ebb), about E. and in a line with the middle of the rock, or small island, near *Ardslignach Point* in *Ardnamurchan*. This rock is avoided on the W. side, by keeping the E. side of *Calve Island* at *Tobermorry* S. ½ E. or by sailing within half a mile of the shore of *Mull*. It is avoided along the S. side, while *Coll Island* is hid by *Rudhaver Point*; or the *Red-rocks* appear in one with the *Point of Ardslignach*. To avoid it along the N. side, keep the *Red-rocks* open to the S. of the rock near *Ardslignach*.

Harbours and Anchoring-places in the Sound of MULL *and adjacent Main.*

HARBOURS and ANCHORING PLACES.

LINNHELOCH.

Linnhe-loch is a large and safe arm of the sea, extending from the S. entry of the Sound of *Mull* eastward about fourteen miles, to *Loch Leven* and *Lochaber*, which are narrower lochs that branch eastward from it. *Linnhe-loch* is sufficiently land-locked, and the bottom all strong good ground, but the water too deep for convenient anchorage; except in *Loch Arkeg*, on the N. side, which is a very fine safe harbour; in the Sound of *Shona*, which is fit for small vessels; and the bay on the W. side of *Ru-na-gall Point*, where ships may ride in moderate weather. The first and last of these places require no description, or direction, but the draft. (Loch Arkeg harbour. Bay W. of [illegible] Point.)

The Sound of *Shona* is a safe Creek for small vessels; but to sail in through the W. entry they must have at least half flood, and keep about one-third from the Main, or starboard side, to avoid a ledge which extends about a cable's-length southward from the W. end of *Shona Island*. In this entry there is not above three feet of water at low spring-tide: at high-water there are twelve or fourteen with neap-tide. The best anchorage is in a small bight, near the west end of the island, within a cable's-length of the shore, eastward of a little house, which stands near the high-water mark. In sailing for *Shona* between the east end of *Lismore* and *Port-na-cros*, keep near the middle between the Main and the small islands off the end of *Lismore*, to avoid a shallow bank of sand, which lies between *Port-na-cros* and *Castle Stalker*, and extends a quarter of a mile from the shore; or, to avoid this shoal, keep some part of *Ben-[illegible]* in sight by the N. end of *Craig Island*, till you are about a cable's-length or two from *Shona*, then shut in *Ben-[illegible]* quite on *Craig Island*, and sail in through the *Narrow*, keeping nearest the Main side. (Sound of Shona harbour. Sand-bank near Castle Stalker.)

LOCH LEVEN.

Loch Leven is a fine well-sheltered harbour, capable of large ships; but they must have flood-tide to go in with, and such as draw above twelve feet should not sail in till near half-flood; for there are not above twelve feet in the entry at low spring-tide; and the stream, when strongest, runs about three miles an hour. A little before you enter the *Narrow*, there is a ledge that extends above a cable's-length northward from the [illegible], which must be avoided by keeping nearest the larboard shore. The best anchorage is above the *Narrow*, in the middle. (Ledge near the Narrows.)

There is a reef which extends westward from *Coilchrene*, going towards *Loch Linnhe*, near half a mile. (Reef off Coilchrone.)

LOCH-ABER.

There is good anchorage for large ships in any part of the north side of *Loch-aber*; smaller vessels will find a more moderate depth, and better shelter on the E. side of the *Corran*, or *Narrow*, about two cables-length from the shore; or off *Camusnagaul*, at the head of the Loch, about one cable's-length from the shore. In sailing up through the *Corran*, take flood-tide, or slack-water; spring-tides there run about four miles an hour when strongest: and avoid a sandy shoal, which lies between *Ru[illegible] Point* and the *Corran*, above a cable's-length from the shore, on which there is but nine feet at low spring-tide. (Tide. Shoal near Corran.)

LOCHIEL.

If any ships have occasion to go into *Lochiel* harbour, they must take flood tide, sail between the two first islands at *Camusnagaul*, and anchor above a mile northward of the entry; for nearer to the entry is all rocky ground on both sides; and spring-tides in the *Narrow* run four miles an hour.

Anchorage in the Sound of MULL.

LOCH DUART.

Loch Duart, on the E. side of *Mull*, as you enter the Sound from the south, is a convenient place to stop in in the summer, or in moderate weather; but it is not safe to continue in it in winter or harvest. The north side of the bay is the safest anchorage; a little more than a cable's-length from a small point, on eight or ten fathoms, *Duart Castle* in a line with the top of *Cruachan-ben Hill*, or nearly so.

ARTORNISH *Bay*.

In *Artornish Bay* a vessel may stop a tide, in moderate weather, a little eastward of the ruinous castle, a little more than a cable's-length from shore, on five or six fathoms clean ground.

LOCH ALIN.

This harbour is well-sheltered against all winds, the ground good, and the water of a moderate depth. The inconveniency of it is, that the entry is narrow, and requires a leading wind, which, on some occasions, may confine a vessel, though the wind may otherwise be favourable. In the middle of the entry there is only twelve feet of water at low spring-tide, and only six feet near the S. side.

SCALASDIL *Bay*.

Scalasdil Bay (by strangers called *Macalister's Bay*) is pretty well sheltered, good ground, and sufficiently deep for any ship. This is a convenient place to stop in. Drop anchor any where above a cable's-length from the shore, except near the S. side of the Bay, where it is shoal for more than a cable's-length from the high-water mark. The most commodious place seems to be near half a mile northward of the village Scalasdil, off a small brook, on six or seven fathoms.

CORANINENACH *Bay*.

In this Bay vessels may stop a tide, or ride in summer, on good ground, about a cable's-length from the shore, on six or seven fathoms water. Large ships may stop farther out, on sixteen or eighteen fathoms.

Aras

MULL, TIRI, *and* COLL *Islands*.

ARRAS *Bay*.

Arras Bay is pretty good anchorage; for it is sheltered from all winds from the westerly quarter, which are commonly the most frequent and most violent winds; and the ground is good. A vessel may anchor any where in this bay, above two cables-length from the shore; the most convenient seems to be, where the castle bears W. or W. by N. To sail into this anchorage from the S. along the west side of the small islands, which lie in the middle of the Sound, keep a cable's-length from them, to avoid a shoal that lies about the middle between these islands, and the *Point of Galenbury*, before described; or you may sail as near these islands as you please. There is nothing to fear on the E. side of them.

TOBERMORAY *Harbour*.

Tobermoray Harbour is a very fine place for large ships; for it is sheltered from all winds, the ground good, and the depth moderate. Large ships may anchor any where above a cable's-length from the shore. Small vessels may ride more commodiously on the W. side, about a cable's-length eastward of the southmost house.

LOCH SUNART.

Loch Sunart is a long arm of the sea resembling a river; except that there is no current, and very little stream of tide in it. It is quite well sheltered, the ground almost all of it clean and good, and capable of several hundred sail of the largest ships. The greatest inconveniency of this harbour is, the narrowness of the entrance, which is little more than a cable's-length wide in the best channel. Small vessels, to ride in a moderate depth, must lay one anchor on shore, except at the head of the Loch; but large ships may anchor almost any where above a cable's-length from the shore.

Rock near Ardilyenach Point. The rocks to be avoided in coming in, are a rock about half a mile westward of *Ardilyenach Point*, which dries about half-ebb, and is before described; a small shoal in the middle between *Ewreska* and *Ben-torran*, on which the least water is six feet; to avoid it, keep nearest *Carna*.

The small island near *Dowrgadan* is shallow near a cable's-length southward.

Ledge and Shoal near Camisfern. There is a ledge that extends southward from the eastmost of the two largest islands near *Camisfern*, which dries two hours before low-water; and a sandy shoal, which extends about a cable's-length W. from the island at the point east of *Camisfern*.

Sand off Strontian. Off the town of *Strontian*, there is a sand-bank which extends above a third over to the opposite side; the S. end of which is always below water, and has twelve feet the least water over it.

Anchorage in S. Sound in Oronsey. *Kylyfinnan*, on the S. side of *Ben-Oronsey*, is an extraordinary good place to ride in; being well-sheltered, the ground good, and the depth sufficient for any ships. The bight on the E. end of this island is also good anchorage, about a cable's-length from the shore.

Near Glenmore. On the E. or W. sides of the *Point of Glenmore*, on the N. side of the entry, a vessel may ride safe in the summer-time, about a cable's length from the shore, and in a moderate depth.

Off Camisfern. Between the two largest islands off *Camisfern*, there is good anchorage on seven or eight fathoms water. Also on the W. side of the point and island south-eastward of *Camisfern*.

Off Strontian. At the head of the Loch, on the south side over-against *Strontian*, there is good anchorage and moderate depth.

LOCH MINGARY, *on the N. side of* MULL.

In this bay a small vessel may shelter and ride on two fathoms of clean sand. In going in, keep the middle, or somewhat nearest the E. side, and anchor a cable's-length above the entry.

LOCH ACKUNE.

In the summer-time a vessel may stop in the mouth of this Loch off the *Point of Quinish*, but should not continue long there; for there is no shelter against N. and N. W. winds, which raise a great swelling sea on this part of *Mull*. There is a rock in the middle of the mouth of this bay, and three or four more farther up on the W. side, which dry about the first quarter of ebb.

A Description of the Tides, Rocks, Shoals, Channels, Anchoring-places, and Harbours, on the West Side of the ISLAND MULL, *and in* TIRI *and* COLL.

C H A R T XXIII.

TIDES.

Tides on the West Side of the ISLAND MULL, *and in* TIRI *and* COLL.

Time of High-water in Mull, Tiri, Coll, Isolabeal, and Ross. It is high-water on the W. side of *Mull*, and on the shores of *Tiri* and *Coll* at five o'clock, on the full and change-days of the moon; but on the shores of *Ross*, in *Mull*, and *Isolabeal* opposite to it, at 5¾.

Rise of the Tide. On this part of the coast ordinary spring-tides rise ten or eleven feet perpendicular; extraordinary tides fourteen or fifteen; ordinary neap-tides five or six feet.

Direction of the Stream. The stream of flood along the W. side of *Mull* comes from the southward, and runs northward on both sides of *Isolabeal*; from thence to the *Treshanish Islands*, and along the W. side of *Ardnamurchan* on the Main of *Scotland*. The flood, some leagues westward of *Mull*, sets in from the south-westward, passes along *Skerryvore Rock* toward *Tiri Island*, divides into two branches off the W. end of that island; one of which runs eastward along the S. side of it and of *Coll*, the other runs eastward along their N. sides.

Velocity of the Stream. The stream of tide along the W. coast of *Mull*, and along the rocks and islands of it, runs not above two miles an hour when strongest, except between the *Treshanish Islands* and *Rutrshanish* (the N. W. head of *Mull*), where spring-tides run about four miles an hour when strongest.

Rocks

Rocks and Shoals on the West Side of MULL ISLAND, *and along* TIRI *and* COLL *Islands.*

ROCKS and SHOALS.

Dubartach, Torran, and other rocks westward of *Ross* in *Mull*, have been described in Chart twenty-first, to which we refer.

On the W. side of *Staffa Island* there are several rocks; the outermost of which lies near a mile from that Island, and is always above water.

About the middle of the *Treshanish Islands*, between *Fladda* and *Lunga*, there is a reef of rocks partly under water, and that partly dry, and are covered each tide.

Skerivore Rock lies S. W. about four leagues from *Tiri*; it is always above water, about a quarter of a mile long, and may be seen four or five leagues off from a ship's deck. There is a reef which extends near half a mile eastward from the E. end of *Skerivore* rocks that dries at four hours of ebb; and a small rock near a mile eastward from it that dries about half-ebb; and a rock which lies W. S. W. ½ W. from it about 1½ miles, which dries about half-ebb likewise.

Boinshi Rock lies about two leagues N. E. from *Skerivore Rock*, and is never dry, except, perhaps, with extraordinary low tides; but may always be perceived by a swell, or breakers on it.

Skerrialough Rocks lie north-westward from the *Point of Cragagh* in *Tiri*; *Dubhere*, the outermost, is about two miles from the shore, and is always above water.

There is nothing to be feared in sailing within a mile of *Dubhere* on any side, excepting a small rock that lies about half a cable's-length south-eastward from it, and dries at half-ebb.

About a mile westward from the *Point of Cragagh* there is a rock which dries about half-ebb.

Almost every point in *Tiri* has a ledge, or rocks, lying a cable's-length or two, or three from it; particularly *Hynish* and *Rabranish Points* on each side of *Travey Bay*; *Kyles*, on the S. and N. sides; and the W. end of *Gunna Island*.

On the S. side of the Sound of *Gunna* (which is the safest channel between *Tiri* and *Coll*), and about two miles E. from the S. side of *Kyles*, there is a small rock which dries with spring-tide only. It bears S. E. ½ E. from the W. end of *Gunna Island*. This rock is avoided along the S. side, when *Bonbyrgh Hill* (at the S. W. end of *Tiri*) is without, or southward of, the rock that resembles a hillock on the extremity of the *Island Soay* in *Tiri*; it is avoided along the N. side, when that rock bears on the middle of *Bonbyrgh*.

To sail through the Sound of *Gunna*, keep near the middle, or about one-third from either side of the channel.

To sail along the S. side of *Tiri*, keep at least half a mile from what is always above water, and all the rocks will be avoided, except the spring-tide rock eastward of *Kyles*, already described.

Along the N. and S. sides of *Coll Island*, there are no rocks that lie above a quarter of a mile from the land, except one a little more than half a mile S. from the W. end of *Coll*, near the Sound of *Gunna*, which dries about half-ebb: one about half a mile W. from *Soay*, near *Lochachasfid*, which dries about half-ebb: *Baderrik*, on the E. side of the mouth of *Lochachasfid*, that dries with spring-tide only, and is little more than a cable's-length from a rock near the *Point Ranfinch*; a leading-mark to this rock is *Ranfinch Point* on the top of *Bonill Hill*, which stands at the side of the bay on the opposite side of the island, and has a small kern on it: a rock that dries about half-ebb, about a mile eastward of *Baderrik*: and *Cornaliach Rock* off the E. end of *Coll*, which lies near a mile N. N. E. from *Ben-more*, and dries about half-ebb.

Anchoring-places and Harbours on the West Side of MULL, *and in* TIRI *and* COLL ISLANDS.

ANCHORING-PLACES and HARBOURS.

LOCH LAICH.

Loch Laigh is open to the N. near two points of the compass, and therefore cannot be reckoned a good harbour, but there is no danger in sailing into it; the ground is all clean, and toward the head of the bay holds pretty well; so that in summer it may be reckoned a safe harbour, but not in winter. The safest anchorage is near the head of the bay, on the W. side of *Ben-nam*, on four or five fathoms water.

LOCH SCRIDAN, *or* LOCH LEVEN.

Loch Scridan is a large and safe harbour, of easy access, capable of the largest ships; it is pretty well sheltered, the ground all good, and of a moderate depth. The best anchorage for large ships is within a mile of the head of the bay, on from nine to sixteen fathoms water. There is nothing to be feared in sailing to this anchorage with a leading wind; but in turning in, or out, the three following rocks, that lie near the S. side, must be avoided.

On the S. side of *Loch Scridan*, near the mouth, and above a cable's-length north-eastward of the rocks or small islands of *Arinn*, there is a rock that dries with spring-tide only; which is avoided while any part of *Inchkeniel* is seen to the northward of the small islands.

About half a mile eastward of the point of *Oranfig*, there is a small rock which is covered only at high spring-tide, called *Coragie*.

Skerrachdomag is a rock near *Kilmany*, the middle of which is always above water, and has a little grass on it; and the E. extremity is covered about high-water only. To avoid the extremity of it, keep the point of *Bawy* shut on *Inchkeniel*.

There is a small rock, which dries with spring-tide only, that lies about half a cable's-length from that part of *Skerrachdomag*, which is half between the grassy part of it, and the N. E. extremity, and about two cables-length south-eastward from the grassy part there is a rock which dries partly at half-ebb, and partly with spring-tide only. A leading-mark to the north-eastmost part of this rock is the grassy top of *Skerrachdomag* in one with the highest hill of *Inchkeniel*.

The safest anchorage for small vessels in this Loch, is between the rock last described, and the middle of *Skerrachdomag*, on four or five fathoms water.

The mouth of *Kilfinechan Bay*, opposite to *Skerrachdomag*, is good anchorage. Also in the bay eastward of *Oranfig*, about 1½, or two cables-length southward of *Coragie Rock*.

LOCH-NAKAEL.

Loch-nakeal has good ground in most parts, and is sufficiently sheltered by the islands in the entry; but it is liable to hard squalls of wind from the hills, when it blows fresh between the N. E. and N. W. points: the S. side of this harbour is not so good ground for anchorage, nor so clean as the N. side.

West of MULL, *and the Islands* TIRI, COLL, ULVA.

Rocks near the entry. [illegible] The rocks to be avoided sailing into this harbour are, a reef that extends northeastward, near half a mile from the E. end of *Inshchainach Island*; and *Re-megary Rock*: the reef is avoided by keeping the middle between *Gisfeal Island* and *Inshchainach*; or one-third part of *Ameyiere Island* on the highest hill of *Inchkeal*.

Beamegary Rock. *Re-megary* dries with spring-tide only, and lies about one-third from the E. end of *Ulva*, and two-thirds from *Sand-Ban*. It is avoided along the S. side, while any part of *Ameyiere Island* is in one with the middle of the highest hill in *Inchkeal*. To avoid it along the N. side, keep the northmost point of *Ameyiere* southward of the S. end of the highest hill of *Inchkeal*; or keep within a cable's-length of the E. end of *Ulva Island*.

Rocks near the head of Loch-na-keal, on the S. side. On the S. side of *Loch-nakeal*, about a mile and a half from the head of it, there are rocks that dry partly at two hours of ebb, and partly at low-water. To avoid them, keep *Ilan Earsa* shut, or nearly shut, on the low part of *Tergeneg Head*.

Rock near Calfa on the N. side. On the N. side of the harbour, right opposite to the last-mentioned rock, there is a rock about a cable's-length from the shore, which dries about half-ebb.

Anchorage. The best anchorage in *Loch-nakeal* is, on the E. end of *Ilan Earsa*, about two cables-length from the shore. In the summer-time a ship may ride any where above *Ilan Earsa*, in the middle, or nearest the N. side of the Loch, on from six to eleven fathoms water.

KYLESAVER CREEK, *in* GOMETRA ISLAND.

Kylesawa is a small Creek between *Gometra* and *Ulva* islands, where there is pretty good shelter, good ground, and sufficient depth of water. The anchorage is about two cables-length above the entrance, on four fathoms water.

Rock near the entry. About two cables-length southward from the point of *Gometra* at the entry, there is a rock that dries two hours after high-water, which must be taken on the larboard-hand going in.

Rock, above the anchorage. About half a mile up the Creek, there is a rock which dries at half-ebb, which shelters the anchorage on the N.

ACHERSTY-VORE CREEK, *in* GOMETRA ISLAND.

Achersty-vore Creek is on the N. side of *Gometra*, at the W. end, and is a very good place for a small vessel that draws not above seven or eight feet water. About half up this Creek there is a rock always above water, near the W. side, at which the sand dries each spring-tide: anchor on the E. side of this rock, with one anchor on shore.

CRADAO BAY, *in* ULVA ISLAND.

Cragag Bay, is a Creek on the S. side of *Ulva*, where small vessels may ride safe in summer within the small islands, on five fathoms water. The entry is on the E. side of *Heninike* (on which there is a small kern to point it out), between it and the small islands near it eastward, and reaching to the point of *Tormore*. In sailing towards this creek, keep *Calfa Island*, and three rocks, always above water, that lie between it and *Heninike*, on your larboard-hand; these rocks lie in a straight line with *Hen-inike*, and serve as a direction to it. Anchor about a cable's-length northward of *Heninike*, where there appears to be most room.

Sound of ULVA ISLAND.

Rock in the entry. This is a Creek at the E. end of *Ulva*, which is only fit for small vessels that draw not above seven or eight feet of water; but it is well sheltered, the anchor-ground good, and soft to lie on, in case a vessel shall happen to take the ground. The entry to this harbour is from the S. About the middle of the narrowest part of the entry, as it turns towards the anchorage, there is a rock that dries one hour after high-water, either side of which is sufficiently deep: anchor on the S. W. side of this rock, about half a cable's-length from it.

LOCH TUA.

Loch Tua, being wide in the entry, and not sufficiently sheltered from the westerly winds, cannot be called a safe harbour in the winter-time. The safest anchorage is in the bay of *Sorby*, on the N. side of *Ulva*, where there is good ground and sufficient depth for any ship. Go up that bay till you are land-locked by the west point of the bay on *Treshinish Point*, and there drop anchor.

Mara Rock. In sailing into this anchorage, avoid *Mara Rock*, which lies off the mouth of it, near half a mile from the shore; a leading-mark to which, is *Fladda Island* (one of the *Treshinish* isles), just hid by *Ulva*. To avoid it on the S. side, keep *Kerobuig Island* half out by *Ulva*. To avoid it along the N. side, keep *Fladda Island* half out by *Ulva*. In moderate weather a ship may stop almost any where within two miles of the head of the Loch on either side, about a cable's-length from the shore.

LOCH ACHAMICH.

This Bay is only fit for stopping in the summer-time. The only clean part to anchor on is, near the head of the Loch, about two or three cables-length from the sand.

Reef off [illegible]. In sailing in, avoid a reef of rocks, that dries about low-water, and extends from the point of *Inroay*, about two cables-length.

Anchorage in TIRI ISLAND.

In *Tiri* there is no safe place of anchorage; only in summer a ship may stop on clean ground in *Vrory Bay*, almost any where above two cables-length from the shore. Or on the W. side of *Kirkabol Bay*, on three or four fathoms, about two or three cables-length from the shore. Do not steer northward for this anchorage, till two ruinous chapels, which may be seen near the houses of *Kirkabol*, bear N. W. by N. and, to avoid the rocks in the middle of the bay, steer nothing to the northward of that course.

Acharsfginchan Creek. A small vessel, with a pilot, may go into *Acharsfginchan Creek*, about high-water, and lie aground safe on mud.

Anchorage in COLL ISLAND.

Loch-[illegible]. There is no good anchoring-place in this Island. In the mouth of *Lochorbasil*, above *Suey*, a ship may stop in the summer-time on five or six fathoms water, and clean sand, about one, or two cables-length from the shore.

Loch Tiin. In *Loch Tiin* a vessel may stop, in moderate weather, on the E. side of the Island that lies half a mile up the bay, on three or four fathoms, about the middle of that Island.

NAUTICAL DESCRIPTIONS

OF THE

WEST COAST

OF

SCOTLAND,

FROM

ARDNAMURACHAN *in* ARGYLESHIRE, *to* CAPE WRATH *in* STRATHNAVER.

A Description of the Tides, Rocks, Shoals, Channels, Anchoring-places, and Harbours from ARDNAMURACHAN, *near* MULL ISLAND, *to* SKY *and* CANA ISLANDS.

CHART XXIV.

Tides from ARDNAMURACHAN *to* SKY *and* CANA ISLANDS.

TIDES.

ON this part of the coast of *Scotland* it is high-water, on the full and change days of the moon, at 5½, or 6h.

Ordinary spring-tides rise eleven feet perpendicular; neap-tides five or six feet.

The stream of flood sets in from the south and south-westward, and runs not above one mile an hour when strongest; except along the W. side of *Ardnamurachan*, where it runs about two miles an hour when strongest; and in the Sound of *Cana*, and near *Hyskir*, where spring-tide runs about three miles an hour, and neap-tide above half a mile when strongest.

Rocks between ARDNAMURACHAN *and* SKY, *and* CANA ISLANDS.

ROCKS.

On this part of the coast there are no rocks or shoals, but what are near the shore, or near harbours, excepting *Bo-afhadil* Rock, which lies about three miles northward of *Faskadil* in *Ardnamurachan*, and dries with spring-tide only; and some rocks and shoals about half a mile south-westward from the W. end of *Hyskir*, part of which dry with spring-tide only. The weather did not permit me to examine *Bo-afhadil* particularly. The bearing of it was taken from *Mull Island* only.

There are some rocks said, on pretty good authority, to lie about four or five miles S. W. by W. from *Hyskir*, that dry with low spring-tide. These rocks did not appear in winter, when *Hyskir* was surveyed, and there was no pilot to be had that could bring the vessel to them.

Anchoring-places and Harbours between ARDNAMURACHAN *and* SKY, *and* CANA ISLANDS.

ANCHORING-PLACES and HARBOURS.

LOCH MUDART.

Loch Mudart is capable of small vessels only, and fit for them only in the summer-time. The entry is dangerous without a pilot.

In sailing toward this harbour, along *Ardnamurachan*, avoid *Bo-afhadil*, formerly mentioned, by keeping within a league of the shore. Avoid also a rock which lies about two cables-length N. from the point of *Ardnamush*, and dries about half-ebb.

Near the W. end of *Ilan-tana* there are several rocks; the outermost of which lies within a quarter of a mile of the shore, or of the rocks which are always above water.

About

South Coast of SKY ROM.

[illegible] About a cable's-length N. W. from the point, or rock, on the S. side of the entry, there is a small rock that dries with spring-tide only. To sail along the N. side of this rock, take the point last-mentioned in one with the houses of *Inverie*. *Inverie* is a village at the head of the Loch below a gap, or deep sink, in the hill: the houses are ranged in a semicircular form along the upper side of the corn field.

To sail up this loch. In sailing up *Loch Nadort*, there are several rocks always above water; keep the middle between them as near as you can, and anchor any where nearest the same side.

LOCH AYLORT.

Loch Aylort is not sufficiently sheltered for vessels to ride long in, in the winter-time; but in summer they may ride safe on the S. side of the bay, about a cable's-length or two eastward of *Ilan-gour*, on four or five fathoms water. Or on the N. side of the bay, about two cables-length eastward of the island, near that side. The first anchorage is the best.

LOCH NANUACH.

Loch Nanuach is all good ground, and the depth fit for the largest ships; but being open to the W. it is not safe in the winter-time, except to small vessels, which may anchor within the small islands of *Druminderid*, on the N. side of *Ilan-Cabber*. Large vessels may anchor, in summer, any where eastward of *Ilan-Cabber*, on the N. side of the bay, about two cables-length from the shore; but this anchorage seems too much exposed in the winter-time.

Rock near Ilan-Toan. In sailing into *Loch Nanuach*, if you happen to be near *Ilan-Toan*, avoid a small rock which is dry with spring-tide only, and lies about a quarter of a mile southward of the westmost of three remarkable rocks always above water, on the W. side of that island.

Channel to Druminderid Creek. The best channel into *Druminderid Creek*, is along the E. side of the cluster of small islands and rocks that shelter it on the west: keep about a cable's-length from them, till you are near the northmost rock, which is always above water, and about a quarter of a mile W. from *Ilan-Cabber*; then keep one-third from that rock, and two-thirds from the island, to avoid a rock which dries about half-ebb, and lies near the middle between them.

Channel along the E. side of Ilan-Cabber. If the wind will permit, a vessel may sail into this Creek along the E. side of *Ilan-Cabber*. In sailing this way avoid a small rock, which dries with spring-tide only, which lies above half a cable's-length, S. W. from the S. end of *Ilan-Cabber*; and give the N. E. point of the island a moderate birth; to avoid a rock, dry with spring-tide only, which lies about one-fourth from the island, and three-fourths from the point of *Druminderid*, nearest to the island.

LOCH NAGAUL.

There is very good anchorage near the head of this bay, but the mouth of it is so full of small islands, rocks, and sand-banks, that it requires a pilot particularly well acquainted to bring a vessel in; and no directions without one ought to be relied on. If a vessel is under any necessity of going in here, take as much of the flood-tide as can be done; sail along the S. side of *Ilan-Langay*; keep within a cable's-length of the starboard shore, and anchor any where off *Keppoch*, on the S. side of the bay. The Draft will exhibit the rocks and shoals plainer than any description can make them.

LOCH NEVISH.

Loch Nevish (opposite to the point of *Slate* in *Sky*) is a large, well-sheltered arm of the sea, the bottom good, and capable of a fleet of the largest ships; but the water, at a sufficient distance from shore, is too deep for ordinary vessels, being from forty to fifty-eight fathoms.

[illegible] About the middle of the entry (which is above two miles wide), and above half a mile S. S. E. of *Bowmen*, there is a rock called *Bowen*, which dries at low spring-tide only: to avoid it along the S. side, keep *Inverie House* in sight by the point of *Rarand*.

[illegible] *Heviadeveg* are two small rocks that lie near the shore, between *Rarand* and *Scotas House*, and dry about half-ebb.

Ledge E. from [illegible] There is a rocky ledge that extends eastward, about a cable's-length from *Rarand Point*, the W. end of which dries about half-ebb.

Anchorage. The only safe anchorage in *Loch Nevish*, is in that arm, which extends south-eastward; any part of which is safe, but requires a great deal of cable out, or one anchor on shore.

Small vessels, in the summer, may stop on a more moderate depth in the bay of *Inverie*, off the house *Scotas*, above which it shallows fast; drop anchor in from twenty to eleven fathoms water.

LOCH EYSORT in SKY ISLAND.

Loch Eysort is the east side of a large bay, between the *Aird of Strath* and *Slate*, which divides into two branches. The mouth of this Loch, for above a mile up, is all good ground, sheltered sufficiently from all winds, excepting the west and S. W. and the depth is sufficient for the largest ships. This part of the *Loch Eysort* is very fit for ships or vessels in the summer-time, except when it blows fresh from the W. or S. W. which then makes a great sea and hard riding. In the winter vessels must take a pilot, and go above *Ilan-heast* to ride safe.

Rocks in Loch Eysort, Tarskervag Rocks. The rocks to be avoided in sailing up *Loch Eysort*, are the rocks off *Tarskervag*, which dry about two hours after high-water, and extend westward about half a mile from the S. side of that bay.

Ord Rocks. The rocks near *Ord* dry before half-ebb, and extend from the shore below the house of *Ord*, northward, near half over, toward *Berreg*. They are avoided, by keeping the E. end of *Ilan [illegible]* open with the small island, near the old castle of *Ord*.

Berreg Rock. *Berreg Rock* extends southward from that shore near half a mile: the middle of it is always above water. To sail along the S. end of this rock, keep *Ilean-[illegible]* W. ½ S. or a large [illegible] open with the N. end of *Rum*.

Channel to Ilan-heast narrow. Sailing from *Berreg* eastward to *Ilan-heast*, the water is shallow on both sides, so as to leave the channel where narrowest, not a cable's-length wide. To sail in the channel, keep the middle as near as possible, or take a pilot, for no distinguishable land marks are to be seen.

Rock [illegible] On the S. W. side of *Ilan-heast*, a little more than half over, towards the highest part of the hill, which is covered with bushes of wood, there is a small rock always above water, except at the height of spring-tide.

Stopping Places. Near the mouth of *Loch Eysort*, stop nearest the N. side, on from twenty to ten fathoms. On the E. side of *Berreg Rocks*, stop about two cables-length eastward from these rocks, and as far southward of the E.

end

end of *Brorag*, on six or seven fathoms water. On the E. side of *Ban bagh*, anchor on from seven to eleven fathoms.

LOCH SLEPIN.

Loch Slepin, which is within the same entry with *Loch Eyshort*, is a very good place for ships, or vessels, of any burden to stop in with any wind but the south; for being open on that quarter, a great swell sets in when it blows fresh from the south, and makes hard riding there. In blowing weather, and in winter, it is safest riding at the head of the Loch, nearest the W. side of that harbour.

Rocks and shoals to be avoided in failing up *Loch Slepin* are; a ledge extending eastward above a cable's-length from the point of *Rona-bordan*, near the *Aird of Sleath*: a shoal, partly rocks, partly sand, near the S. side of *Kilmore Bay*, which extends a quarter of a mile from the shore. The least water on that shoal is twelve feet. — Rocks and Shoals near Loch Slepin.

Near the head of *Loch Slepin*, before you enter the proper harbour, about half a mile from a low green point that makes the W. side of the entry, there is a rocky shoal which extends eastward, almost half over to the opposite side: also there is a rock lying off the low head of *Terrin*, part of which dries at two hours of ebb, and part with low spring-tide. To avoid these two shoals, having passed *Kilmore Bay*, keep the middle as near as you can, till you have entered the harbour, then drop anchor nearest the W. side, for the E. side is shallow a good way off. — Near the Harbour.

LOCH SCAVIG.

There is no safe anchorage in this Loch, or rather bay, being liable to violent squalls of wind from the *Culin Mountains*, and the bottom rocky in many parts; only there are two very small creeks at the head of it, close to the foot of the mountains, where small vessels may lie safe at a land-fast, or with one anchor on shore. Each of these creeks is sheltered by a small Island, but they are of such difficult access, that none ought to attempt them without a pilot. The least water in the eastmost creek is one fathom, and in the westmost two fathoms.

SOA ISLAND *Anchorage*.

With southerly winds vessels may ride near the N. E. end of *Soa Island* in from seven to ten fathoms water, above a cable's-length from the shore. When the wind is any thing northerly, very violent gusts of wind come suddenly from the mountains.

Near the W. end of *Soa* there are several rocks; that farthest from the shore is about half a mile off, and is always above water; and has a ledge extending about a cable's-length southward from it, which dries at low spring-tide only. — Rocks near Soa.

LOCH BRITTIL.

Within this Loch the ground is all clean; but being open, and much exposed to southerly winds, it is fit to stop in only in the summer-time. Anchor nearest the N. side of the bay, on seven or eight fathoms water; or near the head on five or six.

LOCH SKRESORT *in* RUM ISLAND.

Loch Skresort is the only part in the *Island Rum* that may be called a harbour; but being open to the east, and liable to squalls from the hills near it, it does not seem sufficiently safe in harvest or winter. The best place of anchorage is on the S. side of the bay, about half way to the head, on three or four fathoms, where *Bruncrey Hill*, or the hill near it, bears S. W.

On the S. side of this bay, almost half up, there is a rocky ledge which dries with spring-tide only. It begins between two houses, near each of which there is a little corn-ground, and extends about one-third right over. — Rocky ledge on the S. side.

At the head of the bay the water is shallow above two cables-length from the high-water mark; so that a vessel must not run too far up before the anchor is drop. — Shallow at the head.

EGG ISLAND *Anchorage*.

In the small bay on the W. side of *Ban-bagh*, a vessel may stop in moderate weather, on four or five fathoms water, but it is not safe to lie here long, because it is exposed to W. and S. W. winds, and there is very little room to spare off cable.

Also in the summer-time a vessel may stop in the bay of *Laig*, about two cables-length from the shore, taking care to avoid two ledges that are on the E. side of the bay, and extend a cable's-length from the shore.

ISLAND MUCK.

There is no place of anchorage in this Island proper to be recommended; only, there are two creeks, one on the N. W. side, the other on the S. E. where, if a small vessel had any business, she might venture to lie a few days in the summer season. The first is the bay of *Galanich*, on the E. side of which there is a ledge that extends near two cables-length north-westward; between which, and the W. side of the bay, there are two small rocks that dry with spring-tide only. To avoid these rocks, it is necessary to have a pilot; or to go in at low-water with spring-tide, when they may be seen. Anchor within the innermost rock, about a cable's-length from the shore. A small vessel may go in after half-flood, by keeping about half a cable's-length from the land on the starboard-side. — Galanich Bay.

The other creek, on the S. E. side of *Muck*, is much safer once a vessel has got in. On the W. side of the entry to this small bay, there is a rock always above water, on the S. end of which there is a rock that dries at two half ebb, and lies about half a cable's-length from it; eastward of these two rocks, and within half a cable's-length of them, there is a reef which dries with spring-tide only. The channel in, is close along the E. side of the first-mentioned rock, which is always above water. Anchor in the mouth of the bay on six fathoms water. — Creek on the S. E. side.

On the N. side of *Muck*, about three quarters of a mile from shore, there is a rock always above water; on the N. and E. sides of which there are ledges that dry with spring-tide only, that extend above a cable's-length from it. — Rock and ledges.

CANA ISLAND *Harbour*.

The harbour of *Cana* is small, but pretty well sheltered, and commodiously situated for vessels bound either northward or southward; and on that account is more frequented than any of the harbours in that neighbourhood.

CANA ISLAND, SKY ISLAND.

larboard. The best place of anchorage in this harbour is, nearest the W. side of the bay, when Coraghan Point bears E. on three or four fathoms at low-water.

[illegible] On the S. side of the entrance of Cana harbour, there is a rock lying off a small cove in Sandy Island; the N. E. end of this rock is covered at high-water only, and may always be perceived. Above a cable's-length westward from this rock, and S. S. W. from Coraghan Point, there is a small rock within half a cable's-length of the shore of Sandy Island, which dries with spring-tide only. You are past this rock on the W. side, when the westmost house of Coraghan, at the end of the Sandy Bay, is hid by the point of Coraghan; and nearly abreast of it when that house is seen fairly by the point.

[illegible] On the W. side of Coraghan Point, within the harbour, and about a pistol shot from the shore, there is a rock that dries at half-ebb; this rock must be avoided in riding here with a S. W. wind.

Tide. It is high-water in the harbour of Cana at six, full and change days: in the sound of Cana (between Cana and Rum) the stream of ebb begins half an hour later.

Stream. The stream in the sound, near Cana, when strongest, runs about three miles an hour: on the Rum side it is not so strong. The flood along the W. end of Cana runs northward about two miles an hour when strongest. Near Hyskery it runs about three miles an hour.

[illegible] The rocks off the W. end of Hyskery extend south-westward about half a mile, and dry in several parts with spring-tide.

For the other harbours along the S. side of Sky, see the next Chart.

A Description of the Tides, Rocks, Shoals, Channels, Anchoring-places, and Harbours in the S. E. Part of SKY *and the adjacent Main.*

CHART XXV.

TIDES.

Tides along the South Part of SKY.

[illegible] On the S. part of Sky, and the adjacent main, it is high-water at six; on the full and change days of the moon, near the head of long bays, or lochs, it is about half an hour later.

[illegible] The stream of flood sets in from the southward, and runs northward, as far as the several bays and channels it runs into will permit.

[illegible] Ordinary spring-tides here rise eleven feet perpendicular, neap tides five or six.

[illegible] Along this part of the coast the stream of tide is scarce sensible, except in narrow channels, or near headlands crossing the direction of the main stream. In Kyle-rea, in the inner sound, spring-tide, when strongest, runs seven miles an hour; neap-tide one. In Kyleakin, near Kyle-rea, spring-tide, when strongest, runs five miles an hour; neap-tide 1½.

ROCKS.

[illegible] There are no rocks, or shoals, along this part of Sky and the main, but what lie in, or so near the lochs and sounds, that they will be described along with them: except Sheraes Rock, which lies about two miles S. S. E. from Crymahow Head, westward of Loch Bracadale, and is always above water; northward of Sheraes, there are two small rocks which dry about half-ebb; one is very near it, the other about half a mile from Sheraes.

ANCHORING-PLACES and HARBOURS.

Anchoring-places and Harbours in the South Part of SKY *and adjacent Main.*

Loch Nevish on the main, and the Lochs and anchoring-places on the S. E. coast of Sky, from Slate to Loch Brittil, having been described with the former Chart (to which we refer), we now proceed north-westward to

LOCH EYNORT.

In Loch Eynort a ship that draws twelve or fifteen feet of water may ride almost quite land-locked, about a cable's-length from the low green point of Glenynort, on three, or 3½ fathoms. The largest ships may ride about half a mile lower, off Crakenish, on six or seven fathoms, good ground, but a little more open to westerly winds, which set in a great sea when it blows fresh.

[illegible] Dufforn, which lies off the entrance of this Loch, about half a mile from the shore, is always above water, and steep too almost quite round.

Ledge. At the north point of the entry there is a small ledge, extending about half a cable's-length southward, which must be avoided failing in or out.

LOCH BRACADALE.

Loch Bracadale is a large bay, containing several branches, or lesser Lochs within it, that make exceeding good harbours; particularly Loch Harport, the E. side of Ilan-Heversay, and Loch Harlosh.

Loch Harport. Loch Harport is a large arm of the sea on the S. side of the bay, capable of several hundreds of the largest ships, quite land-locked, neither rocks nor shoals within it, or near it, the water of a moderate depth, and the ground extraordinary good. Ships may stop in the mouth of Loch Harport on either side, between Ilan-Ornsay and Bracadale; and may ride all weathers any where from Bracadale to the head of the Loch.

[illegible] Heversay anchorage is fit for small vessels only; the place being enclosed by a reef of rocks on the N. E. side, which dry partly about half-ebb, and partly at low-water spring-tide. The rock which lies nearest the N. E. point of Ilan-Heversay, is dry two hours before low-water: the large rock next to Colbost dries about half-ebb; the southmost of these rocks bears E. N. E. from the middle, or highest part of Ilan-Heversay.

Loch Harlosh. Loch Harlosh is on the E. side of the peninsula of Balmore, and is sheltered by that point, and by the Islands Harlosh [illegible] The safest anchorage is above Balmore House, on five or six fathoms water.

[illegible] There are two rocks on the starboard-hand going in here; one of which, called Stornbury, is always above water: about a cable's-length northward of it, there is a small rock that dries with spring-tide only. To avoid this last rock, keep Stornbury and Tamborigh open of each other. Within Loch Harlosh, near its head, there is a rock that dries with spring-tide only.

SKY ISLAND.

On the W. side of *Loch Poltiel* there are several rocks which ſtrike the ordinary anchorage, the northernmoſt of which is always above water, and the ſoutherneſt dries about half-ebb: in failing in, when you can clear the rock always above water, by the ſame courſe the reſt will be cleared likewiſe. There is ſome foul ground near the anchorage, on which no diſtinct mark could be found.

Loch-eagelo and *Loch-Vorlig*, being open to the S. may be reckoned ſtopping-places, rather than harbours: the ground is all clean, and no danger in the way to them.

Loch Eagelo, and Loch-Vorlig.

The Inner Sound of SKY.

The Inner Sound, is the channel between the E. end of *Sky*, and the main of *Scotland*, which, as far northward as *Kyle-rea*, the narroweſt part, has neither rock, ſhoal, ledge, nor ſenſible ſtream of tide in the way of ſhipping. The ground is all good for anchorage, excepting a few parts near the land where it is rocky; but the water in the open channel is generally too deep for ordinary merchant-ſhips to ride in, except within two cables-length of the ſhore: the *Sky* ſide is the ſafeſt to ſtop on. The *Lochs*, or harbours, in the Inner-Sound are the following:

LOCH NIVISH *is deſcribed above.*

LOCH HOURN.

Loch Hourn, in *Glenelg*, on the main, is a large, well-ſheltered, arm of the ſea, of eaſy acceſs, the ground good, and capable of a numerous ſleet of the largeſt ſhips. They may anchor any where from *Rafer* to *Barisdale*, only avoiding a ſpring-tide rock on the N. ſide, which is a little eaſtward of *Arnisdale*.

In the mouth of *Loch Hourn*, near the middle, there is a ſmall rock always above water; the water is ſhallow, about half a cable's-length eaſtward of this rock: it is avoided while *Ardnaſlignaich Point* is on, or near, the point of *Slate*.

Rock in the Entry.

Near the E. point of *Arniſdale Bay*, there is a ſmall rock always above water: about a quarter of a mile eaſtward from this rock, there is a rock that dries with ſpring-tide only. To avoid it failing up, keep the middle, or at leaſt one-third, from *Glenelg* ſide, till you are about a quarter of a mile from the two ſmall iſlands next eaſtward.

Rock near Arniſdale.

Small veſſels may ride in a moderate depth in the bay of *Arniſdale*, between the rock off the E. point and the ſhore, on nine or ten fathoms water; or on the E. or W. ſide of the two ſmall iſlands laſt-mentioned, about a cable's-length from them.

Anchorage.

ILAN-ORONSA, *or* LOCH-INDAAL.

Loch-Indaal, or *Ilan-Oronſa*, as it is moſt commonly called, from the peninſula at the mouth of it, is a ſmall bay in *Sky*, oppoſite to *Loch Hourn*, where ſhips of any burden may ride ſafe, particularly on the S. W. ſide, under ſhelter of the peninſula. Go not far up this bay.

LOCH DUICH, *and* LOCH LOUNG.

Loch Duich lies at the N. end of *Kyle-rea*, or narroweſt part of the channel, between *Sky* and the main. It is quite well-ſheltered, the ground good, and being above three miles long, and half a mile broad, at a medium, is capable of a great number of the largeſt ſhips.

To ſail into *Loch Duich* from the ſouth, it is neceſſary to go through *Kyle-rea*, in which the ſtream is for the moſt part very rapid, and therefore requires flood-tide. In this ſound ſpring-tides, when ſtrongeſt, run about ſeven miles an hour; and neap-tides above two. *Duncan Bay*, near the entry of the *Kyle*, is a convenient place to ſtop in for the tide. On the W. ſide of the entry of *Kyle-rea*, near *Laiter*, there is a rocky ledge that extends from the ſhore eaſtward, about two cables-length. You avoid this ledge, while *Sandy Point*, at the mouth of *Loch Hourn*, is open of *Duncan Point*.

Kyle-rea.
Strong Tide.
Ledge near Laiter.

At the N. end of *Kyle-rea*, and about a cable's-length from the *Point of Sky*, there is a ſmall rock, called *Caileach-ſtone*, which is covered a little before high-water; to avoid this rock along the N. ſide, keep *Duncans Hill*, in *Raſa Iſland*, on any part of the corn-field oppoſite *Kylerhea*.

Caileach-ſtone.

Sail into *Loch Duich* with flood-tide on the N. ſide of the ſmall iſland, which lies near the entrance, and avoid a ſmall rock about a quarter of a mile above that iſland, which lies about a cable's-length from the ſhore on the ſtarboard-ſide. The ſtream between the iſland and the ſhore, on the N. ſide, runs about five miles an hour when ſtrongeſt.

To ſail in.

Loch Loung is a narrow branch of *Loch Duich*, which muſt be entered with flood-tide, and not before half-flood; becauſe the entrance is ſhallow, having only ſix feet of water in it at low-water. Anchor in the broadeſt part, near half a mile up.

Loch Loung.

KYLAKIN *Channel.*

Kylakin is that part of the inner Sound which runs weſtward between *Lochalſh* and *Sky*. Spring-tides here, towards the W. end, when ſtrongeſt, run about five miles an hour. The flood ſets in from the north-weſtward, and meeting the ſtream from the ſouthward off the mouth of *Loch Duich*, both together run eaſtward up that Loch.

Tide.

There is a rocky ledge that extends from *Caſtlemorfaring* northward, almoſt half over to the ſmall iſlands. To avoid this ledge, keep the middle, or neareſt the ſmall iſlands.

Ledge off Caſtlemorfaring.

About half a mile weſtward from the weſt end of *Kylakin*, there is a rock that dries about low-water, and lies about two cables-length from the ſhore of *Sky*. To avoid this rock, keep *Caſtlemorfaring* in ſight by *Kylakin Head*.

Rock W. of Kylakin.

LOCH CARRON.

Loch Carron is large, ſeemly ſheltered, and the ground very good; but the way to it is incumbered with very ſmall iſlands, or rocks, and the entrance narrow, ſo that it is not to be attempted with ſafety by a ſtranger. Two or three perches properly placed would make the beſt channel ſufficiently plain. As it is at preſent, the ſafeſt channel for a ſtranger is, at the laſt quarter of flood to ſail in within a cable's-length from either ſide of the two ſmall iſlands, or rocks, called *Staringwhark*; from thence ſail eaſtward, about a mile, for another ſmall iſland that lies about a cable's-length from the ſhore of *Rarig*, and ſail between that iſland and the ſhore, keeping neareſt the *Rarig* ſide (in this channel there is not above three or four feet at low ſpring-tide); from *Rarig* ſail in through the middle of the narrow entrance; and to ride on a moderate depth,

SKY ISLAND.

anchor on the S. side, just as you have past the narrow: or on the E. side of the peninsula, about 1½ mile up. This last is for small vessels only, as it is shallow pretty far out.

There is a reef of rocks that lie near half a mile south-eastward of Steinigeadh; the top of the southmost of them is always above water; the top of the northmost is covered at high-water only. A vessel may stop a tide on either side of these rocks.

Small vessels may ride in the mouth of the bay of Plock, S. of Steinigeadh. They must go but a little way in, for it shallows soon.

LOCH KISHORN.

In Loch Kishorn there is good holding-ground, and water for the largest ships, but it is not sufficiently sheltered for vessels in the winter-time. The best anchorage is near the head of the bay, on eight or ten fathoms; or between the island on the S. side of the entry, and the point near it, on from 5½ to six fathoms water.

CROULIN ISLANDS Harbour.

Small vessels near the N. E. end of Sky, may find good shelter by running in between the two islands of Croulin; where they may either lie a-ground on soft sand, or be kept afloat by land-fasts on each side, on eight or ten feet the least water. This creek may hold three or four small vessels. The best and deepest part to ride on, is a very little S. of the minister's house. Directly off this house there is a bank of soft sand, which is dry at low-water with spring-tide. Enter Croulin on the N. side; for the S. entry is dry at half-ebb.

TUSCAO Bay.

Tuscag is a small bay on the main, opposite to Croulin Islands, sheltered from all winds but the south. In the entry, near the middle, there is a small rock dry with spring-tide only: by keeping nearest to either side this rock may be avoided. Here the ground is clean, and the depth sufficient for any ship.

APPLECROSS Bay.

In moderate weather a ship may stop on clean ground in Applecross Bay; but must not go farther in than till she is abreast of the cluster of small houses, which are on the S. side, where there are five or six fathoms at low-water; for it shoals suddenly above that.

KYLESCODO Harbour.

Kylescodo is a very safe harbour, between Scalpa Island and Sky, of easy access, and fit for ships of any burden; only, like all other places in the neighbourhood of high mountains, it is liable to violent squalls when the wind blows from them. Sail in along the N. end of Scalpa, for the south entry dries at low spring-tide. A large vessel failing in about low-water, when she is past the beachy point of Kameraberach in Scalpa, must give the shore below Dunerne House a moderate birth, to avoid a sandy shoal that extends about a cable's-length from it, on which there are but two fathoms, or 1½ at low spring-tide.

Sheriatrafan rocks lie near half a mile northward from Sheriaderik Island, on the E. side of Scalpa, and are dry at half-ebb. They are avoided along the E. side, while Longa Island is seen eastward of Sheriaderik; they are avoided along the W. side, while Castlemoyle in Sky is hid by Longa.

LOCH EYNORT.

Loch Eynort is a well-sheltered bay, near to Kylescodo, the access is safe, the ground good, and the water of a moderate depth. The only inconveniency in this harbour, is the sudden squalls of wind that come from the mountains in blowing weather. On the S. side of this Loch, from the entry to Lusgrineveg, there is a sand-bank reaching about one-third over, on most of which there is but twelve feet at low-water, and on the upper end only six. Large ships may anchor any where nearest the north side, smaller vessels may anchor on the S. side, above the before-mentioned sand-bank, where the depth is less.

LOCH SLIGACHAN.

Loch Sligachan in Sky is well-sheltered, good ground, and the water sufficient for the largest ships; but the channel in the entrance is narrow, and requires a leading-wind and flood-tide, or slack water. In sailing into this harbour from the E. there are three shoals to be avoided; the first lies a quarter of a mile eastward of Scasser House, is partly rocks, and partly sand, and extends about two cables-length from the shore; and is avoided by keeping the top of Scor Hill in Trotternish (the highest visible along that coast, with a ragged top) in sight, eastward of Ardtoranish Point, till the house of Scasser bears S. W. by W. then steer on that house, and keep within half a cable's-length from the shore till you open the Loch fairly, then fall in; by which you will avoid a ledge that extends south from Balmeran Point across the entry. The third shoal is a rocky ledge, which extends about a cable's-length eastward from Tormore Head: this is avoided, while Rameburnis Point in Uig parish is seen out by, or eastward of, Ardtoranish Point.

The best anchorage in Loch Sligachan is about a quarter of a mile above the entrance on the S. side, along a cable's-length from the shore. This Loch is liable to violent squalls of wind when it blows fresh from the south or west.

CLACHAN BAY in RASA ISLAND.

This Bay is sufficiently sheltered, good ground, and a moderate depth of water; but subject to sudden squalls of wind, like other places on the E. side of Sky, when it blows hard from the S. or W. quarters. You may ride in any part of the bay, about two cables-length from the shore, on five or six fathoms water.

It is high-water in this neighbourhood at six, full and change days. The stream of flood sets in from the north; and between Clachan in Rasa, and Ardtoranish Point in Sky, runs about two miles an hour when strongest: in other parts it is scarce sensible.

PORTREE Harbour.

The Bay of Portree, off the houses, is an exceeding good harbour for a few ships of any size; it is well-sheltered, the ground good, the depth from five to fourteen fathoms, and nothing to fear coming in but a rock, about half a cable's-length from Airdmarthy Point on the starboard as you enter the anchorage, part of which is always above water.

A D[illegible]

A Description of the Tides, Rocks, Shoals, Anchoring-places, and Harbours in the North Part of Sky Island, Rona, Raza, and adjacent Main.

CHART XXVI.

On the north part of Sky, on Rona, Raza, and the adjacent part of the main of Scotland, it is high-water at six o'clock, on the full and change-days of the moon; but as far westward from the coast as Margaretta's Rock the stream does not turn till eight.

The stream of flood along this part of the coast sets in from the southward, and turns eastward along Galtrigil Head, Vaternish Point, and between Fladdahuan Island, and Sky; from thence it runs along Ben-trodda northward, between Sky and the islands Rona and Raza, till it meets the flood coming through the inner sounds off Loch Kishorn in Applecross, where both turn northward, and run with a gentle motion along the coast of the main.

On this part of the coast, ordinary spring-tides rise eleven feet perpendicular; extraordinary thirteen; ordinary neap-tides six or seven.

The stream of tide along this coast has very little strength, except near the head-lands, Galtrigil, Vaternish Point, and Rubanish, where spring-tides, when strongest, run about three miles an hour; and near Margaretta's, where they run about five miles an hour when strongest, and neap-tides one and a half, or two.

The rocks that lie off this coast are Fasker, which is a remarkable rock always above water, near the mouth of Loch Snizort.

Margaretta's is a small rock, not thirty yards long, which lies about a league N. by W. from the S. end of Fladdahuan Island, and bears from the highest part of the Shiant Islands in the Lewis S. W. ½ S. and from the E. end of Stalpa, or Lan-glass, in Harris in Long Island, S. E. ½ S. This rock dries about half-ebb. To avoid it along the N. side, keep about one-third from the island Fladdahuan, and two-thirds from Stalpa in Harris. To avoid it along the E. side, keep the island Altavay (at Loch Staffin in Sky) out to the E. by Ben-trodda in Kilmore parish in Sky: to avoid it along the W. side, keep Rubanish Point in Kilmore parish out to the W. of Fladdahuan Island. When Margaretta's is seen, a ship may sail within half a cable's-length of it on all sides.

Sheramenis Rock lies about a mile and three-quarters eastward of Fladdahuan, is about a cable's-length long from N. to S. The S. end of it is covered with spring-tide only; the N. end dries at half-ebb, and the middle with spring-tide only. There is a small spring-tide rock that lies about a cable's-length southward from the S. end of Sheramenis. You avoid Sheramenis on the N. side, when Walamore Island (the highest of the small islands, near Fladdahuan, like a hill) is on the point of Vaternish; or when Hewal (a remarkable hill in N. Uist) appears southward of Walamore Island.

Within half a mile of the N. end of Rona Island there is a number of rocks always above water; about half a mile from the outermost of these there is a rock, called Gamarhan, that dries at low-water only. You avoid this last along the W. side, when the mouth of Portree harbour is open of Rona.

Anchoring-places and Harbours in the North Part of Sky, in Raza, and Rona, and the adjacent Main.

Loch Polteel in Sky Island.

Loch Polteel, near Galtrigil Head in Sky, is a very good bay for ships or vessels of any burden to stop in with moderate weather, or when the wind is off shore, for the ground is good, and the depth of water moderate; but being open to the W. and N. W. there must be hard riding with such winds. At the head of this bay, on the S. side, there are two rocks near the shore; one lies on the E. side of the small low point, and its top is always above the water; the other is about a quarter of a mile eastward from this, and dries only at low spring-tide. Small vessels may ride pretty safe within the first-mentioned rock.

Loch Foliart.

Loch Foliart is a very fine bay for ships to run into; there being no rocks or shoals in it but what are very near the shore. In the wide part of this Loch, from Galtrigil Head to Tegort Point, the water is rather too deep for anchorage, being about fifty fathoms above two cables-length from the shore; but at the head of the Loch, in Dunvegan harbour, or within the small islands on the W. side of it, there is fine shelter, a moderate depth, and safe riding for a great many ships of any size.

In sailing for Dunvegan harbour, give the extremity of Tegort Point, and the middle from that to Grumbler Island, which is on the E. side of the entry, a moderate berth; for a ledge extends above a cable's-length north-westward from the Point; and there is a shoal, or foul rock, that lies near the small rock, which is always above water, on which shoal there are but four feet at low spring-tide: to avoid this shoal, keep Galtrigil Head open with Tegort.

On the W. side of the entrance of Dunvegan harbour, there is a small sunk rock, on which the least water is six feet: it bears W. by S. from the middle of Dunvegan Castle. To avoid this shoal along the E. side (which is the safest side), keep Tegort Head, and Berrey Head five, or in a line.

In sailing for the anchorage on the S side of the islands Grund and Shoandis, keep near the middle, between Grund Island and Ligmis, to avoid a rock which lies about two cables-length S. E. from Grund.

Eastward from the middle of Ben-firandis, there is a sunk rock, which lies about half a cable's-length from that Island, on which the least water is nine feet. Anchor any where above Ben-firandis, on five, or four fathoms, the least water.

Loch Bay.

Loch Bay is a branch of Loch Foliart, and is capacious, good holding-ground, of easy access, and, near the head on the S. side, sufficiently sheltered from all winds. Enter between Ilanise and Ardmore Head, but keep

Rona Island, Gairloch, on the Main.

keep above a cable's-length from the N. point of *Ramsa*, to avoid *Skerraburn Rock*, which lies about that distance from the extremity of the island, and dries at two hours of ebb.

There are two rocks between *Ramsa* and the point of *Groban*, the southmost of which is called *Skerragorab*; it lies near the middle, and dries about half-ebb; the other dries with spring-tide only.

Skerrabhig is a rock whose top is always above water, and is deep quite round.

There is a ledge which extends about two cables-length S. W. from *Ian-lamby*, and dries at low-water.

If there is any necessity of sailing into *Loch Bay* through the S. channel, keep about one third from the starboard, or *Gorban*, side; or keep the little *Ilan-lamby* in a line with *Borrery Head*, till the *Kirk of Trumpan* (a remarkable house, about a mile above the bay of *Ardmore*) is seen to the eastward of the smallest *Ramsa Island*, then steer straight in for the anchorage.

Loch Snisort.

Loch Snisort is a spacious arm of the sea, of easy access, a moderate depth in most parts, well sheltered in the proper anchorage, and the ground good; several fleets of the largest ships may ride in it in safety all weathers.

There is a small rock, whose top is always above water, that lies about half a mile eastward from the middle of *Ilan-Aferith*.

The principal anchoring-places are the bay of *Uig* at the head; in passing the narrowest part, keep the middle, or nearest the starboard-side, to avoid a ledge which extends about a cable's-length from the N. shore, and dries about low water. Anchor eastward of this ledge, about a cable's-length from the N. shore, on from three to five fathoms water; or stop any where in the bay.

In that long arm, which goes up from *Lienall* to *Iarnagh*, ships may anchor any where, particularly off *Clachamish*, or above *Eary Borough*. This arm is strictly *Loch Snisort*

In sailing into *Loch-Greshornish*, avoid two rocks, one of which lies a cable's-length north of the extremity of the *Ard*; and another on the south side of *Ard*, about half a cable's-length from the high water mark; both dry about half-ebb. Go about a mile up before you drop anchor, to avoid foul ground in some parts below.

Duntulim Harbour.

Duntulim harbour is the channel between *Ilan-tulim* and *Sky*. It is pretty well sheltered, the ground clean, and the water sufficient for large ships; but being narrow, it is therefore fit for small vessels only; and these require to have one anchor, or a land-fast, a-shore on the island, so as to ride out of the stream of tide, which runs pretty quick in the middle of the Sound.

Two Rocks. Vessels may enter this harbour either along the N. or S. end of the island; but the north entrance is best. In this last entrance there is a rock always above water, except with extraordinary high-tides, which lies nearest the *Sky* side; take this rock on the larboard-hand, and you may sail within half a cable's-length of it, or nearer if you please; for it is deep close to it. Give the N. end of the island a birth of above half a cable, to avoid a rock that lies off it, and dries about half-ebb. Take ebb-tide to sail in at the north entrance, and flood to sail in at the south.

S. Entrance, a ledge. In the south entrance there is a ledge that extends S. E. from the extremity of the island, about one-third over the channel, which must be avoided in sailing in or out this way. *Anchor* about the middle of the island.

Kilmaluik Bay.

Kilmaluik bay is about three miles eastward of *Ilan-tulim*, has clean ground, and a sufficient depth of water in it; as it is open to the north, it is not safe to lie long in it, especially in winter; but in moderate weather, or with the wind off the shore, vessels may stop conveniently in the mouth of this bay. About a cable's-length from the shore, on the S. side of the entrance, there is a rock which dries with spring-tide only.

Loch Staffin.

Loch Staffin is for the most part clean ground, and the depth of water sufficient for any ships; but being open to the north, it cannot be reckoned safe anchorage, except in the summer-time. The best part of the bay to ride in, is off *Flodda* in *Sky*, on six or eight fathoms. In sailing in avoid *Clachwater Rock*, which lies off the point of *Flodigary*, and is covered about high-water only. *Altevig Island*, shut with *Flodda Island*, clears this rock along the E. side.

There is a long narrow rock, which is always above water, which lies along the E. side of *Altevig Island*. It is shallow about a cable's-length from each end of this rock.

Creek in Rona Island.

Near the S. end of the island *Rona*, there is a small creek, sheltered by a little high island in the mouth of the bay, in which small vessels may ride very safe on about three fathoms water. There are two channels leading into this harbour, one on each side of the small island, both very narrow, which therefore require a leading-wind; the northmost channel is the best.

N. Entrance. Near the middle of this entry, there are two rocks always above water, except with extraordinary high-tides: the best channel here is to take the southmost of these rocks on the larboard-hand. If you enter on the north side of these two rocks, keep nearest the *Rona* side, but avoid a spring-tide rock, near this entrance, a little from the shore of *Rona*.

S. Entrance. The south channel is all clear, except a small rock covered at high-water only, which lies off the point on the starboard-hand as you turn in towards the anchorage. When this rock is visible, you may sail on either side of it, by keeping the middle.

On the N. E. side of the anchorage, there is a small island near the shore, and two rocks near this island, the westmost of which dries at two hours of ebb; the southmost with spring-tide only: when the wind is S. or S. W. spare out off so much cable as to ride over these rocks.

Loch Terridon.

Loch Terridon is a long arm of the sea, of easy access, well sheltered, and almost all of it good holding-ground; several hundreds of the largest ships may ride in it in safety all weathers.

There is nothing to be feared in sailing into, or up this Loch, but one small spring-tide rock, which lies about two cables-length northward of *Rumansbeg Point*, on the S. side of the entrance; *Ilan Horistram*, on the N. side, is always above water, and deep close to it on all sides.

The

LOCH YEW, LOCH BRIEM.

The best anchorage for large ships is in *Loch Shielding*, between the two *Narrows*, any where nearest the S. side of that large bason; or any where above that, in what is properly called *Loch Terridon*. Anchorage.

The coves, before you enter the *Narrows*, where single ships, or a few small vessels may ride in the summer-time, are, *Loch Tries* on the N. side of the first *Narrows*; *Loch Ardrakin*, and *Loch Bay* over-against it, with an anchor ashore on each side; and within the S. end of *Ron-garoder* under along the S. end of *Ron-garoder*. Stopping-places.

LOCH GERLOCH.

Loch Gerloch is a large bay, sheltered almost on all sides, with clean ground in all parts of it, and good holding-ground in the principal anchoring-place, and capable of a fleet of the largest ships. There are no rocks or shoals to be feared either in it, or near it. Ships may ride in any part of this Loch, when it does not blow hard from the W. or S. W. particularly on the E. side of *Band* [illegible]. The best part in winter is any where between *Ron-Horisdale* and *Flowerdale*, on from nine to twenty fathoms water. Anchorage.

Small vessels may anchor in winter on the W. side of *Ron-Horisdale*, on the S. E. side of a rock in the Sound, which is always above water.

A Description of the Tides, Rocks, Shoals, Anchoring-places, and Harbours on the N. W. *Coast of* SCOTLAND, *from* RUBRA *in* GERLOCH, *to* CAPE WRATH *in* STRATHNAVER.

CHART XXVII.

Tides from RUBRA *to* CAPE WRATH.

TIDES.

From Rubra in *Gerloch*, to *Ru-more* in *Cogiach*, it is high water at 6½, on full and change-days of the moon; from *Ru-more* to *Cape Wrath* at seven. Time of High water.

Spring-tides along this coast rise about eleven feet perpendicular; neap-tides rise six or seven. Rise of the Tide.

The stream of flood runs north-eastward along the coast; but its strength is scarce sensible, except near *Ru-stair of Assynt*, where it runs about one mile and a half an hour when strongest; or in narrow channels that lead into wide bays, where it sometimes runs a mile, or a mile and an half an hour at most. Direction and Strength of the Stream.

There are neither rocks nor shoals lying any where along this part of the coast, without the head-lands or islands. Such as are near the harbours will be described with them. No ROCKS or SHOALS off the Coast.

LOCH YEW.

HARBOURS.

Loch Yew, in *Gerloch*, is a large well-sheltered bay, of easy access, a moderate depth of water, good ground for the most part, and where fleets of the largest ships may ride in safety at all times.

The best places to ride in are, on the E. side of *Ilan-Yew*; and in the bay of *Ferny*, on the E. side of the bay; off *Inveraspaidale*, and off *Pluckart*, near the head of the *Loch*.

LOCH HAMISCANICH.

Loch Hamisconich, or *Camisconich*, being open to the north, is fit for ships only in summer, or to stop in moderate weather.

The best places of anchorage here are, on the E. side of *Ilan-Grainard*, above a cable's-length from the shore; off *Udrigil*, or *Sand*, above two cables-length from the shore; off *Sand* try the ground before you let go the anchor, for there is some foul ground there. Anchorage.

Off *Mellon*, on the west side of the mouth of this bay, there is a rock about a quarter of a mile from the shore, which dries about half-ebb; between which, and the land on the shore, some rocks appear about low-water. Hidden Rocks.

LOCH-BEG, *or little* LOCH BRIEM.

Loch-beg is an arm of the sea, above two miles long, well-sheltered, and good ground, capable of a fleet of the largest ships; and nothing to fear in it but one rock in the entry, near the W. side, which dries with spring-tide only. It lies near half a mile above the W. point of the entrance; one third from that point, and two-thirds from the point of *Scoray* on the opposite side. To avoid this rock, keep the middle, or nearest the E. side. Rock in the Entrance.

The best part of this Loch to anchor in, is within a mile of the head. Small vessels will need to lay out an anchor on shore, in order to ride on a moderate depth. Anchorage.

LOCH-MORE, *or* LOCH BRIEM.

Loch Briem is a large and safe arm of the sea, capable of hundreds of the largest ships, and no rocks nor shoals within it, but one ledge on the E. side off *Ulapoole*, which extends above a cable's-length from that shore; which is avoided by keeping one-third from the *Ulapoole* side. Ulapool Ledge.

The best places in this Loch to anchor in are, in *Ulapoole Bay*, on fourteen or fifteen fathoms water, above a cable's-length from the shore; and any where above *Logie Point*, on from thirteen to twenty-four fathoms. Anchorage.

In sailing between *Corniskere Ilands* and *Rubanderril*, give *Rubanderril Point* a birth of above a cable's-length, to avoid a rock called *Neals*, dry about half-ebb, which lies off that shore. Hidden Rock.

LOCH KENORT.

Loch Kenort is a harbour on the E. side of *Ilan-Martin*, about a mile northward of the mouth of *Loch Briem*, in which vessels may ride very safe on four or five fathoms water, good ground, and well-sheltered.

There

LOCH ESHIBBERY, LOCH INIVER, LOCH RO, LOCH NITT.

N. Channel. There are two channels leading into this harbour; one along the N. side of *Ilan-Martin*, the other along the S. side of it; that along the N. side is quite clean and deep water, but liable to squalls from the hills when the wind is northward; on which account it is not so much frequented by those who are acquainted with the other. S. Channel. In the S. channel there is a rocky ledge on each side to be avoided; the one extends south-eastward from the point of *Ilan Martin*, which is on the S. side of the bay; the other extends northward from the point of *Ardvore*, on the opposite side, near two-thirds over. The depth between these two ledges, at low spring-tide, is not above nine feet. To sail through this channel, take a leading-wind, half-tide, and keep, as near as you can, one-third from the point of *Ilan-Martin*, and two-thirds from the point of *Ardvore*. Anchorage. Anchor in any part of the bay of *Ilan-Martin*; or if there are more vessels than there is room for in the bay (which often happens when there are herrings there), small vessels may ride along the shore of the island north-eastward, with one anchor on shore; for without the mouth of this harbour the ground is foul in several parts, and does not hold well.

ILAN-HADERRA, or the SUMMER ISLANDS.

All the islands between the points *Ru-more* and *Ru-keanderrik*, are called *Ilan-haderra*, though it is strictly the name of the largest only. The rocks not always above water, and most in the way of ships sailing through these islands, are the following:

Rock off Pattengach. Off the S. end of *Rona-mach*, there is a rock which extends about a quarter of a mile southward from it. That end, which is about a cable's-length from the island, is covered at high water only: the outmost end dries with spring-tide only. It is avoided as the next rocks.

Rocks of Ranteugs. About a cable's-length W. by S. from *Ru-duart* (near E. of *Rona-mach*), there is a small rock that dries at half-ebb. Somewhat more than a cable's-length northward from this rock there is another, which dries with spring-tide only. To avoid these along the S. side, and likewise the rock off the S. end of *Ilan-mach*, keep the N. end of *Ilan-a-na Glasfrich-nanglerach Island*. *Glasfrich* is a low green island.

Rock off Dorny. Near one third from *Dorny*, on the main, and two-thirds from *Ilan-haderra*, there is a rock which dries with spring-tide only. To avoid it keep about the middle, between the main and *Ilan-haderra*.

Ledge off Rue. There is a rocky ledge that extends from the point of *Rue*, in *Ru-more*, about one-fourth over towards *Molgrach Island*. To avoid this sailing from the north, keep *Ru-fair* in *Assynt* in sight by *Ru-more*, till you are one-third over toward *Molgrach*.

Anchoring places in Sandwater, Kale Yord. There are no harbours in the *Haderra Islands*, but two small creeks that are fit only for small vessels; viz. *Skenderry*, and the *Kale Yord*. The *Kale Yord* is a cove in a bay, on the E. side of *Ilan-haderra*, which is sheltered on the N. E. by two small islands, or rocks; within which is the best anchorage, on four fathoms good ground, and between these rocks is the channel in. In southern weather a vessel may ride without these two islets, in the bay on the N. side of them.

Skenderry. *Skenderry* harbour is the Sound between *Ilan-Rishil* and *Ilan-tanerd*. A small vessel may ride safe here on three fathoms water, clean ground; but she must sail in along the S. side of the island. A vessel coming from the northward, may stop in the bay of *Rishil*, on the E. side of the island, on three fathoms clean sand.

LOCH ESHIBBERY.

Eshibberly is a small, but very safe, harbour, eastward of *Ru-more*; the ground holds well, and the depth is sufficient for the largest ships; but, as the bay is narrow, it may be convenient to lay one anchor on the shore. On the S. E. side of the islands, near the entrance of this harbour, any ship may ride in moderate weather, on clean sand.

LOCH INIVER.

Loch Iniver, above the little island *Glasfarb*, which lies in the middle of it, is well-sheltered, good ground, of a sufficient depth for the largest ships, and nothing to be feared in sailing in along the S. sides of *Soya Island* and *Glasfarb*.

Rocks near Soya Island. On the E. side of *Soya Island*, there is a reef of rocks extending north-eastward from the E. point of *Soya*, about half way to the main; the eastmost of which dries two hours before low-water. To avoid these rocks along the S. side, keep any part of *Clout Island* in sight by *Soya*. To avoid them along the N. side, keep within one-third of the main, and two thirds from *Soya*: or keep the low point at the extremity of *Ru-fair* covered, or nearly so, by *Ru-ru*.

Kierlag Rock. About half a cable's-length northward from the point of *Kierlag* there is a small rock, which dries about low-water. This must be avoided in running in, or out.

Glasfarb Ledge. On the N. side of *Ilan-glasfarb*, in the middle of the bay, there is a ledge, which extends northward, about one-fourth over toward the main. It is avoided by keeping the middle, or nearest to the main side.

Anchorage. Rock near Caigy. The best place of anchorage in *Loch Iniver*, is on the E. side of *Caigy Point*, about a quarter of a mile from *Fliin*, on five or six fathoms water. About a ship's-length from the point of *Caigy*, there is a rock that dries about low-water.

LOCH RO.

Loch-Ro is a small very narrow creek, of difficult access, but very safe, once a vessel has got into it; but it is not safe for a stranger to attempt it. The best anchorage is above the *Narrow*, and eastward of two rocks, which lie near the point, on the larboard-side going up.

ILAN-OULDENAY *Anchorage*.

A small vessel may anchor on six or eight fathoms on the S. side of *Ilan-ouldenay*, in the narrow Sound. Rocks near Crona. Sail in along the S. side of *Crona Island*. On the E. side of *Crona*, there are several rocks always above water; and half between these and the N. end of *Crona* there is a rock, which dries at half-ebb.

LOCH NITT.

Loch Nitt is well sheltered, the ground good, and the depth sufficient for any ships; but, being very narrow, is not fit for large ships.

Rock in the mouth of it. In the mouth of *Loch Nitt*, nearest the W. side, there is a rock always above water; and one about a cable's-length S. from that, which is covered at high-water only. To avoid this last rock, keep the eastmost of the *Ailsan Islands* in sight by the other rock.

At the S. side of the point that forms the narrowest part of this harbour, it shoals about a ship's-length westward; which should be attended to in running out or in. *Ledge at the Narrows.*

The best part of this Loch to anchor in is off the small islands, a little above the narrowest part, in four fathoms water. *Anchorage.*

LOCH ARDVAR.

Loch Ardvar is a small, but quite safe harbour for small vessels, between *Loch Nut* and *Kyles-cough*. In the proper anchorage there is water for the largest ship to ride on; but in the narrowest part of the channel leading towards it, there is not above three feet at low-water with spring-tide; so that a vessel that draws above nine feet cannot go above the *Narrows* with deal draughts, even at high-water. *Channel shallow.*

In the mouth of this Loch, near the middle, there is a rock, which is not covered till about high-water; the channel on each side of this rock is sufficiently deep for any ship; but that on the E. side, or starboard-hand, seems broadest. On the N. or outside of this rock, it shoals near half a cable's-length northward. *Rock in the Entrance.*

When you are about a quarter of a mile within the mouth of this Loch, the channel turns eastward. At the narrowest part there is a point on the starboard hand, from which a rocky ledge extends north eastward almost quite cross the channel; here is the shallow water before-mentioned. To sail through it therefore, take half-flood, or high-water, according to the size of the vessel and time of the moon, and keep about a ship's-length from the shore, on the N. or larboard-side; and anchor on the N. side of a small green island, on from five to seven fathoms water. A vessel may stop a tide within the entrance, in the bight on the starboard-side. *Ledge at the Narrows.* *Anchorage.*

LOCH KYLES-CODOR.

Kyles-cough is a large, well-sheltered arm of the sea, of easy access, and where fleets of the largest ships may ride safe all weathers. For above two miles within this Loch, the water is rather too deep for ordinary vessels to anchor on (being from thirty to fifty fathoms), except one anchor is laid on the shore: but above *Dean-Ranit*, where the contracted channel begins to widen, ships may anchor any where. In the narrow channel the stream, at spring-tide, runs about one mile an hour. *Anchorage.* *Stream of Tide.*

The only rock, near this Loch, necessary to be mentioned, is one that lies near the island *Calvay-vel*, about a quarter of a mile W. S. W. from it, and dries about low water. It is avoided along the S. side, while *Rama-chasson Point*, in *Ilan-coldrimy*, is on the extremity of *Ra-fair*. *Dangerous Rock.*

This Loch may be distinguished at sea by its position from *Ra-fair*.

LOCH SARK.

Loch Sark, at the N. side of the entrance of *Kyles-cough*, is a fine creek for a few small vessels; but the entrance being dry at low spring-tide, they must have half-tide at least, before they can go in, or out.

LOCH CALAWAY.

Loch Calaway, near *Loch Sark*, is a small bay, where the ground is good, and the depth sufficient for any ship; but being open to the N. W. it is not thought safe in the winter-time.

LOCH BADANBUIL.

Loch Badabuil (sometimes called *Badcall*) is a bay well-sheltered by a number of small islands. The ground in it is good, and the depth sufficient for the largest ships. The best channel into it is that through the middle of the islands, between a row on each hand, which extends east, and will appear plainer in the draft than by a description. Give each island and rock in the way a moderate berth, and anchor near the middle of the bay, on ten or twelve fathoms.

ILAN-HANDA.

In the summer-time a ship may ride in the *Sound of Ilan-Handa*, off a sandy bay in the island, about a cable's-length from the shore, on five fathoms clean sand. On the E. side of this anchorage, there is a narrow spit of sand, which extends about half over from the island to the main; the least water on it is twelve feet. *Sand bank.*

Off the S. point of the *Sandy Bay*, near the middle of the channel, there is a small rocky shoal, on which the least water is nine feet. In sailing through the S. W. entrance of this Sound, this shoal must be adverted to about low-water. *Shoal in the S. W. Entrance.*

Off the eastmost point of *Ilan-Handa*, there is a rocky ledge that extends above a cable's-length from the shore E. S. E. and dries at low-water. *Ledge off the E. point of Ilan-Handa.*

The rocks, near the W. end of *Ilan-Handa*, lie near two cables-length from the shore, and dry about half-ebb. *Rocks near the W. end.*

LOCH LUSFORD.

Loch Laxford (sometimes pronounced *Lusford*) is a capacious very fine harbour; there is nothing to fear coming in, but what is always above water; except an half-tide rock, about a cable's-length W. from *Dufkers*; the ground and shelter are good, and the depth moderate for ships of all sizes.

The best anchorage is above *Ilan-ardi* any where; or nearer the mouth of the *Loch*, on the S. side, between *Ilan-ard*; and *Finadd*. *Anchorage.*

There are four very small islands westward of *Ilan-ard*; the channels between them are deep and safe; only on the S. side of the second, from the entrance, a ledge extends near half a cable's-length from it southward. *Channels between them.*

This Loch may be distinguished at a distance, by *Arkal Hills*, *Stack Hill*, and *Ilan-Handa*. *How distinguished at a distance.*

LOCH HINSBOLT.

Loch Hinshort has a safe entrance, is well-sheltered, the ground good, and the depth of water moderate for ships of all sizes. Sail up till you are land-locked, and anchor toward the N. or E. side.

This Loch may be distinguished at a distance by *Arkal Hills*, or by *Ilan-Handa*. *How distinguished at a distance.*

LOCH ARDICAAL.

This is a creek with a sufficient depth of water, and the ground clean and good, but there is hard riding in it in winter, when the wind blows from the westward.

NAUTICAL DESCRIPTIONS

OF

ILAN-FAD,

OR

LONG-ISLAND;

FROM

BARA HEAD *to the* BUTT *of the* LEWIS.

A Description of the Tides, Rocks, Shoals, Anchoring-places, and Harbours in the S. Part of LONG-ISLAND, *between* BARA HEAD *and* BENBECULA ISLAND.

CHART XXVIII.

Tides between BARA HEAD *and* BENBECULA.

TIDES.

Time of High-water.

ON the shores between *Bara Head*, in *Berneray Island*, and *Benbecula Island*, it is high-water on the full and change-days of the moon at 5½.

Rise of the Tide.

Ordinary spring-tides, on this part of the coast of *Long Island*, rise eleven feet perpendicular; neap-tides rise five or six.

Direction of the Stream.

The stream of flood sets in from the S. S. W. toward *Berneray*, which is the southmost of the *Bara Islands*; and about a mile from *Dun-owraway*, or *Bara Head*, divides into two branches; one of which runs along the E. side of *Bara Islands*, the other along the W. side of them, and sets in through the several Sounds, or channels between the islands, from the westward, with a considerable velocity; in some of them it runs five or six miles an hour with spring-tide, when strongest; neap-tides run about 3½. Along the open coast, the strength of the stream is scarce sensible; except about one mile southward of *Berneray*, where it runs about three miles an hour when strongest.

Velocity.

ROCKS.

There are no rocks or shoals along the E. side of this coast, but what lie in, or so near to the bays and harbours, that they will be described with them: nor are there any without the points and promontories on the W. side, that lie above half a mile from the shore, till you come to the northmost part of *South Uist*, near *Benbecula*, where there are several rocks that dry about half-ebb, or before low-water.

Bays and Harbours in the BARA ISLANDS.

ANCHORING-PLACES and HARBOURS.

VATERSAY BAY.

Vatersay Bay is on the E. side of the *Island Vatersay*; it is land-locked on all sides in the anchorage, excepting two points of the compass, between the E. and S. E.; the ground in most parts is clean sand, the depth from four to seven fathoms at low-water. The rocks to be avoided in sailing into this bay are, one near the N. side, about half a mile westward from *Sandyhaveal Island*, which dries about half-ebb, and is in the way of ships turning out or in only. On the S. side of the bay, about half up, there is a rock that dries at low-water, and lies about a cable's-length from the point of *Quier*. The best anchorage is a little above this rock; opposite to which rock, on the N. side, and about half a cable from the shore, there is a small spring-tide rock. There is a sheep-fold, or small enclosure, near the point of *Quier*, by which that point may be known.

Rock on the N. side.

Rock on the S. side.

Best Anchorage.

LONG ISLAND, BARA, SOUTH-UIST.

If a ship is under any necessity of sailing between *Vatersay* and *Sanderay Island* from the W. she must keep nearest to the *Vatersay* side, till she passes the point, where there is a small sandy cove, to avoid a rock in the middle, which dries at low-water; then sail between the black rocks and *Sanderay*. [illegible]

BA-CHISAMIL.

Ba-Chisamil, or *Chisamil Bay*, is good holding-ground, safe anchorage, and the water sufficient for the largest merchant-ships; but in sailing into it there are some rocks to be attended to.

If you sail into *Chisamil Bay*, between *Muldonich Island* and the E. point of *Vatersay*, there are two rocks near the middle, that dry with spring-tide only, to be avoided. To avoid these, keep within two cables-length of the rocks always above water near *Muldonich*, or within two cables-length of the rocks near the point of *Vatersay*. You may sail within half a cable's-length of *Muldonich Rocks* if necessary. Rocks between Muldonich and Vatersay.

If you sail in along the N. end of *Muldonich*, then *Sheep Rock*, rocks along the point of *Vatersay*, and a ledge and shoal near *Orasay Island*, are to be avoided.

Sheep Rock lies about one-fourth from the S. side of *Bara Island*, and three-fourths from *Muldonich*, and dries about low-water. A leading-mark to it is, the rock always above water near *Orasay*, in one with the westmost point of *Bara*, opposite to *Kebs*. To avoid *Sheep Rock* along the S. side, keep *Sterks Rock* (which is near the W. point of *Chisamil Bay*) open with *Kebs Point* in *Vatersay*. To avoid *Sheep* on the north side, keep within two cables-length of the shore of *Bara*; or keep *Sterks* appearing on the W. end of *Bara*. Sheep Rock.

About a cable's-length S. from *Orasay Island*, there is a rock always above water, from which a ledge extends southward about half a cable's-length. Westward from which rock, and S. from the point of *Orasay*, there is a rocky shoal, on which the least water is five or six feet. These rocks are avoided along the S. side, and the mixture of rocks and sand along the point of *Vatersay* along the N. by keeping *Sterks Rock* a little open of *Kebs* in *Vatersay*, or appearing on the point of *Bara*, opposite to *Kebs*. The shoal which lies south from the W. point of *Orasay*, is avoided along the W. side, sailing into the anchorage, while the top of a small rock, which is about a cable's-length W. from *Orasay*, is in a line with *Castle-chysamil*, or open to the E. of it. Ledge [illegible]

Anchor in *Chisamil Bay*, where the castle bears N. E. somewhat more than a cable's-length, on four fathoms water. Anchorage.

On the E. side of *Bara* there is a round point below [illegible] *Hills*; above a quarter of a mile eastward from that point there is a rock that dries with spring-tide only; and three between it and the shore that dry about half-tide. Rocks near the E. Side of Bara.

Near the N. E. point of *Bara*, opposite to *Curachan Rock*, there is a small rock always above water; and a reef of rocks extending about half a mile south-westward from it, which dry about half-ebb. Rocks near the N. E. Point of Bara.

BA-HIRAVAH.

Ba-hiravah is a small harbour, on the E. side of *Bara Island*, sheltered by *Wia* and other islands, with good ground and water sufficient for any ship, but fit for small vessels only, because of its small size. The channel is between *Curachan Rock*, which lies above a mile from the shore, and the islands *Hellisay* and *Wia*, is wide and nothing to be feared in it, only a ledge that extends about half a cable's-length eastward from a rock always above water, which lies near the shore of *Bara*, half a mile before you enter the proper anchoring-place.

OTTER-VORE ROAD.

Otter-vore is that part of the channel between *Bara* and *South Uist*, which is almost surrounded with islands, rocks, and shallow sand-banks. In this road several hundreds of the largest ships may ride safe in the former-time; but though there can be no great sea in it, yet the anchor-ground is not strong enough to hold sufficiently in blowing weather, in the winter half of the year. The best entry to this road is between *Gigay* and *Eriskay Islands*, there being nothing to be feared in it. In the S. channel, between *Flattay* and *Hellisay*, there is a rock about half a cable's-length southward from the W. end of *Hellisay*, that dries about half-ebb: and a ledge that extends westward, about half a cable's-length from a more northerly part of that end of the island. S. Channel and Rock near Hellisay.

The most convenient anchorage, in moderate weather, is any where northward of the small *Island Crisamil*, between *Gigay* and *Fuda Islands*, on from four to seven fathoms water. With easterly winds anchor about two cables-length from the W. side of *Hellisay*; with westerly winds anchor half a mile eastward of the S. E. point of *Fuda*. Anchorage.

The rocks near this anchorage are, two between *Crisamil Island* and *Hellisay*, nearest the former: the top of that next *Crisamil* is always above water, the other dries about half-ebb, and reaches near half-way to *Hellisay*. Rocks near the Anchorage.

There is a rock and shoal that extend southward from the S. E. end of *Fuda*, above a quarter of a mile. Rock near Fuda.

If a ship is to sail to the westward from *Otter-vore Road*, the safest course is to keep about two cables-length from the N. E. corner of *Fuda*, and then to steer N. N. W. till *Fuevay Island* bears W. S. W. by which course the spring-tide rock, which lies about half a mile E. of *Fuda*, the shallow water between *Fuda* and *Fuevay*, and a half-tide rock near the middle, between *Fuda* and *Orasay Island*, will be avoided. Course from Ottervore to the westward.

Between the islands *Wia* and *Flattay*, a ship may ride safe all weathers, on from four to eight fathoms the least water. Sail in between *Flattay* and *Hellisay*. Fuevay Harbour.

Harbours in SOUTH-UIST.

ACHERSYT-VORE, *in* ERISKAY ISLAND.

South-Uist.

Acherset-vore, on the E. side of *Eriskay*, is a small creek, and requires a leading-wind in and out, but very safe for small vessels after they have got in. In entering this harbour, there are two rocks to be avoided (and between them a rock always above water): the first lies about a cable's-length northward from *Maclean's Head*, on the larboard-hand, as you enter the harbour's mouth and dries at low spring-tide only. Rock in the Entry.

About two cables-length westward from the spring-tide rock, there is a rock right in the middle that dries at half-ebb. To avoid these two rocks, give *Maclean's Point* a birth of a cable's-length, then steer in for the south side of the entrance, and keep about one-third from it, and two thirds from the opposite shore. When the half-tide rock is covered, there are eight or nine feet of water over the spring-tide rock, which can-

not

one them less dangerous for small vessels. If the half-tide rock is seen, the spring-tide rock may be avoided, by keeping the former in one with the top of a green hillock, which stands in the middle, at the head of the bay, a musket-shot above the shore.

[illegible] About half way between *Calve Nes* (which is always above water), and the mouth of this harbour, there is a small shoal, on which the sea often breaks in blowing weather: the depth on it could not be sounded for the breakers, but it is judged six feet may be the least water over it. A leading-mark to it is *Calig*, in a line with the eastmost point of *Baro*.

LOCH BOISDALE.

Loch Boisdale is an arm of the sea, where a fleet of the largest ships may ride in safety all the year round. The ground holds well, and the depth is from four to twelve fathoms. The best anchorage is toward the head of the bay, near the W. end of the low island, which lies about the middle of the broadest part; but large ships may ride any where above *Ilan-cubay*.

[illegible] In failing for *Loch Boysdale* from the south, avoid a rock, dry at low-water, which lies near half a mile off the point *Rona-bordag*. When the Sound of *Ilan-cubay* is open, or nearly so, you avoid it along the N. end.

[illegible] The W. end of *Ilan-cubay* shoals above half a cable's-length westward.

[illegible] Near half a cable's-length eastward from the low island before-mentioned, in the broadest part of the Loch, there is a small rock, which dries with spring-tide only.

[illegible] Northward from the west end of this low island, and about half a cable's-length from the opposite shore, abreast of a rill of water that runs down the end of the hill, there is a rock that dries with spring-tide only. This rock is avoided, while the extremity of *Ilan-cubay* is a little open with the land on the N. side of the Loch.

LOCH EYNORT.

Loch Eynort, in *South Uist*, is a large arm of the sea, of easy access, well-sheltered, good ground, moderate depth, and capable of a fleet of the largest ships. The upper part of it, above the *Narrows*, is called *Loch-Arinakin*.

Anchorage. The best anchorage for large ships is about the middle of *Loch Eynort*, where it is broadest, on from six to twelve fathoms water. Vessels that go up to *Loch-Arinakin* should take flood tide, or slack-water, for spring-tides in the *Narrows*, when strongest, run about three miles an hour. They must also avoid a rock that lies near the *Narrows*, on the larboard-side, that dries about low-water: you avoid it by keeping nearest the starboard-side.

LOCH SKIPORT.

Loch Skiport is a spacious harbour of easy access, good ground, a moderate depth of water, and well-sheltered, where several fleets of the largest ships may ride in the greatest safety at all times. Take *Ourasb Island* on the larboard-side going in, and anchor either on the north, the south, or west side of *Ilan-Skilley*. In the basin, on the S. side of *Ilan-Skilley* (which is called *Loch Peumbarestag*), about the middle, and one-third from the E. end of this anchorage, there is a small patch of sand, on which the least water is six feet: this must be avoided in anchoring here. Enter this anchorage along the west end of the island.

In Loch Peumbarestag a Sand bank.

Two Rocks near the Anchorage. Near the anchorage, on the west side of *Ilan-baly* (the small island, half a mile above *Skilley*), there is a small rock on the S. W. side, that dries at half-ebb; and another on the west side, about half a cable's-length from the shore, which dries with spring-tide only.

Loch [illegible]. The entry of *Loch Gamasbrtan*, farthest up, being narrow, the stream of tide runs pretty quick, and therefore must be favourable in failing in or out. Keep nearest the W. or starboard-side of this entry; for the E. side has not above six feet in it at low spring-tide; but on the W. side there are eighteen at least.

How distinguished. *Loch Skiport* may be distinguished at a distance by *Heckla Hill*, which is remarkable, and the highest in this neighbourhood.

LOCH KYLESLEWSA.

Loch Kyleslewsa is small, but a very safe harbour, on the W. side of *Ilan-lewsa*, near the mouth of *Loch-Skiport*; where twenty or thirty vessels may ride, as if in a pond, on from three to six fathoms water, good ground. It may be entered at either end, but the channels are so narrow, that a stranger ought not to attempt either of them without a pilot.

Among the islands between *South Uist* and *Benbecula*, there are many good harbours, with a sufficient depth of water; but the rocks and islets are so numerous, that except conspicuous beacons, or perches, were put on some, no directions will be found sufficient for failing through them, without a person minutely acquainted with the places.

A Description of the Tides, Rocks, Shoals, Anchoring-places, and Harbours in the Middle Part of LONG ISLAND, *between* BENBECULA *and* HARRIS.

CHART XXIX.

TIDES. Time of High-water, Rise, Direction, and Velocity of the Tide.

On the shores of *Benbecula*, and *North Uist*, it is high-water on the full and change-days of the moon at 6½. Ordinary spring-tides rise eleven feet perpendicular; neap-tides five or six. The stream of flood sets in from the south-westward, and runs along the coast with little velocity, not above one mile an hour when strongest.

ROCKS and SHOALS. There are no rocks or shoals that lie off this part of *Long Island*, on the E. side, but what are so near the harbours, that they will be described with them. The rocks along the west coast are so many, and so little in

Rocks near Hyskere. the way to harbours, or in the track of shipping, that a particular description is unnecessary. As *Hyskere* is the remotest island, we shall observe, that near it there are several rocks covered, and uncovered, daily by the

 tide,

side, some of which seem to be two miles from it; and that no ship should sail within a league of it on the west side; nor sail at all between it and North-Uist, or Causamul isles: if they are under any necessity to do so, the best rule is to avoid the breakers.

The rocks along the N. W. coast of North Uist, will appear sufficiently plain in the draft.

LOCH LOIP.

HARBOURS in North Uist.

Loch Loip (between the islands *Wia* and *Benbecula*) is a very safe harbour, after a vessel has got into it, the ground good, and the depth sufficient for any ship; but there are several rocks right in the middle of the entrance, which require close attention to avoid. This reef extends from east to west, about half a mile. The eastmost rock is always above the water, looks whitish, and lies near the south point of the entrance; the westmost lies south from the north point of the entrance, over the middle, and is always above water; between each of these rocks and the adjacent shore, the channel is sufficiently deep for any ship. Rocks in the Entrance.

The easiest channel in, is close along *Wia*, between the first mentioned whitish rock, and the south point of the entrance; keeping *Galrigal Head*, in *Sky*, over any part of that rock, till you have sailed half a mile up, when you will be past all the other rocks. South Channel in.

If there is not a leading wind for the S. channel, keep about half way between the point of *Wia* and *Ron-Greinabil*, and steer on the north point of the entrance, until you are about a cable's-length from it, then stand in between the point and the black rock, which is always above water. North Channel in.

In the mouth of the first cove, on the *Wia* side, which is near half a mile above the rocks, there is a small rock that dries about half-ebb. Anchor any where in the harbour, avoiding this rock. Small vessels may ride in this cove, within the rock. Rock in a Cove of Wia.

LOCH KEREVAH.

Loch Kerevah, which is about half a mile northward of *Loch Loip*, is of easy access, good ground, well-sheltered, and the depth in the anchorage sufficient for any ship; but it is narrow, and at low-water with spring-tide, there are only twelve feet of water in the narrowest part, near half a mile up.

There is a ledge which extends about half a cable's-length from the south side of the entrance of the harbour, about a quarter of a mile westward of a rock which is always above water. There are also ledges, which extend eastward about a cable's-length from the north point of the entrance; these must be avoided. Anchor in the broadest part, half a mile up the Loch. Ledges near the Entrance.

LOCH USKEVAGH.

Loch Uskevagh is a large arm of the sea, near a remarkable round hill, called *Benbecula*; in the upper part, which is the widest, there are a number of small islands and rocks, that exclude shipping from anchoring above a mile within the harbour. The anchorage is at the W. end of a chain of islands that lie along the N. side of the entrance, where the water is six fathoms deep at low-water; but in most other parts there are only three. There is nothing to be feared going in, if you avoid what is always above the water; only near the anchorage there is a rock that dries about half-ebb, which lies on the N. side, about half a cable's-length southward of two small islands; and a ledge in the bay opposite to it, on the S. side, which extends northward about a cable's-length: anchor so as not to ride over either of these. Rocks near the Anchorage.

LOCH KYLESWIAVEG.

Kyles-Wiaveg is a creek adjacent to *Uskevagh*. It consists of two parallel branches; but the southmost is shut up by small islands and rocks along the coast leading to it, and to the mouth: the northmost only is accessible, and it is so narrow, that very small vessels only should attempt it, though the water is sufficiently deep. The channel is close along the north shore, taking all the isles on the larboard-hand: anchor at the west end of them, on five fathom water, with one anchor on shore. Channel.

LOCH-BANACAPLICH, in RONA ISLAND.

HARBOURS in N. Uist.

Banacaplich consists of two small bays, both of them well-sheltered, good ground, and the water a sufficient depth. There is nothing to be feared coming in but what may be seen. As these creeks are small, it may be convenient to lay one anchor on shore.

LOCH-RUEVAL.

Loch Rueval is a very good harbour, at the south-east point of *North Uist*, sheltered by the island *Flota-mor*, and other islands near it, where above a dozen of large ships may ride in safety; but the channels to it are narrow, and require a leading wind, and favourable tide.

There are two channels leading in; the first is along the S. side of *Flota-more*, which is the safest. Between the west end of *Flota-more* and *Rona*, keep mid-channel, or nearest the starboard-shore, to avoid a rocky ledge which extends near half over from *Rona*. Spring-tides in this channel, when strongest, run about two miles an hour. South Channel.

The north entry to this harbour is narrower, and shallower, than the other, having but two fathoms in it at low-water with spring-tides, and requires flood, or slack-water, to go in. There is a ledge just as you enter the harbour, on the starboard-hand, which reaches half-way over; so that it is necessary to keep the south side pretty close, till you are above half a cable's-length within the harbour. North Entrance. Ledge in it.

This harbour, lying at the S. end of *Hecval Hill*, which is remarkable, and next northward of *Benbecula*, may be distinguished at a distance by them. How distinguished.

LOCH EVORT.

Loch Evort, in *North Uist*, is an arm of the sea that extends five or six miles into the country; but the anchorage is in the innermost part, about a mile up, where it is well-sheltered, the ground good, and the depth fit for ships of any size, but there are two rocks near it to be avoided, one on the north side, and another on the south side.

The rock on the north side of the place of anchorage dries two hours after high-water; and is avoided on the S. side, by keeping the mouth of the Loch open, or very little shut, till the house Vatabeay bears N. N. E. then you are to the westward of the rock; or till the E. end of a small green island, which lies about half a mile southward, is in a line with the top of *Purival Hill*, which is the next highest hill to *Hecval*. Rocks near the Anchorage.

LONG-ISLAND, HARRIS.

Anchorage.

The rock on the south side of the anchorage lies about half a cable's-length from an islet, or rock always above water, near the point of a creek that runs eastward. The best anchorage is on the N. side of the harbour, north-westward from the first-mentioned rock.

Entrance.

Enter the mouth of this Loch, on the north side of the rock that lies off it, which is on the S. side, and always above water; and give the south side of the entrance above that rock a moderate berth.

LOCH NAMADDY.

Loch Namaddy (or *Loch Maddy*, as it is called by strangers) is a large bay, with a multitude of islands in it, under the shelter of which, on the south side of the bay, fleets of large ships may ride in safety at all times. In the summer, ships may anchor any where along the south side, after they are half a mile within the mouth of the bay, on from seven to four fathoms water: in winter it is safest and best riding above the *Rider Islands* on four fathoms.

Ledges and Rocks.

In running in, or out of the anchorage of *Loch Maddy*, there are several ledges to be attended to; but none of them extend above a cable's-length from the shore. On the W. side of the small island, which is near north of *Ardnamaddy Point*, there is a ledge which extends westward, near a cable's-length.

Off the E. end of *Fibvar Island*, there is a ledge which extends southward, about half a cable's-length; and one on the opposite coast, which extends about a cable's-length from the shore northward.

The westmost of the *Rider Islands*, on the end, shoals near half a cable's-length southward.

On the south side of the bay, which is half a mile S. W. from the westmost of the *Rider Islands*, there is a rock about half a cable's-length from the shore, which dries with spring-tide only. At this rock *Rulander Head* appears in the middle, between *Maddy-mo Rock* and the E. end of *Rider Island*.

About a cable's-length westward from the W. end of *Fibvar Island*, there is a rock which dries with spring-tide only. To avoid this rock in sailing between *Fibvar* and *Ilan-Hamersay*, keep the middle, or keep *Ardnamaddy Point* in sight by *Fibvar Island*.

Off the west end of *Ilan-Hamersay*, there is a rock that lies about a cable's-length from it, westward, which dries about half ebb.

Loch Partan is a creek on the north side of *Loch Namaddy*, in which small vessels bound southward sometimes take. The channel into it is very narrow, and hazardous except to such as are very well acquainted; and there is not room in it for more than three vessels at a time. To sail into it, take *Ilan-Fladda* on the larboard-hand, and avoid a rock on the *Rulander* side, over against the middle of *Fladda*, that is covered at high-water only, and is about half a cable's-length from the shore. When you are near the narrow part of the channel, keep the middle as near as you can, till you get through it, and anchor in the mouth of that arm, which runs eastward, taking care to anchor clear of some rocks that lie there, so as not to ride over them; and not to give out much cable, especially with E. or S. E. winds.

BA-CHAAID, or CHEESE BAY.

Ba-Chaaid is a harbour at the N. E. point of *North Uist*, in the Sound of *Harris*, sheltered on the E. and N. sides by the island *Greneta*, and a great many other islands and rocks westward of them. There is room, and depth of water in it, for a fleet of the largest ships to ride in safety. The anchorage is between *Ilan-Crudey* and three small islands, near a mile north-westward of it: or in *Loch Hermetra*, within the islands near west of *Hermetra*, on eight fathoms water. Keep along the S. and W. sides of the little high island, on the south side of this anchorage. Between this little island and *Hermetra*, it dries at low spring-tide. This place may also be entered from the N. by keeping the middle between *Hermetra*, and a rock which is always above water, that lies near a quarter of a mile northward of the point of *Hermetra*. In this channel there are but twelve feet at low spring-tide. On the other side of the rock there is deeper water, but the channel is not so straight. Small vessels may ride on the W. side of the three small islands before-mentioned, on from three to eight fathoms.

The best channel into this harbour, is between *Hermetra Island*, and island *Crudey*, giving the shore of *Hermetra*, and the W. end of *Crudey*, each of them a birth of at least a cable's-length, for there are ledges and shoals that extend that distance from *Hermetra*; and a rock at the W. end of *Crudey*, that lies above half a cable's-length from the shore, which dries at two hours of ebb. This rock is avoided along the N. side, while *Bruchalis Hill* (the northmost visible in *North Uist*) is seen along the N. side of the three small islands mentioned before, that lie in the middle of this harbour, near a mile west of *Crudey*. About half a cable's-length south-westward from the middlemost of these three islands, there is a rock that dries with spring-tide only; which must be avoided in sailing this way. Also a rock on the W. side of the anchorage here, near a cable's-length from the shore, which dries at two hours of ebb.

There are two rocks that lie above a cable's-length north-westward from the westmost of these isles, the eastmost of which is always above water; the other dries with spring-tide only, and must be avoided in anchoring in this neighbourhood.

The Sound of HARRIS.

The Sound of *Harris*, on the *North Uist*, or south side, is so full of rocks and shoals, that no vessel ought to attempt a passage through it along this side of the channel: along the main of *Harris* is the only safe course, though it too is very difficult, until one is particularly acquainted. The remarkable points, rocks, and islands first to be inspected in the draft, and attended to in sailing through this channel, are *Ru-rough Point*, *Milesfore Rock*, *Stroms Islets*, *Dufsère*, and *Saramaraia Island* near it; *Ilan-Seglay*, *Ilan Stromay*, and a rock near it, always above water, the sandy bay of *Drymachaird*, and *Coppay Island*.

The rocks to be avoided in sailing through the Sound of *Harris*, in the common channel, are as follow:

From *Dunevan Island* and *Milesfore*, to *Rumaderdach* islets, the channel is all clear and deep water. About a quarter of a mile N. W. from *Rumaderdach*, lies *Rumaderdach Rock*, which dries two hours before low-water; and is avoided along the W. side, while a kern in *Stone Islet* is in a line with the top of *Bruchagrival Hill* or *Tar Head*: or any part of *Coppay Island* in sight to the westward of *Seglay Island*.

About a mile westward from *Rumaderdach*, and S. from *Dufsère*, there is a rock that dries with spring-tides only. Leading-marks to this rock are, *Coppay* about a sail's breadth open to the W. of *Shelinas* or *Tar Head* appearing along the E. side of *Saramaraia Island*: therefore, *Coppay* open to the E. of *Dufsère*; or *Tar Head* open of *Saramaraia*, clears this rock along the E. side.

Between the island *Ensay*, and *Ilan-Seglay*, near the middle, there are two rocks near each other, that dry with spring-tide only. These are avoided along the E. side, by keeping somewhat nearer to *Seglay* than to *Ensay*. Have avoid also a ledge, which extends a cable's-length southward from the S. end of *Seglay*.

There

LONG-ISLAND, HARRIS.

There are two spring-tide rocks that lie eastward from the N. E. point of *Ensay*, and near half-way between it and *Stromay Island*. To avoid them along the E. side, keep nearest to *Stromay*; or from *Seghay* steer on, or a very little westward of the black rock that lies at the W. end of *Ilan-Stromay*.

Rocks between Ensay and Stromay.

Near the middle, between *Seghay* and *Stromay Islands*, off a small point at the ferry-house, there is a spring-tide rock. To sail along the W. side of it, keep the black rock, near the W. end of *Stromay*, in a line with *Coppay*. To sail between it and *Harris*, keep any part of *Stromay* on *Coppay*.

There are four rocks between *Ilan-Stromay* and the head of *Harris* to be avoided; one about a quarter of a mile north of it, which dries with spring-tides only; the second is *Sherinerinach*, a spring-tide rock, near a mile N. N. W. from *Stromay*: the third is three quarters of a mile west of *Sherinerinach*, which dries at four hours of ebb; the fourth is *Grueagach*, about half a mile westward of *Rodelnesa Point*, and dries with spring-tides only.

To sail along the W. side of *Sherinerinach*, having past the black rock at the west end of *Stromay*, keep *Ru-Ranish Point* (the S. point of *Harris*) in sight by the W. side of *Seghay Islands*.

To sail along the E. side of the rocks that lie west from *Sherinerinach*, keep *Dunaaran Island* open of *Ensay*.

To sail along the west side of *Grueagach Rock*; keep the black rock at *Stromay* in a line with *Dunaaran Island*.

To sail from the E. end of *Stromay*, between *Grueagach* and *Sherinerinach Rocks*; keep about two or three cables-length from the shore of *Harris*, till you are near the S. end of the sandy bay of *Drumcheinil*, then steer W. or W. N. W. half a mile, or a quarter of a mile; and then steer for *Coppay Island*, or between it and the head.

To sail through the Sound of HARRIS *from the S. or E.*

Take ebb tide, for ebb sets northward in this channel, and flood southward: enter between the main of *Harris* and *Dunaaran Island*; steer between *Dusbere* and *Rennaderdach*; and to avoid the spring-tide rock, which lies southward from *Dusbere*, take *Coppay Island* and *Dusbere* in one, or *Coppay* open to the E. of *Dusbere*; or *Sounasnair Island* open of the *Head*; and sail about two cables-length from *Dusbere* and *Sounasnair Island*, keeping them on the larboard-hand; giving the N. end of the latter a birth, sail between it and *Seghay*, and keep about one-third, or one-fourth from *Seghay Island*; and two-thirds, or three-fourths, from *Ensay Island*. When you have past *Seghay*, steer for the west side of the black rock, at the W. end of *Stromay*; and to avoid the rocks off the north end of *Ensay*, keep *Ranish* hid by *Seghay*, or just appearing along the south side of it: take *Stromay* on the starboard-hand, and having past the black rock, keep *Ru-ranish Point* in sight by the E. side of *Seghay*, or the north end of *Seghay* southward of the black rock of *Stromay*, to avoid *Sherinerinach* on the starboard-hand; then steer freely toward *Coppay Island*.

The channel between *Ilan-Stromay* and *Harris* is sufficiently deep, but the stream of tide runs quicker in it than in other parts of the Sound of *Harris*. To sail through it, follow the before-mentioned course and directions, till you are within half a mile of *Stromay*, then stand eastward for the channel, or Sound of *Stromay*; keep near the middle going through it, and sail along the *Harris* coast, till you are near the sandy bay of *Drumcheinil*, then stand from the coast westward, or W. N. W. till the black rock at *Stromay* is in a line with *Dunaaran Island*; and keep these two on till you are past *Grueagach Rock*, then steer between *Coppay* and the head.

Stromay Channel.

Between *Berneray Island* and *Harris*, the stream of flood runs southward, and ebb northward; but the stream begins to turn southward one hour and a half before it is low-water on the shore; and the stream of ebb begins an hour and half before high-water on the shore. From about the 20th of *March*, till the 20th of *September*, the northward stream is scarce sensible between *Berneray* and *Ensay*, during eight days of neap-tides; but the southward stream is very sensible: from about the 20th of *September*, to the 20th of *March*, during neap-tide, there is little or no southward stream, but the northward stream is very sensible.

Streams of Tide very irregular.

Some of the inhabitants of *Berneray* say, that during the first six months, that is, while the sun has north declination, neap-tides run all day southward, and all night northward; and while the sun has south declination, that neap-tides run all day northward, and all night southward. This I had no opportunity of confirming by my own observation. But as spring-tides here do not run above one mile an hour when strongest, neap-tides must be very slow; when their boats, or fishing-lines, driving a little with the wind, may give occasion to people, fond of the marvellous, to mistake in a matter that requires care and nicety in the experiment.

ROWDIL *Harbour.*

Rowdil is a bay at the S. W. point of *Harris*, about a mile long, and above a quarter of a mile wide, of easy access, the ground in it all clean, and the depth of water sufficient for the largest ships. As the anchorage is not sheltered from all winds, but open to the S. and to a point or two on each side of that, other harbours in this neighbourhood are preferred to it in the winter-time. About a pistol-shot from the shore, on the W. or larboard-side, as you enter this bay, there is a small rock that dries with spring-tide only, which must be avoided in turning out or in.

As the head of this bay there is a creek where small vessels may lie aground on clean sand, and very safe with all winds. The entrance to it is dry at low spring-tide. Sail in here about high-water, and keep nearest the point[s], or small point on the starboard-hand. This creek is esteemed a convenient place for cleaning a vessel's bottom.

Creek at the Head of Rowdil.

FINNIS *Bay.*

Finnis Bay is well sheltered, the ground good, and is capable of holding twelve or fifteen large ships at anchor.

About half a mile from the head of this harbour, nearer to the E. than to the W. side, there is a rock that dries about half-ebb, on which, in 1755, a perch was placed: this rock shoals about half a cable's-length from the S. end of what dries at low-water with neap-tides.

Rock near the Head.

Enter this harbour between the two islands that lie in the mouth of it; take the small island, which is a quarter of a mile farther up, on the starboard-hand, and anchor any where above it in four fathoms water, avoiding the before-mentioned rock.

Directions.

Loch Lebrod is the open bay next E. of *Finnis Bay*: it is full of rocks, and therefore not fit to drop anchor in.

5

Loch

LOCH PULLATOICH *and* GEOCROP.

Theſe are two ſmall harbours within the *ſame* bay, ſeparated by a peninſula; and though the water in each, particularly in *Geocrop*, is ſufficiently deep, yet their ſize makes them only fit for ſmall veſſels.

There are rocks on each ſide to be avoided before you enter this bay: one lies eaſtward, near half a mile from the narrow point of *Loch Lanbrod*, and about that ſame diſtance, S. by E. from a green iſland near that point. On the E. ſide of the entrance is *Dyſcre* (a remarkable rock, always above water, except with extraordinary high-tides), and ſeveral that lie two cables-length weſtward from it; the weſtmoſt of which dry about half-ebb. Keep above half a mile from the point, on the W. ſide of the entrance, and above a quarter of a mile from *Dyſcre*, and the rocks on each ſide will be avoided.

In the middle of the *Narrow*, as you enter *Pullapick* harbour, there is a ſmall rock that dries at half-ebb. The channel on the W. ſide of this rock is deepeſt and ſafeſt.

Near the entrance of *Geocrop* harbour there are two rocks always above water; the channel between them is ſufficiently deep; the weſtmoſt is the largeſt and moſt remarkable; between which and the point of the peninſula next northward, there is a ſhoal which reaches half over to that ſhore. Therefore, in ſailing through this channel, keep nearer to the peninſula than to the rock.

LOCH-STOKENISH.

Loch Stokeniſh is ſheltered from all winds, the ground is good, and the depth ſufficient for the largeſt ſhips; but the entrance is narrow, and requires a leading-wind. The channel is between *[illegible] Iſland*, and *[illegible] Rock*, keeping about one-third from the iſland, and two-thirds from the rock, to avoid a ſpring-tide rock, which lies neareſt to *Dyſcre*.

Between *Dyſcre* and the point of *Loch Geocrop*, there are ſeveral rocks that dry about low-water only.

In paſſing *[illegible]* (the ſmall iſland, a quarter of a mile north of *[illegible]*) give the north end of it a birth of at leaſt half a cable's-length.

About a quarter of a mile ſouth from the *Iſland Maaliſkel*, there is a rock which dries at two hours of ebb. To avoid this, and the other rocks on the W. ſide of this bay, keep the E. ſide of the [illegible] of *[illegible]* in ſight, by the E. ſide of *Maaliſkel Iſland*.

Loch Stokeniſh may be entered along the eaſt ſide of *[illegible]*; the leaſt water in it is twelve feet. Near the narroweſt part of this channel, abreaſt of a ſmall houſe, keep the middle, or neareſt the larboard-ſide going in; for it ſhoals a little from the other ſide. The beſt anchorage is above the iſland *Maaliſkel*, on from nine to twelve fathoms water.

Harbours on the North-weſt Coaſt of HARRIS.

Weſt LOCH TARBOT.

Weſt *Loch Tarbot*, including the leſſer lochs or harbours on the north ſide of it, is a ſpacious well-ſheltered arm of the ſea, where ſeveral hundreds of ſhips of all ſizes may ride ſafe in all weathers, for in the proper anchoring-places it is quite land-locked, the depth is moderate, and the ground holds well; but weſterly winds, eſpecially in winter, ſet a great ſwell into it. The beſt parts of this Loch to anchor in are the following:

Anchor any where above *Ilaniſa*, on from eleven to five fathoms.

In ſailing in paſt *Soa Iſland*, avoid a reef of rocks that extends from the S. E. above half way to *[illegible]*; the eaſtmoſt of which lies off the mouth of *Loch Meavag*, and is always above water; the next to that is covered at high-water only; another is dry at low-water only; and near the ſhore of *Meavag* is one which dries with ſpring-tide only. Alſo in ſailing along the N. ſide of *Taranſay Iſland*, avoid a ledge that extends above a cable's-length from the north-eaſt point of that Iſland.

If you enter along the S. ſide of *Ilaniſa*, give the S. E. point of the Iſland a birth of about a cable's-length, to avoid a ledge that extends ſouthward from it.

Loch Bunavoneader creek, oppoſite *Ilaniſa*, has good ground, and five fathoms the leaſt water in the middle. Enter between *Ilaniſa* and the black rock, which is always above water, above a quarter of a mile north of it; for on the north ſide of the rock there is a rocky ſhoal that extends from it half way to the ſhore, on which ſix feet is the leaſt water.

Loch Meavag is a narrow creek, half between *Soa Iſland* and *Ilaniſa*, in which ſmall veſſels may lie aground on ſix feet water and clean ſand. Go not above the houſe on the ſtarboard-hand. Sail in along the S. ſide of the reef of rocks that extend S. E. from *Soa*, and take the eaſtmoſt of them, which is always above water, on the larboard-hand.

Loch Leiſavagh is a very ſafe creek for veſſels that draw not above twelve feet of water. Anchor in the middle on three, or 3½ fathoms.

Carigan Rocks are always above water, and one of them remarkably higher than the reſt.

Between *Clargan* and *Scarp Iſland*, there are three ſmall rocks that dry with ſpring-tide only; they lie a little nearer to *Scarp* than to *Clargan*, and may be perceived at any time either by the breakers, or by a ſwell on them, even in the calmeſt weather. Theſe may be avoided along the weſt end, by keeping the weſt end of *Taranſay Iſland* a ſhip's-length out to the W. by the higheſt of the *Clargan Rocks*.

If a veſſel has occaſion to ſail into *Loch Tarbot*, along the ſouth ſide of the *Iſland Taranſay*, ſhe muſt keep the middle, or neareſt the larboard-ſhore, to avoid *Bountſal Rock*, which lies above two cables-length from the ſhore of *Paibel*, in *Taranſay*, and dries at low-water only.

Langarad Rock, between *Paibel* and *Iy* in *Taranſay*, lies about two cables-length from the ſhore, and dries at half-ebb.

Near the head of the bay of *Iy*, there is a rock always above water, within which a ſmall veſſel may ride ſafe on three or four fathoms of water. Anchor within a cable's-length of the rock.

A veſſel may ſtop off the E. end of *Taranſay*, between *Ra* and *Laſtrans Point*, on three or four fathoms clean ſand. Anchor neareſt to *Taranſay*, but avoid a ſhallow bank that extends above two cables-length from the ſhore of *Ra*, on which the leaſt water is ſix feet.

The

9

The Channel between SKY *and the* LEWIS.

CHART XXX.

That part of the *Island Sky*, which is included in this Chart, is described page 53, with Chart XXVI. That part of *Long-Island*, which is included in it, follows next with Chart XXXI.

A Description of the Tides, Rocks, Shoals, Anchoring-places, and Harbours in the N. E. *Part of* HARRIS, *and in the* LEWIS, *or* N. *Part of* LONG-ISLAND.

CHART XXXI.

TIDES. Time of high-water, between all shore.

On this part of the coast it is high-water on the shore about 6h, on the full and change-days of the moon; but the stream, about a league off the coast, from *Harris* to the *Shiant Islands*, turns two hours later; and three hours later in the middle, between *Harris* and the *Island Sky*.

Rise of the Tide.

Ordinary spring-tides rise ten feet perpendicular; and neap-tides four.

Setting of the Stream.

The stream of flood, both on the E. and W. sides of the *Lewis*, runs northward along the land, and both meet off the *Brogh Rock*, a league or two south-eastward of the *Butt*, or northmost point, of the *Lewis*.

Velocity of the Stream.

Between *Scalpay Island* in *Harris*, and *Shiant I*sl., the stream, when strongest, runs about two miles an hour; between *Ilan Shiant* and the *Lewis* it runs three; from thence to the north eastmost part of the *Lewis*, it does not run above one mile an hour off the coast; nor does it run more than that along the west coast, except along the *Butt*, where it runs two miles an hour when strongest.

ROCKS.

There are no rocks or shoals that lie above half a mile from the coast of *Lewis*, except *Sheriner*, on the S. E. side of *Scalpay Island* in *Harris*, and *Bo-barton*, a sunk rock off *Barvas*, on the N. W. of the *Lewis*, and such as are within, or near harbours or bays, and will be described with them.

Sheriner Rock.

Sheriner is a rock, about half a cable's-length long, which dries with spring-tide only, and lies S. E. ½ S. from the highest hill of *Scalpay*, or *Ben-glas* (as strangers call it), and W. ½ S. from the middle, or highest hill of *Shiant Islands*; the water is sufficiently deep quite round it, within half a cable's-length from what dries at low-water with spring-tide, except on the W. end, where it shoals about that distance from it. A leading-mark on it is, *Galtamore Rock* or *Shoal*, about two ship's-length open of *Garivelan*. When *Galtamore* is only a sail's-breadth open of *Garivelan*, or shut on it, you are then at least a mile northward, or westward of *Sheriner*, and sail between it and *Scalpay Island*, or the *Lewis*. When the highest of the small islands, near *Fladdahuan* in *Sky*, is in a line with the top of a little hill, which is next S. of *Scurnary Hill*, you are then abreast of it; keep that little highest island on any part of *Scurnary Hill*, and you clear it along the S. side: keep the island on the second top, or rising, southward from *Scurnary*, and you clear *Sheriner* along the north-east side.

Leading-mark to it.

Bo-barton Rock.

Bo-barton is a rocky shoal that lies off the parish of *Barvas*, about a mile northward from the shore, at the [illegible] of *Barvas*. The least water on it is said to be fifteen feet. The weather did not permit to sound the water over it.

Galtamore.

Galtamore is the greatest of the rocks that lie near the *Shiant Islands*: about a quarter of a mile north-west from it there is a rock that dries about half-ebb, which must be avoided in sailing near *Galtamore*.

Harbours along the E. Coast, from HARRIS *to the* BUTT *of the* LEWIS.

HARBOURS.

LOCH CRASSAVAGH *in* HARRIS.

Loch Craisavagh is a large bay, with good ground, and the water sufficient for the largest ships; but being open to the south and south-east, it is not thought safe anchorage in the winter-time; except close to the head of the bay, where a small vessel or two may ride within a rock.

Rocks on the W. side.

On the west side of this bay there are two rocks that lie about a quarter of a mile from the shore, and the northmost of them more than a quarter of a mile northward from the two small islands in the mouth of the bay: that near the islands dries with spring-tide only, the other about half-ebb.

Anchorage.

Sail into this Loch on the E. side of the two islands, anchor any where clear of the two fore-mentioned rocks, on from nine to twelve fathoms water. But if a vessel is to go up to the head of the bay, in passing a rock, or islet there, which is always above water, she must keep close along the west side; for there is a ledge that dries at half-ebb, which extends westward from the rock almost half over. This creek is pretty well sheltered by these rocks.

Rock at the Head.

The S. Harbour of SCALPAY, *or* ILAN-GLASS.

This harbour lies on the west side of *Scalpay*, facing *Ru-grabanish*, is sheltered from all winds, the ground is good, and the depth of water sufficient for any ship; ten or twelve ships of any size may ride safe in it; but requires a leading-wind in and out, the channel being between two islands that are not two cable's-length asunder.

Sheargriddarb Rock.

Near the middle of the entrance, between *Scalpay* and *Ru-grabanish*, there is a rock called *Sheargriddarb*, which dries about low-water: it lies nearest the *Scalpay* side. It is avoided along the S. side, at a considerable distance, while any part of the *Lewis* is seen by *Scalpay*. It is avoided along the W. side, by keeping the middle between *Scalpay* and *Ru-grabanish*. You are past it going in, when *Shiant* is shut with the point of *Scalpay*.

Near the south-west end of *Scalpay*, there is a rock about a quarter of a mile from the shore, which does not dry but with extraordinary low tides. It is avoided while *Ru-ubraish* in *Lewis* is seen by *Scalpay*.

Rock between Rossay and Shiansay.

Near half way between the islands *Rossay* and *Shiansay* (but not in the way to this harbour) there is a rock that dries at two hours of ebb. It lies one-third from the island next west of *Stirpay*, and two-thirds from the middle of the islands on the *Grabanish* side.

To sail into the harbour.

To sail into the S. harbour of *Scalpay*, keep any part of the *Lewis* in sight by *Scalpay*, till you are half way, or nearly so, between *Ru-grabanish* and *Scalpay*, then sail for *Hamersay Island* (on which there is a barn), giving the west point of it a birth, and sail in, in the middle, between it and *Rossay*: as you enter the harbour, give the point on the starboard-hand a birth of half a cable, and anchor abreast of, or a little above, the small islands on the larboard-hand, on from seven to four fathoms water.

3 The

LONG ISLAND, LEWIS, *East Side*.

The North Harbour of SCALPAY.

The north harbour is a creek in the north-west end of *Scalpay*, capable only of four or five small vessels; there being no more than eight or nine feet of water in it at low spring-tide; but is sheltered from all winds, and the ground good. Take ebb-tide going in; for flood runs out, or eastward, and in the narrowest part runs about two miles an hour when strongest; and continues an hour and a half after the water begins to fall on the shore. Sail in between *Scalpay* and *Meleunish*, giving the E. end of *Scalpay* a birth of about a cable's-length; going into this harbour, keep the little island in the mouth of it on your starboard-hand, and sail in the middle, or rather nearest the larboard-side. If there is not water enough to go in, a vessel may ride off the mouth of the creek on ten or twelve fathoms good ground, and pretty good shelter. Avoid a rock about a cable's-length westward from the south, or starboard-point of the entrance, which is covered at high-water only.

EAST LOCH TARBOT.

East Loch Tarbot is that large bay which is on the west side of *Scalpay Island*. In the mouth of it, besides *Scalpay*, there are a great number of lesser islands that break off the sea, and make this a very safe harbour for ships and vessels of any size; a hundred of which might ride in it easily on good anchor-ground, and well-sheltered.

This Loch may be entered, either on the south-west side of *Scalpay* through the islands, avoiding *Sgeirgrlaich Rock*, as before directed, and keeping *Hammersay*, *Raffay*, and *Shirisay* on the starboard-hand, and the chain of islets along *Ru-grabanish* on the larboard, and avoiding the rock off the middle of them that dries at two hours of ebb, described in the last harbour, by keeping the middle, or nearest to the *Grabanish* isles. Or it may be entered along the north side of *Scalpay* along *Meleunish*, which is the easiest for one unacquainted.

When the rock off the island between *Raffay* and *Shirisay* is seen, a ship may sail on either side of that rock, and go in between *Shirisay* and *Siggay* to the anchorage; avoiding a rock, nearest *Siggay*, which is always above water, except at high spring-tide.

About two cables-length eastward of the *Direcleit* isles, and northward of a rock always above water, there is a rock that dries with spring-tide only; and one southward of that which dries about half-ebb.

The best anchorage in this Loch is between *Direcleit* and *Urga*, and from thence to the *Narrow* at the head, on from seven to sixteen fathoms water. Small vessels in winter, may anchor in the *Narrow* with one anchor on shore, on two fathoms: or in the bay at *Direcleit*, keeping near the middle going in, to avoid two half-tide rocks, on the starboard-hand, and one on the larboard; anchor in the south corner of the bay, above a cable's-length from the shore.

HARBOURS in the LEWIS.

LOCH SEAFORT.

Loch Seafort is a large arm of the sea between *Harris* and the *Lewis*, capable of several hundreds of the largest ships. It is almost quite land-locked in all parts, the ground good, the depth of water from five to thirty fathoms; and when *Shriner Rock*, described before, which lies about two leagues southward from the entrance, is avoided, there is nothing to be feared in sailing in, only there must be a leading-wind through the *Narrow*, as you enter the Loch. Anchor any where above *Marwick*. At the west end of *Ilan-Seafort* is the smoothest riding, and most moderate depth of water.

The rock near the entrance on the east side is always above water, and deep quite round. There is a rock on the *Harris* side, that lies about half a mile from the shore of *Meleunish*, and dries at half-ebb. This rock should be attended to in sailing along that shore.

LOCH CLAY.

Loch Clay is of easy access, has good ground, and a moderate depth of water for ships of any size; but being open on the south to two or three points of the compass, it is likely a great swell will set into it when the wind blows fresh from that quarter, especially in winter.

Small vessels may anchor half a mile from the head of this bay, in a cove on the E. side, on six fathoms water; or, nearer the mouth of the Loch, on the east side of the little island, with one anchor on shore: this creek is safe all weathers. It shoals on each side, a little way from the shore, near the south entrance; therefore, in sailing in this way, keep the middle as near as you can, till you enter the *Narrow*, when you are past these ledges.

LOCH VALUMIS.

Loch Valumis is a narrow harbour, fit for small vessels only. In summer they may ride any where along the west side of the peninsula, on three or four fathoms water, for the ground is all good: in winter it is safest riding at the north end of the peninsula land-locked, on nine feet the least water.

Near the mouth of this creek, on the E. side, there is a small rock always above water: north-eastward from which, about two cable's-length, there is a small rock that dries at half-ebb, which must be avoided sailing along that shore.

LOCH BROLUM.

Loch Brolum has good ground, and depth of water for ships of any size; but being open to two or three points of the compass, it is reckoned safe anchorage only in the summer-time; except to such small vessels as can go into the creek at *Brolum House*; off the mouth of which there is a small rock, near a cable's-length westward from the point on your starboard-hand going in, that dries with spring-tide only; and another in the middle of the entrance: this place therefore requires high-water to go in and out.

The best anchorage for large vessels is at the head of the Loch, a cable's-length or two from a small island there.

LOCH SHELL.

Loch Shell is a spacious, convenient, and safe harbour for ships and vessels of all sizes. Ships bound to the southward may ride most conveniently in the bay of *Lemerway*, on the north side of *Ilan-Newart*, or near the north side of that island. In sailing to this anchorage, avoid a rock off the north-east part of the island, which dries at four hours of ebb; and lies about one-third from the shore of the *Lewis*, on the starboard-hand, and two-thirds from *Newart*.

Sailing into the west harbour, near half a mile past *Ilan-Newart*, avoid two rocks on the starboard-side, that dry about half-ebb, by keeping the middle, or nearest the shore on the larboard-side. Anchor a mile or two up this Loch.

This harbour may be distinguished at a distance, by its bearing from *Shiant Islands*.

Loch

Loch Houen.

Loch Houen, or *Loch Durgeen*, is all clean good ground, and the depth sufficient for any ships; but being open to the east in the mouth where it is broadest, and above that narrow, it is only fit for stopping in; or for small vessels to run in the narrow part half a mile, or more, up the Loch.

The Birken Isles.

The *Birken Isles* lie in the mouth of a long arm of the sea, in the parish of *Lochs*, and give name to that Loch. There is good ground, a moderate depth of water for any ships, and safe riding in the summer-time about a mile up the entrance, near the middle, between *Tannay Island* on the north side, and *Cromore Head* on the south, on fourteen fathoms. In winter it is better to go as far up as *Cromore House*, and anchor off the mouth of that bay, on eleven, or nine fathoms. Small vessels may go into the creek of *Cromore*, and ride on two fathoms the least water. Within it there is a small rock, on the W. side, about half a cable from the high-water mark. Take care not to ride over it. Vessels bound to the southward may ride more conveniently, and very safe, on the north side of the *Birken Isles*, between the islands *Tannay* and *Vatersay*, or in the cove at *Ranish*. You may sail in either along the south, or along the north side of *Vatersay*: if you sail in along the north side, keep about half a cable's-length from that Island, to avoid a rock that lies about a cable's-length north from *Vatersay*, and dries about half-ebb. — *Anchorage.* — *Anchorage on the N. side.* — *Rock N. from Vatersay.*

If there was any occasion to go above St. *Colm's Island*, the riding there is very fine, and safe for great numbers of ships of any burthen. The channel up is along the N. side of St. *Colm's Island*: about a quarter of a mile north from the middle of which there is a small green isle, which must be taken on the starboard-hand, at the distance of about a cable's-length, to avoid a small rock that dries at half-ebb, and lies about mid-channel, between the *Green Island* and St. *Colm's*. — *Above St. Colm's Island.* — *Rock in the Channel.*

Loch Grimishader.

In *Loch Grimishader* there is good ground, a sufficient depth of water for any merchant ship, and at the head it is well-sheltered from all winds; but it is so narrow, that there a vessel must have a following-wind up. In the mouth of a small cove, near the middle of this Loch, there is a rock which is covered only at high-water with spring-tides: the deepest water is on the north side of this rock. Anchor off the grounds at the head, on from four to seven fathoms, or any where above the fore-mentioned cove. — *Rock in the Middle.*

Loch Stornaway.

Loch Stornaway is a large and safe harbour, with water sufficient for the largest ships, and nothing to be feared in sailing into it; only in tacking give the point of *Arnish* a birth of a cable's-length; or stand no nearer it than till the west side of the small island within the harbour is in one with the remotest castle a little above it. The point of *Holm*, on the opposite side of the entry likewise, requires a birth between the point and the island next it, to avoid a rock that extends a cable's-length south from the point, and dries about half-ebb. This rock has ten fathoms close to it; and is avoided while the island within the Loch is open off the point of *Holm*. — *Arnish and Holm Points, give them a Birth.*

About a mile up this harbour, on the E. side, there is a rocky ledge that extends southward, near two cables-length from the north point of a small bay. — *Ledge on the E. side.*

The best anchorage in this harbour is above the little island, near the town of *Stornaway*; or along the south side of *Arnish Point*; or any where along the west side, on from four to six fathoms of water. — *Anchorage.*

Loch Tua, or Broad Bay.

Broad Bay has a moderate depth of water, and clean ground almost in all parts, and is a convenient place for ships to stop in in moderate weather.

In the middle, about three miles up, there is a small rock, called *Sheirbey*, which dries with spring-tides only. Leading marks on it are, the kirk of *Aynes*, a sail's-breadth open of *Rabbed Head*; and the point of *Tongue*, in a line with the highest hill of *Barvas*. — *Sheirbey Rock.*

The rocks within *Gress Bay* dry about half-ebb.

Harbours on the West Side of the Lewis.

Loch Resort.

Loch Resort is a long, narrow, arm of the sea, where a numerous fleet of the largest ships may ride in safety all the year round. It is well-sheltered, the ground good, and the depth from twelve to five fathoms, or less, shallowing gradually as you go up. Near the mouth it is subject to sudden squalls of wind from the neighbouring hills, in blowing weather. Off *Tresfall*, where it is broadest, seems the best place of anchorage.

Off the mouth of this Loch, about three-quarters of a mile northward of *Scarp Island*, there is a cluster of rocks, the eastmost of which, and one near the middle, are always above water; the westmost dry about half-ebb. These are avoided sailing from the west, toward *Loch Resort*, by keeping a mile from the W. end of *Scarp Island*, and sailing northward, till *Maleshay Island* bears E. then steering eastward, keeping nearer to *Maleshay* than to *Scarp*, till *Maleshay* bears north; then steer southward for the mouth of *Resort*. — *Dubsker Rocks.*

Loch Hamnevay.

Loch Hamnevay is well-sheltered, good ground, and the depth moderate for ships of any size. A fleet of the largest ships may ride in safety in it all weathers. There is nothing to be feared in going in but *Dubsker Rocks*, between *Scarp* and *Maleshay*, mentioned above with *Loch Resort*, which are avoided sailing from the north, by keeping nearest to *Maleshay*, as is before directed, when sailing from the south.

In moderate weather a ship may stop at anchor on the E. side of *Maleshay*, between it and the main of the *Lewis*, a cable's-length, or two, from the middle of the island, on from five to eleven fathoms water. — *Anchorage near Maleshay by Shore.*

Loch Roag.

Loch Roag, properly, is that long, narrow, arm of the sea, the entrance of which begins about two miles south from *Wuiver Island*, and is so narrow and shallow that only boats, or very small vessels, can go into it. There is also a strong stream of tide that runs in and out, which renders it more difficult and hazardous. But under the name *Loch Roag*, we comprehend the places of anchorage southward of *Wuiver*, and the *Fourteen-penny land*. Along the south-side of the *Fourteen-penny land*, called *Kyle Flodey*; in the creek *Miavagh*, and near the south end of *Lewsa Island*, a great number of ships and vessels may ride at all times, in good shelter, good ground, and a moderate depth of water.

The best channel into these harbours is between *Vacsay Island* and *Wuiver*, taking the small island *Hollshay* on the starboard-hand, and keeping nearer to *Wuiver* than to the *Fourteen-penny-land*, to avoid a spring-tide rock that lies near the middle between them, and east from an isle called *Bun Hedge*, near the latter. — *Channel in.* — *Spring-tide Rock.*

LONG-ISLAND, LEWIS, *West Side*.

Rock near Hartasore. About a quarter of a mile north-westward from *Hartaskere*, there is a small half-tide rock to be avoided.

Rocks near Wiarera Island. Anchorage. The two small rocks that lie about a quarter of a mile northward from the north end of *Wiarera*, are near quite covered with the tide. In *Kyle Flotay*, anchor nearest to the north shore. On the south side of *Lewra*, anchor between it and the south end of *Flotay*. In *Loch Miawagh*, which is at the west end of the *Fourteen-penny-land*, a vessel may ride quite smooth in the hardest gales, on from two to four fathoms of water.

Pabbay Anchorage. Rock near it. A small vessel, in the summer-time, may ride on the south side of *Pabbay Island*, on three fathoms water, about a cable's-length from the shore. In the middle of that channel there is a rock that dries at half ebb; which is avoided by keeping one-third, or one-fourth, from *Pabbay*, and two-thirds, or three-fourths, from the shore of *Kniep*.

Shoal off Pabbay. About two cable's-length south-eastward from the south end of *Pabbay*, there is a small shoal, on which the least water is six feet. This shoal is avoided, sailing between *Pabbay* and *Vacasay*, by keeping nearest to *Vacasay*.

LOCH BURGLOME.

Loch Burglom is the channel, or sound, between the south-west side of *Bernera Island* and *Uig*. This harbour, though of considerable capacity, is fit for small vessels only; for in the entrance, near *Burglom* in *Bernera*, there is not above three feet of water at low spring-tide; and in the widest part of the anchorage only twelve feet. At this place there is a little island, and about a cable's-length E. from it, a rock that dries at half-ebb, and another half a cable's-length north of the island, which must be avoided in sailing and

Anchorage without the Loch. Rocks in the way. anchoring near it. Without the entrance, on the west side, there is very safe anchorage on seven or eight fathoms, good ground, and sufficient shelter; but there are several rocks to be avoided in the most direct way to this place, which is along the E. side of *Wiarera Island*. The first is the half-tide rock, a little from *Hartaskere Island*, which was mentioned before. The second is a half tide rock, above a quarter of a mile westward from *Bosta* in *Bernera Island*. The next is a spring-tide rock in the middle, between the north end of *Wiarera* and the little island next east from it; to avoid which, keep nearest that little island; or keep *Hartaskere* in a line with, or between the two rocks, which are always above water, off the north end of *Wiarera*. The last are three rocks that dry about low-water, which lie about a cable's-length from the shore of *Wiarera*, along the round point where the house stands; to avoid them, keep the middle of the channel, or nearest

Best Anchorage off Tolda. to *Bernera*. The safest channel, however, is along the west side, and south end of *Wiarera*. Anchor off *Toulat* a cable's-length, or two, from the shore, on from six to nine fathoms.

LOCH BERNERA.

Loch Bernera is a large arm of the sea, extending along the E. side of the Island *Bernera*, where a great number of the largest ships may ride in safety in the summer-time, on from eight to twelve fathoms water; and in winter may be quite land-locked, on from three to five fathoms. There is nothing to be feared coming in, but what may be avoided by keeping above a cable's-length from the land.

To sail into Loch Bernera, and avoid the Rocks. At Sandwick. Rock Ben Eadan. Enter on the E. side of *Mahar*, which is the outermost of the small islands; take the rock *Crilar*, which is near the south-east end of *Little Bernera*, and always above water, on the starboard-hand; keep above a cable's-length from the shore at *Sandwick*, on the larboard-side to avoid three small rocks that dry about low-water; and, on the starboard-side, avoid a small rock that dries with spring-tide only, which lies about a cable's-length north from *Ben Eadan*; and is avoided while *Crilar Rock* is in a line with, or in the least open of, *Mellar Island*. Avoid also a small rock that lies about a cable's-length eastward of the little island near the point of

Near Brighkiel, and Bifiagh. *Brighkiel*; which dries at low-water, and one-half a cable north of the point of *Bifiagh*, near *Brighkiel*. These rocks are out of a ship's-way, except when she is turning in, or out of the harbour.

Anchorage. Anchor in summer any where between *Tolda*, on the main of the *Lewis*, and *Vacasay Island*; in winter it is best riding farther up, between *Calvay* and *Brinskiel*, on from five to three fathoms.

LITTLE BERNERA *Harbour*.

Rock in the middle. Small vessels may ride in the Sound of *Little Bernera*, on clean sand, about a quarter of a mile eastward of the house. A little eastward from the house, in the middle of the channel, between two points opposite to each other, there is a rock that dries about half-ebb: a small vessel may sail up on either side of this rock, by keeping about one-fourth from the shore on either side, and three-fourths from the other, and anchor in

Rock on the S. side. good shelter a cable's-length west of the rock. Within the entrance of this harbour, within a small bay on the south side, half a cable's-length from the shore, there is a little spring-tide rock, which is avoided while you do not enter that bay.

LOCH CARLOWA.

Loch Carlowa is a pretty good harbour in the summer-time, and convenient for vessels bound to the westward. In sailing into this harbour, when you are about half a mile up, keep the middle, or nearest the larboard side, to avoid three small rocks that lie off *Doon*, about one-third from the south side, and dry

Rocks on the S. side. when it has ebbed one hour. Anchor in the bay of *Kerwick*, on four fathoms water.

The Place of these Lochs, how perceived at a Distance. The place of the Lochs in this neighbourhood may be perceived at a distance, by the *Bernus Hills*, and more particularly by the appearance of *Garnilan*, which is a large rock rising out of the sea, like a round regular hill, a little without the other lower islands.

F I N I S.

Alterations in the Sand-banks near LIVERPOOL.

Since the Descriptions of the Banks and Channels near *Liverpool* were printed off, the following Alterations have come to the Writer's knowledge.

That part of Hoyle Sand, which lies between the *North-east Buoy* and *Helbry Swash*, has extended about a quarter of a mile northward; the North-west Buoy has been shifted eastward accordingly, and Helbry Swash Buoy taken away altogether, as being now unnecessary.

In the N. entrance of *Hoyle-lake*, where some years ago there were fifteen feet water, there are now only eight at low-water, with spring tide: there is, besides, less room within the Lake for ships to ride in than formerly; so that Hoyle-lake seems to be filling up at both ends.

The channel between *Mockbeggar Sand* and *Burbo* has lately shifted considerably southward, and new buoys and land-marks placed to direct shipping through it.

On the *Point of Ayr*, near Chester Bar in the *River Dee*, a light-house is to be erected, with a view to enable shipping to pass that point at a proper distance in the night time. By what means it will do so, the Writer has not yet learned.

www.ingramcontent.com/pod-product-compliance
Lightning Source LLC
Chambersburg PA
CBHW030027030726
47499CB00008B/3161
9783741183850